Down
to a
Soundless Sea

DOWN
TO A
SOUNDLESS SEA

Thomas Steinbeck

Ballantine Books • New York

A Ballantine Book
Published by The Ballantine Publishing Group

Copyright © 2002 by Thomas Steinbeck

All rights reserved under International and Pan-American Copyright
Conventions. Published in the United States by The Ballantine Publishing
Group, a division of Random House, Inc., New York, and simultaneously in
Canada by Random House of Canada Limited, Toronto.

Ballantine and colophon are registered trademarks of Random House, Inc.

www.ballantinebooks.com

Library of Congress Cataloging-in-Publication Data is available from the
publisher upon request.

ISBN 0-345-45576-2

Text design by Jaime Putorti

Map by Mapping Specialists, Ltd.

Manufactured in the United States of America

First Edition: October 2002

10   9   8   7   6   5   4   3   2   1

This modest volume is dedicated
to
Bill and Luci Post
In memory of
William Brainard and Anselma Post

The deepest roots sustain the greatest trees.

—J. E. S.

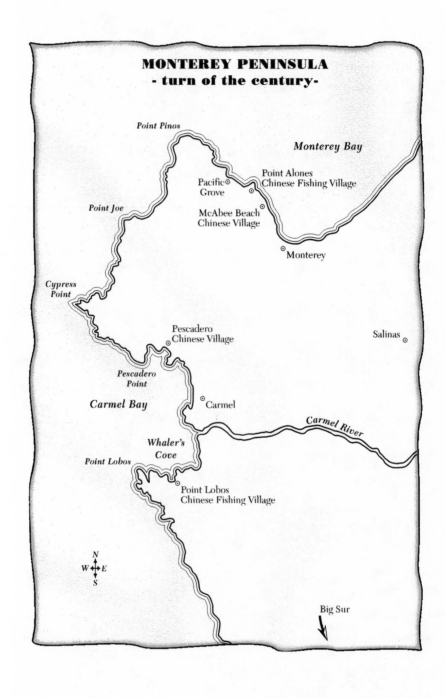

MONTEREY PENINSULA
- turn of the century-

Monterey Bay

Point Pinos

Point Alones
Chinese Fishing Village

Pacific
Grove

McAbee Beach
Chinese Village

Point Joe

⊙ Monterey

*Cypress
Point*

Pescadero
Chinese Village

Salinas ⊙

*Pescadero
Point*

Carmel Bay

⊙ Carmel

Carmel River

*Whaler's
Cove*

Point Lobos

Point Lobos
Chinese Fishing Village

N
W ✛ E
S

Big Sur

CONTENTS

Acknowledgments

First I would like to credit Michael Freed, creator of the Post Ranch Inn on the coast of Big Sur, whose love of that country encouraged him to commission this volume of stories. His respect and admiration for the stalwart souls who settled those broken mountains and rugged shores inspired the author to resurrect and reexamine stories he had heard so often from elders or those who knew something of the anecdotes firsthand.

I would also like to lovingly acknowledge the invaluable contributions of my talented partner and wife, Gail. By the time this volume will have gone to press, she will have read and reread these stories a score of times in aid of correction and clarification. Her inspiration, patient good humor, and fine literary sense has kept this project on an even keel throughout adversities and setbacks that often threatened to halt its completion.

For me the most indispensable assistance comes from a

forbearing and focused story editor. My guide, in that regard, is Professor Leonard Tourney, a marvelous author of historical mystery tales in his own right. It would not be an exaggeration to suggest that I am one of his greatest devotees. It has been a rare privilege to work with someone whose own qualifications create such an inspirational benchmark.

I would also like to express my deepest appreciation to Peter and Patricia Benesh for their efforts in polishing the text. As editors they are true guardians of sentence structure and rational punctuation. I owe them gallons of red ink and a week in Tahiti to recover from the ordeal.

PERTINENT RESEARCH FOR THIS VOLUME CAME from family and local resources, since it was necessary to verify minor details that had been lost in the myriad renditions of stories retold over the years.

There was one particular source that I found most insightful and timely since it edified my lifelong interest in the laboring minorities who first populated California.

Sandy Lydon's exceptional book *Chinese Gold* was an indispensable wellspring of history, maps, names, and topical insights that would have been impossible to compile in the time available. I found Mr. Lydon's history not only meticulously researched, but also illuminating, entertaining, and well written. I look forward to all his future books.

Finally, I would like to thank Elizabeth Winick, my agent at McIntosh & Otis, and Dan Smetanka, my editor at Ballantine Books, for their unwavering faith, support, and hard work.

Author's Note

When I was young I discovered, as all children must, that certain venerable traditions connected to family life required total participation. Most families maintain these fabled customs one way or another and, for the most part, they are obscure in origin. If one is fortunate, these rituals have, at their core, a modicum of wit and entertainment.

My brother and I were particularly blessed with a family convention that involved storytelling. We sprang like noisy chicks from a gaggle of writers, composers, and entertaining raconteurs. My father, the ancient gander of our flock, was particularly fond of a ripping good yarn cleverly and deftly told. Even his taste in friends and acquaintances ran to the tall-tale-spinners and those whose recollections included great and elusive fish.

In our particular rite anyone could play, family or not, but it was understood that the participants had to share in my father's passion for skill. For it wasn't just the story itself that would come under close scrutiny, but also the ability of the storyteller, which often commanded the critical balance in the final reckoning.

Storytelling efforts were usually called forward at the dinner table, though almost any impromptu gathering might inspire an eruption of, "Did your Mom ever tell you the one about cousin Fanny and the King of Tonga?" Family and guests would be cajoled into imparting "that yarn about Grandma Olive and the mountain lion" or "the one about Ernie Pyle and the North African bedbug that won the Purple Heart." It made little difference what the story entailed or whether we had heard it before. The joy of the game always revolved about the mastery of the teller, and of that we never tired.

Like most youngsters, my brother and I always called for stories of far-off ranches, rugged shores, and the inspired exploits of our ancestors. Of course, we loved the funny stories, but there were others that would send us to our beds with chills of foreboding. Like most children, we secretly relished the mysterious, eerie, and hair-raising chronicles best.

I was drawn to stories of my father's youth and the history of the period, anything that depicted the backdrop of his narratives. It became an effortless practice to immerse myself in the details of life in Monterey County from the turn of the century through the 1930s. It appeared to me as a singular time to have lived, and I envied every kaleidoscopic recollection of my father's youthful adventures.

As children we had often visited relatives in Salinas, Monterey, and Watsonville, and in my youth, these places held great charm.

Every craggy mountain, rolling pasture, and rock-bound

cove came alive because of the stories I had heard from native relatives. I discovered in later years that I had accidentally assimilated more knowledge about the Monterey coast and its history than 90 percent of the people who actually lived there. The bulk of this incidental information was metabolized in the form of oral histories that were, for me, pure entertainment.

In this short volume I have attempted to carry on the tradition of telling the old stories, informally of course, as family custom dictates. As in the past, the entertainment is best served with a home-cooked meal and in the company of like-minded listeners. But stories transmitted in an oral tradition have an aura of performance, a flavor of language, and a sense of period that is difficult to reproduce on the printed page. The vernacular of an anecdote being told by a person old enough to remember its origins is quite different from the language employed by those of later generations who retell it. Yet it is the mode and color of the original narration that contributes authenticity, historical bias, and tonality to such annals.

It is, therefore, always a painstaking maneuver to attempt duplication of language used by the original participants and make it ring true for the modern ear. Despite the improbability of success in this arena, I have nonetheless jumped into this linguistic pit armed only with a well-tutored ear and the knowledge that my critics are no better equipped to render judgment than I. There was also the matter of background particulars to be considered. When a story has been told and retold numberless times, the thorny problem of accuracy arises. The tangible *who, where, what,* and *when* of any specific account has a habit of getting mislaid in the excitement of the telling. This problem is often amplified by the number of different versions of the story in circulation.

Any competent police investigator will attest to the persis-
tence of this problem. If there are ten witnesses to an incident,
that investigator is more likely than not to be saddled with ten
different accounts of that same event. Being a writer of historical fiction and not an officer of the law, I have invariably
shown a shameless propensity for the most entertaining and
morally illustrative narratives. But I also respect the underlying
accuracy of detailed facts, and for those I have always gratefully
depended upon the dedicated research of qualified regional
historians.

I encourage my readers to pass along these stories in the
spirit with which they came to me, for they belong to anyone
who finds some small merit in the lessons they impart.

The Night Guide

~⁓

Eighteen fifty-nine was the devil's own year for gales along the Sur coast, but their raucous zenith was registered near the end of April. Crashing up from the south-southwest with piratical ferocity, the cycle of gales unburdened enough water to send the Little and Big Sur Rivers four to six feet over their banks. The runoff from Pico Blanco alone kept the Little Sur at near flood for two weeks.

Sadly, every mortal creature that made the rugged coast a refuge suffered from the shattering blows of an outraged sea. Cresting rollers twenty feet high and two miles long mined into the impenetrable cliffs and rocks for days on end. Inevitably, every rookery, bower, haul-out, and nesting sight on the Monterey coast was swept away. The corpses of every known species of coastal life littered what shore there was left. The sharks enjoyed abundance for days after each gale.

The evidence of destruction was to be had from all quarters. Salmon Creek to Santa Cruz reported roads, byways, and trails strangled in mazes of uprooted and shattered trees. The prodigious rains, sometimes so heavy and horizontal that simple breathing became hazardous, drilled the soil so incessantly that broad landslides were abruptly carved from the mountainsides. Several large rockslides unalterably isolated the more remote mining claims.

It was during a blessed lull between the repetitive coastal tempests that Boy Bill Post moved his wife from Monterey to a newly purchased piece of land bordering Soberanes Creek. His land formed a part of the old San Jose y Sur Chiquito land grant, and he had fixed it in his mind that his acres would be prime for cattle. There appeared to be abundant grazing in the hills and pastures, and the splendid ocean views gave him constant pleasure.

Serious anxiety regarding the recent inclination of weather set Boy Bill Post to hurriedly construct a cabin to shelter his new family. This urgency was magnified by the impending birth of the Posts' first child.

Boy Bill Post had married a handsome Rumsen Indian girl. Her name was Anselma Onesimo and her people had lived along Carmel Valley and its bountiful river for centuries. According to Anselma, her tribe had sprung from beneath the earth on the day of creation. The Rumsen people considered the Sur Mountains as spiritual ground and spoke of Mount Pico Blanco as the navel of the world.

The constraints of time were suddenly made more pertinent by the return of the southern gales. Bill's plans for their cabin were instantly altered to accommodate present needs and it quickly became a slant-roofed, one-room hut near

Soberanes Creek. This proved not to be the most favorable of locations.

The expectant father desperately hand split cedar shakes by the hour without recourse to food or rest. Anselma's lying-in time was uncomfortably close at hand, and Boy Bill Post raced his hammer against the lightning-rent tempest that momentarily threatened to descend upon their heads.

Anselma's cries from within the rude shelter informed Bill Post that his firstborn and the gale might possibly arrive simultaneously. Then a sudden explosive crash of thunder heralded the initial, pelting pebbles of rain. It also proclaimed the welcome cries of his first child.

Post managed to secure the last few cedar shakes to the roof just in time to greet Charles Francis Post. Bill's gift to his burgeoning family was a tight shelter and dry stores. Not much in the way of a defense against the wrath of God perhaps, but better than canvas and poles in those wilds.

March 1, 1859, the day the majestic gales attended the birth, also marked the sad loss of four sound ships. To seal the bargain, the coast of Monterey was sorrowfully altered by rock-grinding waves and carnivorous tides. There were other unique signs accompanying the birth, according to the mother, but it wasn't for some time that anyone realized that young Frank was also the first child born in the high Sur under the American flag.

In any event, the child's nativity was accredited as genuinely auspicious, and it was noted by family members that unusual events occurred on the anniversary of that particular date every year.

By the first of June that same year, Bill Post had built his new family a credible home higher up on the banks of the

Soberanes, and he had begun to move on a few head of livestock to see how they fared before establishing a larger herd.

BILL POST HAD GROWN INTO A MAN of relatively broad experience. He was the son of a successfully retired sea captain
from New London, Connecticut, and the family counted itself
honored to have had ancestors aboard the *Mayflower.* A typical
Yankee, both innovative and practical, Bill always felt equal to
any task he set for himself.

In 1858 Bill Post had had the good sense to marry Anselma, and though he appraised his life as rich in experience,
nothing had quite prepared him for fatherhood. He found himself looking for direct reflections of his own instincts and manner in the person of the child. This seemed only natural to
Anselma, though Bill's observations took on an unsettling character the more he studied the matter. Baby Charles Francis
Post seemed remarkably self-absorbed and uncommonly introspective for an infant.

Anselma quietly insisted there was absolutely no reason for
concern. It was the child's Rumsen Indian blood at play. Indian
babies were rarely clamorous unless soiled or left without
proper attention. Indeed, Anselma exhibited great interest in
her child's reflective temperament. She said it was a sign of
great insight. This did little to assuage his father's concern,
however, and Bill continued focusing closely on his firstborn
for signs of some subtle indisposition.

Bill never ascertained anything beyond his own overanxious
concerns, for Frank bloomed quite normally, though he remained quiet when he had nothing of importance to say. The
child retained information easily and brought a fixed and pa-

tient concentration to every new experience. By the time the boy was three, Bill Post was forced to accept Anselma's elementary appraisal of the situation. Little Frank assuredly perceived and understood more than most tykes his age, but he kept his insights to himself, as did all his mother's people.

Little Frank loved to trail behind his mother as she drifted off into the barrens or high passes on one of her herb and medicine-gathering expeditions. Sometimes they would come across other parties of foraging Rumsen and happily move along together for a day or two exchanging news, gathering pine nuts and birds' eggs, and hunting small game when the opportunity presented itself.

This singular practice made Bill Post extremely uncomfortable from the outset, and he voiced innumerable objections to the custom. But if he thought for a moment he might discourage his wife's basic Indian compacts and traditions, he was pitifully mistaken. Anselma considered foraging as an important part of an ancient and magic family responsibility. The very process required vast knowledge and humble reverence, and heaven help anyone who interfered.

After a while Bill came to see that thorny point for himself and, with his usual Yankee practicality, let Anselma do as she pleased. He just got used to it, as he was meant to. He also became acclimated to little Frank, who sometimes looked at his father as though they had met somewhere else, in another time—a very disconcerting air when adopted by a child.

Bill also became accustomed to his son's long, ruminative pauses when asked a question. Little Frank seemed to ponder every inquiry seriously, regardless of magnitude. He always answered with disarming simplicity and truthfulness. These were not qualities Bill Post necessarily wanted his son to disavow in

favor of thoughtless social spontaneity, so he adopted a circumspect manner when conversing with the child on any important subject.

From little Frank's perspective the whole world made sense.
A moment's balanced reflection always served to place every
reality on an even plane. The truth always made itself brightly
evident to him. Even awash in a sea of distortion, the truth was
easily defined and understood. His reluctance to speak about
all he knew was bred in the bone, as his mother had always
contended. The fixed symmetry evident in all things, spiritual
and physical, was perfectly resolved to little Frank's way of
thinking.

It was with his mother that Frank shared the greatest and
most diverse of dialogues. Oddly, much of it was nonverbal
and needed little in the way of physical inflection to disclose
infinite subtleties. The boy fairly exercised himself in all the
languages at hand without showing much preference for any
one in particular. English, Spanish, and Rumsen phrases were
all the same to little Frank. He would happily express himself
using elements of all three languages simultaneously.

Though he found it peculiar, it never disturbed the child
when his father failed to hear or discern the more enchanted
particulars that always appeared so obvious to the boy, but he
possessed a native discretion and never discussed that part of his
world with anyone but his mother and then only in their own
special dialects. There could be little doubt of Frank's Indian
inheritance, but this was not to say that Bill Post had not left
his mark. The child displayed evident qualities of ingenuity, endurance, and courage typical of a Connecticut Yankee. The boy
even possessed the amiable aspect and rolling gait of a Grand
Banks seaman as irrefutable proof of his father's bloodline.

Little Frank also shared his father's passion broad vistas of the Pacific. Father and son spe watching the sunset beyond the opalescent h gulls wheeled and called overhead. Bill wou what lay beyond the oceans, but his son focused only on what could be seen. It would have been all the same to the boy if nothing whatsoever lay over the horizon. He loved the beauty of the sea for its own sake and asked nothing more of it.

Bill noticed that prolonged contemplation of the bright ocean panoramas occasionally made his son almost giddy. It was then that little Frank would talk mysteriously of the *Ancients* who had once lived in these mountains, the humans who had stared out over those same bright waters before time was recorded. Bill Post often found his son's manner of expression curious; the object of the boy's focus was so unlike that of other children his age.

If Bill Post ever required valid proof of his son's native predispositions, it materialized on a dangerous night in mid-March. It was a night rent with contrary gales, hazardous winds, and lightning that owned the skies for minutes on end. It was a night not unlike that of Frank's birth, with its attendant natal pyrotechnics. The boy was a hardened veteran of tempests of equal ferocity since that auspicious night, but storms inspired curiosity rather than fear in the child. Indeed, little Frank rather enjoyed a really spirited southwester. He would ask his father to take him to watch the monstrous seas cleave themselves against the great rocks of the coast.

On this particular night, little Frank took no joy in the storms, nor in the safety and warmth afforded by his soft bed and downy quilt. His mother had departed on one of her usual hunting expeditions into the mountains three days earlier. She d promised to return before the weather broke. Frank's father had heartily regretted letting Anselma continue with her usual native routines because she was carrying another child. He felt uneasy about the effects her strenuous endeavors and the wilderness might have on mother and unborn child alike.

At any other time little Frank would have thought nothing of his mother's departure except to feel slightly neglected because he could not accompany her. He had come down with a slight cold, and his father had insisted that the boy stay at home until the symptoms subsided.

THE SHATTERING TEMPEST GREW IN INTENSITY, and it was about midnight when Frank heard his father rise, dress, and depart to check the barn and the frightened stock. It was then that a feeling of apprehension and barren anxiety settled on the boy's soul like a wet hide. It made him shiver. Something was wrong, and little Frank was at a loss to know why he felt so distraught. Sitting up, he looked out the rain-streaked window. In the distance, he could see the light of his father's storm lantern moving about inside the barn, so he knew that his father was fine. But he worried sorrowfully about his mother. He was almost sick wondering where she was on such a raging night. The boy closed his eyes tight to drive away the unwelcome images, but he became aware of an even stronger light trying to edge its way past his closed lids to gain his attention.

At first the child thought it was his father's lantern, but when he opened his eyes he realized the light came from a different source altogether. This light shimmered in the corner of his room, shimmered with a gentle luminescence unlike anything the child had ever seen before. He had noticed the wakes of passing ships glow with the same quality in the moonlight, and this pale glow, akin to the water's strange radiance, shed little of itself on the immediate surroundings.

The glow took the form of a tapered pillar at first, but when his eyes became accustomed to the subtle and wonderful color variations emanating from the luminescence, he became convinced that the light was a *who* and not a *what*. This realization infused him with a warmth and confidence that seemed totally natural and admissible. It was as if he had always known about this phenomenon even though he had never experienced it before.

The glowing pillar moved slowly toward the door to Frank's room, and there it waited shimmering with green, blue, and violet pulses of brilliance. The boy nodded with instant comprehension, jumped from his cot, and quickly dressed. A lightning flash suddenly raced across the sky. The crash of its thunder followed almost immediately. Alert to the storm once more, the boy pulled on his boots. Little Frank was not fond of wearing shoes of any description. He was happiest with the soft dirt between his toes, but he obeyed the thought as it came to him.

The glowing pillar floated through the cabin to the front door and waited. Grabbing his jacket and rabbit-skin cap, Frank followed the light out into the storm. There was no sign of his father anywhere, so the boy followed the radiance without further pause. The brilliance guided the boy precisely over well-used paths through the eastern pastures until it reached the mountain. There the guide waited for the boy before slowly ascending a craggy trail that led to the high ridges. Frank had followed his mother over many of those same paths gathering medicinal plants.

As the boy began to climb the trail, the storm, which had

been furious for the past six hours, turned dangerous in the extreme. Lightning fingered across the sky in every direction at once. The explosions of thunder made the earth tremble beneath the child's feet, and the rain pelted down like hail to the point of pain. Faithfully, the illumination never distorted or wavered from the path, so Frank followed without fear. The winds rose to the tenor of plaintive screams, so that every limb and leaf, every blade and bush was helplessly torn and wrenched in obedience to its whims.

As he climbed, Frank witnessed ancient trees cleaved down the center by the stress of contrary winds first raging from the west and then rounding the compass. Sometimes the gusts appeared to sweep from all directions at once. Downed tree limbs and torn vegetation became more dense the higher he climbed, but still the glowing guide remained constant and reassuring, never deviating a degree from the center of the trail, never disordered by wind or the cutting sheets of rain.

Near the top of the track a shallow dale gave spartan shelter to a grove of ancient and distorted oaks. Little Frank struggled over the rise and, clutching his collar against the rain, watched as the light moved to the center of the grove and then stopped. As the boy followed, he noticed a slight alteration in its quality. Changing from the cooler, calming colors, the light now became resplendent with bright streaks of yellow and gold. Vibrant flashes of crimson amplified the sense of urgency. Then, within the briefest moment, the guide flared brilliantly and was gone, leaving only its ghost image imprinted on the boy's eyes. Little Frank waited a few seconds for his vision to clear and then walked to the spot in the grove where the flickering pillar had last stood. Bursts of lightning conveniently illuminated his way so that the path was well defined.

At the bottom of the path little Frank spotted a fallen tree, its great mass of roots exposed and waiting for death. Another flash of lightning and the boy sighted something else: a figure pinned under a lattice of heavy limbs and branches. The boy instantly recognized his mother reaching out and calmly calling his name.

Frank ran to her, gripped her hand, and began sputtering questions in their special dialect. Anselma quieted her son and said that she was unhurt, just trapped. The large limb lying across her back would have to be raised for her to slide free under her own power. The limb was sixteen inches broad and, with the attendant branches, a considerable mass of wood for anyone to move.

Without thinking further, the boy attempted to raise the limb, but his little arms were no match for its girth. Then he remembered watching his father clear tree stumps from the pasture. He looked about until he found a stout broken limb. He wedged the hefty bough under the offending limb in such a manner that, should he have the strength to push the branch up over his head a short ways, his mother might pull herself free. But the weight of the limb precluded a four-year-old boy from doing anything of the kind.

A standard contention of the ages asserts that the bonds between mother and child may easily accommodate the insuperable. So, lacking all sense of the improbability of the task at hand, little Frank pushed up on his makeshift lever and moved forward.

He managed to push the branch up over his head. He repeated the exercise twice more, and before he knew it his mother was standing by his side saying that it was safe to release the limb.

The boy let go and smiled up at his mother. Anselma knelt to see to her son. They were both soaked to the bone, but once satisfied that her child was not injured in any way, Anselma shouldered her bag and shepherded Frank down the steep trail by the incessant flashes of blue-white lightning.

When they at last neared the house, Anselma saw her husband's storm lantern approaching from the direction of the road. Bill Post ran forward, gathered his little family in his arms for a moment, and then quickly ushered them toward the safety of the house. The relief in his eyes almost came to tears. Back under shelter, Bill quickly stoked the fire and went to fetch fresh towels from the cupboard. While Anselma saw to dry garments, Bill retrieved a bucket of rainwater from the overflowing butts on the porch. He hung a small cauldron from its iron hook over the fire and set the water to heat so Anselma might bathe the child and prevent further chill.

Bill Post at last spoke of his anxiety. When he returned to the house and found the front door wide open and little Frank gone, he had not known where to look. He had searched for two hours without a sign. Happily, Bill observed that his wife and child seemed hardly fazed by their wild adventure. So while he fed them honey and warm bread, he asked them to recount what had happened. There was never a note of reproach or recrimination in his voice. Bill Post was far too happy to have his loved ones safe at home for gratuitous displays of troubled indignation.

True to her pure Rumsen nature, Anselma leaned toward the taciturn. Her speech was known for its veracity and brevity, and Bill did not live in hope of a colorful or detailed explanation. She spoke of coming down the trail when a great wind tore a tree from the earth and trapped her beneath its branches.

Then her son found her and helped her escape by shifting the biggest limb. There was nothing more to say for the moment.

Bill shook his head and looked to his son, though he entertained little hope of much help in that direction. Even before his father spoke, Frank piped up with his mixed patois of English, Spanish, and Rumsen. It always took a moment to coax Frank to pick one language and stick with it. The boy told his father that he had been in bed when his mother's spirit had come for him in a light. She had led him up the mountain to move the tree so she could come home. Frank said his meager piece with an air of all-inclusive acceptance, as though this kind of experience was an everyday occurrence. Again Bill shook his head, but he was patient enough to realize that it might take days to secure all the details of the story.

As Anselma tucked her child under his goose-down quilt that night, the boy looked at his mother and asked whether he could someday learn to call her with the light when he was in trouble. Anselma looked at her son, caressed his face, and told him that the light was not something one learned how to do. Love made it happen. Little Frank smiled, blinked once or twice, and fell asleep, content with the answer.

The next day, after the storms had passed well east, Bill Post rode out with the Ortiz brothers to survey the general damage and do what they could to clear the trails. Bill eventually had to rig two mules with a wagon harness to help move the heavier debris.

Later that day and only out of curiosity, Bill and his men rode up the ridge trail to inspect the site his wife and son had spoken of. It was just as they had said, possibly worse to Bill's way of thinking. The local damage was extensive due to the erratic winds.

That evening over supper Bill asked Anselma about the boy lifting the tree to let her escape. Could she by any chance have been mistaken? Could the tree not have moved in the wind? Anselma looked at her husband coolly and shook her head.

Bill continued in a rather abashed manner. With just a tinge of a blush, Bill said he had asked only because it had required the labor of two sturdy mules and a horse just to haul the offending snag a few feet off the trail.

Anselma smiled, shrugged, stroked her husband reassuringly on the forearm, and kissed away the small tears of relief that scrolled down his cheeks.

THE WOOL GATHERER

THE IMMENSE BEAST SLUMBERED upon a wide stone ledge that knifed out from the hillside overlooking the vast expanse of the green Pacific. Ivory-plumed waves crashed almost soundlessly hundreds of feet below cliffs that only marginally accommodated a wagon trail that ran north to south, fifty feet below the ledge. With a massive head resting motionless upon two equally enormous paws, the creature remained so still that one could be forgiven for mistaking the shaggy, gray enormity for a huge boulder.

A closer inspection, though undoubtedly lethal, would have revealed an occasional torpid movement of ancient eyes, or the intermittent widening of cavernous nostrils as itinerant aromas drifted within the creature's orbit of interest.

This primeval megalith of muscle, teeth, and claws had prospered and grown old among the mountains that held back the sea. So old, indeed, that she had outlived all of her clan. It had been many years since the beast had seen or even scented another member of her once-great and ferocious race.

The first, motley tribes of men who came from the north had feared and worshipped her lineage as gods, and both beast and man had thrived with little harm issuing from their mutual tenancy of the land. Life along these rich coasts had been good to all.

Then the shining ones had come from the south. From that time to the present the lineage of god-beasts had suffered continual decimation until nothing remained save bones and brave tales. One or two more summers were all that stood between legend and oblivion for this last matriarchal divinity of the mountains.

A MEANDERING AROMA REFOCUSED the creature's attention. Slowly her half-closed eyes moved to scrutinize the trail below. A short while later a horse, rider, and colt came into view cresting a northern rise that silhouetted their images against sun-backed ocean fog.

The rider was a boy of seventeen, tall and strong for his age. He was mounted on a ruby-roan mare with a white blaze in the shape of a quarter moon. The fractious colt, unwilling to be parted from his dam under any circumstances, traced close behind without benefit of halter or lead.

The youth rode with his right leg hooked lazily around the saddle horn. He sat hunched down in such a way that one would have thought him asleep from a distance. While he traveled, the young horseman blew tunelessly on a small, shrill, tin harmonica. The instrument was a new acquisition, secured in a trade with a school friend for a pocketknife with a broken spring. The boy struggled to teach himself to play the device, and though the resulting cacophony set all creation on edge, the young rider's enthusiasm prevailed.

The boy's saddle and rig were set up to work livestock. An aged, double-barreled coach gun hung in a scabbard under his lariat. His bedroll and saddlebags were tied behind the cantle of a well-seasoned Mexican buckhorn saddle. Like many of the ranch-raised youth of the Salinas valley, the boy had taken a summer job, working cattle for ranchers in the Big Sur. It was hazardous work for man and horse, but boys his age were made of rubber and loved the adventure of being away from home.

Unlike the gentle rolling pastures west of the Gabilans, the ranches of the Big Sur were mountain and sea bound. Every cattle drive was alternately either an exhausting, uphill clamber or a dangerous descent.

Some grazing sections ended precipitously, with long drops to the rocks and waves many feet below the cliffs. If a steer was spooked by an overzealous wrangler at the wrong moment, it often became food for crabs and gulls. The errant cowhand would then return humiliated among his fellows as a "Dutchman's curse," a stamp difficult to amend and impossible to evade.

Though his mount was rigged for working cattle, the boy was not, at least not in the traditional sense. He wore a tweed, slouch-brimmed hat, a brown corduroy jacket with leather patches at the elbows, tan corduroy pants, and low-heeled English riding boots that only covered the ankles. In short, he looked more like an itinerant Irish poet than a cowhand, but that was his kit of choice, and God help any plug-ugly who sniggered at it.

Suddenly the mare caught wind of something dangerous. Her head came up, her eyes widened in fear, and her nostrils flared with rushes of hot vapor. She stopped for a moment, tensed her muscles for flight, pawed the ground in an agitated manner, and then whinnied a shriek of distress to her colt. The boy, harmonica still clenched in his teeth, drew snug on the reins to maintain control and looked about for the source of danger. He trusted the mare's instincts more than his own.

The colt bucked and kicked up its heels in mock defense but stayed close at hand, depending on its dam to signal the next move. The boy, still biting the harmonica, reached for the old shotgun but did not pull it from the scabbard. The young wrangler scrutinized the hillside and trees for a big cat. Then he looked up to the rock escarpment high above and froze. There he saw the immense head and shoulders of the beast. The coal-dark eyes gazed down on the boy with a look so ancient, so fearsome and sad, that the boy stopped breathing. His heart pounded and his sinews seized in fear. He knew at once he was looking into the face of a prehistoric and wrathful god.

Time and space began to swell like a bubble until they encompassed everything the boy had ever known. Small bursts of insight evolved, matured, and then were gone. The boy watched in amazement, expecting at any moment to have the huge animal transform itself into Zeus or a flock of butcher-eyed ravens or maybe even an Indian wizard. But nothing happened. The creature did not move, did not threaten with gesture or sound.

The boy's attention returned to the increased agitation of his mare. She was not about to countenance the present danger to herself or her colt. The mare whinnied, rolled her eyes, and tossed her head. Her intolerance and fear grew more pronounced by the moment. Yet the mammoth creature never moved a muscle or showed a claw. It simply gazed down at the boy's predicament with complete indifference. An aura of weary apathy was enhanced by a cavernous yawn and half-closed eyes.

Now aware of the sounds his excited breath made through the reeds of the little mouth harp, the boy removed the instrument but never took his eyes from the beast above.

The boy had read accounts of Indian holy men who altered form to accomplish their magic, like Merlin casting spells over the eyes of credible men. These images, resurrected from childhood daydreams, did little to quell the boy's anxiety. He could almost feel the hair rise on the back of his neck.

As if to validate the boy's mystical speculations, the shaggy mountain slowly rose to stand on its hind legs. The image appeared to grow more massive every moment. All dimensions expanded until its upright carriage blotted out the morning sun and cast a broad shadow across the trail.

This was sufficient to provoke the mare, and she immediately took charge of a strategic withdrawal. She reared on her hind legs, whinnied a piercing alarm to her offspring, and bolted headlong down the trail at a gallop. To the boy's amazement, the colt kept abreast of the race, taking the flats almost neck and neck with the mare.

It required a half mile of dangerous riding for the boy to recover any semblance of control over his mount. It was another quarter mile before the mare stopped prancing and snorting at every little sound and movement. The strain and exertion of their recent ordeal rendered horse and rider well lathered with fear and fatigue. Only the foal, carrying no burden, seemed willing to continue the contest, though after a sharp nip from the mare it obediently shadowed her once more.

★   ★   ★

THE WORKING HEART OF THE POST RANCH LAY in a protected
basin between the high cliffs of the ocean to the west and the
broad, stony mountains to the east. It was about noon when
the boy at last spotted his destination. From a distance he
could see the large barn with its corrals, outbuildings, and apple sheds.

A dozen riders were gathered about the corrals adjusting
their tack in preparation for an afternoon of hard wrangling.
Some were permanent hands or neighbors from the local
ranches, but others were Monterey or Salinas boys like himself.
They too had made the long ride from home in order to work
the ranches of the Big Sur during their summer vacations.

It was hard work, but it promised good money for hands
that knew which end of a horse gets the bit. Ready cash was
always a reliable incentive for young men in need of the where-
withal to help finance their educations or families or marital
ambitions.

When the young man finally rode up he was greeted by
name. Most everyone present knew him, liked him well enough,
understood his habits and skills, but thought him a trifle preoccupied with worlds of his own invention. He habitually carried books in his saddlebags instead of food and was easily
lured into reading on the trail while his horse plodded on.

The sarcastic and diminutive Lupito Morales, a Salinas pal,
shouted out from the open hayloft, "Where you been keeping
yourself, John? We expected you last night. You missed another famous Post breakfast. Grilled venison, baked apples with
honey, and lots of eggs."

John's school pal Billy Witt piped in with an embarrassing

question. "What have you done with that mare? She looks like Uncle Pepe's mule after ten acres on a hot day. What did you bring her colt for, food?"

Benny Ramirez laughed and winked. "Perhaps some pretty señorita gave John a cool drink and soft eyes and he could not drag himself away."

Lupito piped out from the loft, "Then he remembered us, in a weaker moment, of course, and rode like hell to be at our sides." The ranch hands within earshot began to chuckle. John blushed with boyish mortification and dismounted. He loosened his saddle cinch and led the mare and foal to the water trough.

The Old Man himself, Joe Post, came out of the barn leading his big sorrel. When he saw the tardy arrival, he handed the halter to Ramon Castro with instructions to saddle the brute "before sunset." He then walked over to John and began to chide him for keeping bankers' hours. John blushed again, but he met the old Indian's eyes with a certainty of purpose.

"Where you been, John? You know damn well we begin work around here at sunup. You've already missed the morning sweep. Now listen, son, it's going to be a short season because of the rains, and I can't spare even one man, not even a daydreaming book hound like you. How's your mother and father getting on, by the way? God love 'em. Is Olive still working up a storm? Probably damn happy to see the tail of your horse leave the paddock for a while. Speaking of horses, you better tack your saddle to the buckskin in the last stall. Your mount looks pretty well spent. What happened?"

Old Joe Post was not prepared for the look in John's eyes when he turned to speak. It was as if his eyes had aged years beyond the rest of the boy. John looked directly at Mr. Post, but the old man got the definite impression that John was looking through him to some distant vision. At first John seemed reluctant to speak, but he squared his shoulders, prepared to receive the impact of disbelief.

"I saw a bear," John said slowly. "The biggest bear the Almighty ever created! Bigger than any grizzly I've ever heard of. Bigger than anything I've seen in books. It was resting on that great flat rock just south of the springs where the trail comes close to the cliffs. I swear that bear was big enough to take down a horse and rider with one stroke, but it didn't. Just stared down at me like Saint Peter. Then it reared up on its hind legs, as big as a barn. I almost soiled my pants, by God. The mare spooked like a scalded cat. Can't say I blame her much with the colt in tow. I swear she almost flew. It was all I could do to bring her in check before she took a header and killed us both."

Joe W. Post looked at John hard and long and then looked at his mare. A broad grin broke across his wise old face and he laughed. "Pig's feathers! Son, there haven't been bears like that in these parts since my father was a boy, all killed off years ago. My grandfather said one of those monsters could pick up a whole steer and walk off with it still kicking. You couldn't have seen a Great Sur Bear, John. They're all dead, son; take my word for it. You've been daydreaming again. Now you go saddle up that buckskin like I told you. You're holding up the parade." Ramon Castro brought up Joe Post's saddled horse and the old Indian mounted, calling his schoolboys, wranglers, and vaqueros to follow his example.

John took no offense from Mr. Post's words. He knew what he had seen, of that there was no doubt, but he wasn't about to make himself look ridiculous by arguing the point with a respected Sur veteran like Mr. J. W. Post. John took the mare's reins and started toward the barn to do as he'd been told. The colt happily followed.

John heard Joe Post call after him. "This is going to be a tough season, John. If you don't cut down on the woolgathering and keep your mind on your job, those pretty Salinas girls will find you with empty pockets come the fall term." John nodded politely and led his mare into the barn.

No one enjoys being called a liar, not in so many words, and John relished the stamp less than most. He also knew the futility of heated debates with experts. Cattle, water, and fresh grass would certainly take precedence over John's illusory bear. In any event the whole incident was soon forgotten. Forgotten by everyone, that is, except John.

Without making it obvious, he was determined to find some evidence of his doubted discovery before the season was out. To that end, he even purchased some plaster of Paris from a local blacksmith to make castings of the bear's prints, should he be lucky enough to pick up the bear's trail again. He was most careful not to divulge the plaster's intended purpose, wanting to avoid any further homespun ridicule.

The phantom bear had become John's secret "questing beast." Like King Pelinor and his dragon, John was determined to find proof of his own fabled beast. Unfortunately, there had been intermittent rains that washed the game trails clean every few days. He was also burdened with having to work remote sections of land that were far from his last sighting of the bear. This led John to initiate clandestine forays away from work. Despite his supposed secrecy, these sojourns hardly went unnoticed by Joe Post or the other hands.

Though little was said at the time, John found the point

well taken every payday when he discovered his salary docked for this or that. But with his honor at stake he thought the sacrifice worth the expenditure. The discovery and exhibition of the truth possessed a potential glory beyond the value of money. John believed exoneration was a feast best enjoyed by the light of another's blushing embarrassment.

To John's way of thinking, the search for the great bear had become as unique and important as Arthur's Grail. Consequently, he redoubled his efforts by riding out on long evening searches. His dedication, however, to the romantic vision of his own vindication almost cost him his horse and his life one night.

While following a steep game trail north of the ranch, John's mare lost her footing, and both horse and rider tumbled down a rocky embankment. The rider was bruised, bent, and embarrassed; but his mare was cut up, and for that he felt truly guilty and ashamed. The penalty for his error involved a painful extrication for horse and rider to regain the trail and then a long, slow walk leading the injured mare.

John then had to face mocking rebukes. Leading home an injured mount indicated carelessness in the extreme. Callow cowhands were a dime a bushel, but good horses were worth more than hard money in this country. The fact that the mare belonged to John didn't count for much since it meant he'd now have to use one of the ranch mounts for the duration of the job. His own mare would be unfit for the trail for some weeks.

This incident curtailed John's nocturnal quests for a while, but not permanently. He was always secretly on the lookout for his quarry. Every day he carried his casting plaster, tin mug, and extra canteen in the hope of finding just one mighty paw print to verify his account to Mr. Post and the other skeptics.

★   ★   ★

AT THE END OF THE SEASON the inevitable happened. John found his wages docked into nonexistence, with never a sign of his mythical bear to show for it. First he had to reimburse the Posts for the care of his horse. The farrier was called in lieu of a veterinarian, but that wasn't cheap either. The resultant diagnosis and treatment meant two things. One, John's mare and her colt could not possibly travel back to Salinas for weeks, with all that implied in care, board, and feed. And two, John was broke. He couldn't even afford the stage fare back to Salinas. Old Joe Post had been right. Those pretty Salinas girls would find John with empty pockets come the fall term.

The Posts had a broad reputation as a hospitable and compassionate clan, given to forbearance where youth and folly were concerned. John's antics were barely a passing diversion to people who had seen just about every kind of addlepated eccentric who ever mounted a horse.

On the last day of work the Posts laid out a lavish farewell feed as a token of gratitude for the hired and volunteer labor. It was a traditional Post roundup fiesta. Mrs. Post engineered an enormous feast of roasted wild boar and vegetables, baked pigeons in currants and cream, abalone steaks grilled with green onion and chiles. Other local delights included wild mountain honey cakes and quarts of pickled quails' eggs, acquired in a trade with the enigmatic Sing Fat. Everything looked truly marvelous; everything except John's immediate future.

After a dessert of hot apple pie with thick ginger cream, Mrs. Post approached John and handed him a small, brown envelope accompanied by a pat on the cheek. She said the Ranch hoped to see him again next season. The little manila packet contained four dollars, exactly the price of the stage fare back to Monterey. From there he was on his own. Mrs. Post knew John would jump a local freight to Salinas like the rest of the boys. He would find his way home in good order, and that was all that really mattered. Next year, she hoped out loud, John would keep his mind on his job.

UNHAPPILY, JOHN RETURNED HOME without ever collecting the least evidence of his bear. But that was just as well as far as he was concerned. The less said about the incident the better. He was already tied up in knots trying to think of a way to explain to his folks what happened to his mare. To reveal more than was absolutely necessary would only cause him further embarrassment. The stage ride to Monterey gave him plenty of time to think about the numerous distressing alternatives to the truth.

But John never forgot his Great Sur Bear, the mountain wizard, the God of generations. For John, if for no other living human, the immortal beast was as alive and real as he was, and that was all that really mattered.

When he got home, John was faced with the immediate problem of scraping together four dollars to repay Mrs. Post's generosity. It was imperative that he unburden himself of that obligation as soon as possible to regain his sense of honor, if not pride. Two of the dollars he pulled from his tin strongbox, which was hidden behind a loose board in his closet, but the last two greenbacks he had to borrow from his father. Happily his father asked no questions, but he required the two dollars be paid back by the end of the month.

John went to the Bank of Salinas early the next day to have

a check drawn up. He knew hard cash would never arrive at its destination. He wrote a short letter to accompany the funds and tried to make it sound as mature and businesslike as possible to cover his youthful chagrin.

John's letter was addressed to Mrs. J. W. Post, Big Sur, California, and dated August 12, 1920. It began, "Esteemed Madame, Enclosed find check for stage fare from Post Ranch to Monterey. Distance thirty-eight miles. Rate ten cents a mile. Total four dollars. Hoping that I have not inconvenienced you by my delay." It closed, "I beg, my friend, to be allowed to remain, yours very respectfully, J. E. Steinbeck Jr. P.S. Kindly forward a receipt." The return address indicated was 130 Central Avenue, Salinas, California. John kept that receipt for years to remind him of his bear and the expense incurred by magic visions.

Blind Luck

~~~

An outsider would have said that young Chapel Lodge was truly a creature fashioned by the hand of the Almighty for the purpose of testing the human bounds of endurable loneliness. His father was a traveling man who was always on the shy side of making a decent living for his family. His mother doubled in brass when it came to sharing her husband's borderline schemes for success. As a result, she rarely had time for her only child, whom she considered an impediment to her future prosperity.

The poor child's family had lived under so many roofs, in so many towns, that the boy was ignorant of the meaning of the word "home." Since a real home was the one thing he could not have, it became the one thing he longed for most, even if a tangible intuitive definition eluded him.

As a young boy Chapel spent most of his time desperately

alone. Every so many weeks or months he would be hauled up by his pants loop, loaded with the shabby baggage into the back of a dusty buckboard, and invariably plunged into curious and even more peculiar domestic arrangements. The experience always left him feeling remote from the world and very helpless. His formal education was spotty at best, thanks to his parents, and in later years he would laugh and count himself lucky to be able to read and write with any skill whatsoever. Chapel's enforced solitude in a long register of "cheap and cheaper" boardinghouses presented scant diversions. The most readily available distractions were the page-worn periodicals and lurid dime novels left behind by departing boarders.

In a world in which the fates and their mercurial favors move with the subtle regularity of the tides, it would follow that even Chapel should have secured his share of good fortune at some time, but such was not the case. In fact, Chapel's whole life was an atlas of "from bad to worse." Good fortune was not to be had at any price or from any quarter, so he stopped expecting it.

When he was only fourteen, Chapel's indifferent parents deposited their youthful "dilemma" with a brutish old skinflint of an uncle who lived near Fresno. His father had puffed up, thumbed his glaring suspenders like a ward heeler, and exclaimed that he had made important business connections back East that needed addressing, or so he said, and that a train trip to Kansas City was an imperative move toward success in these matters. Chapel's parents casually assured their son that they would return by spring, wreathed in greenbacks and robed with dazzling prospects. Meanwhile, "Hey you! Boy!"—which Chapel once mistook for his own first name—

was to obey his uncle in all things and make himself useful for once.

After secretly reappropriating the $125 they had settled on the old man to care for the boy, Mr. and Mrs. Lodge boarded an eastbound train and disappeared over the horizon. They never returned. They never even sent so much as a note of explanation. They just vanished, leaving not the least trace of their existence save a gaggle of angry creditors and a veritable turnpike of unpaid bills. No one ever saw or heard from the Lodges again. The rabid old uncle didn't seem unduly surprised by the deceitful nature of his brother's desertion, though he happily took every opportunity to denounce the theft of the money due him. As far as the old panther was concerned, the most damnable, unrepentant scoundrels were usually found close to home, or in it. Chapel's parents and their chicanery remained a thorn under the old man's blanket, and he refused to abide the outrage gracefully. But he would get his money's worth, even if he had to take it out of the boy's hide for the going price of a strong cottonwood switch.

Chapel's very existence, already a portrait of sad neglect, soon became a standing irritation to the old man. He obviously took no joy in the responsibility and reminded the boy of his indignation with every oath he swore. The old bully had eventually taken to smacking the boy around until Chapel had learned to dodge the blows. After that, the brutality became verbal, but no less painful for all that. Chapel began to spend as much time away from his uncle's house as feasible, and that seemed to accommodate everybody's interests.

Unsupervised, floundering, and broke, Chapel launched himself into various categories of willful mischief, but as was to be expected, his dismal attempts at novice criminality were habitually doomed to exposure and punishment. It required a considerable amount of good fortune to be a marginally successful criminal and, of course, Chapel Lodge had no such luck and everyone knew it.

There came a time when Chapel discovered that he had burned a few too many bridges on his old stomping grounds, and he quickly decided to test pastures farther north. San Francisco might offer the silver-lined pockets and the requisite anonymity necessary to a petty thief. Having spent most of his youth in agrarian settings like Santa Maria, Paso Robles, and Stockton, Chapel had an itch to see how the big city eagles lived. Life with the sparrows held no further appeal. He'd been a sparrow all his life, and he hated it. Perhaps San Francisco would also prove less precarious to his liberty. He had already done plenty of time for vagrancy and petty theft, and he didn't look forward to repeating that experience. He was sixteen and ready to strike out alone, for alone was all he knew. He somehow felt he could handle any eventuality if just left to his own devices. How he supported this cheerful illusion of his future success remained a mystery even to him.

So one day, at approximately three in the morning on the edge of town, Chapel Lodge lay hidden near a railroad siding on which a slow, northbound freight wheezed patiently. It was waiting for the fast night express to pass before pulling back out on the main line. Chapel watched the fireman make his inspection of the cars to roust out bindle stiffs from the support rods under the cars. When the commotion had moved on down the tracks, and just before the freight pulled out, Chapel crept out from the underbrush and dashed for a tarpaulin-covered flatcar loaded with heavy machinery. He vaulted aboard and ducked under the stiff, oil-stained canvas. There he made a nest for himself between the crates. Using his packed bedroll as a pillow, Chapel lay back and went to sleep. Lulled by the slow and steady counterpoint of the rails' joints, he rested peacefully for hours.

Visions of fast times and easy living spun through Chapel's dreams like dust devils in dry fields. He awoke to the jolting switches in a shunting yard on the outskirts of San Jose. Barely managing to evade watchful firemen and railroad cops, Chapel at last located and jumped aboard the market train for San Francisco. This time he was forced to sling-ride the truss rods under a freight car filled with iced fish. This mode of travel proved uncomfortable, odorous, and dangerous in the extreme for a newcomer to the sport.

Chapel at last achieved his destination and was wonderfully impressed with the size and power of it all. San Francisco was certainly a treat to behold for a boy with dreams. He had never seen anything like it. Beautiful houses graced the hills; the bay boasted a forest of ships' masts, and scores of steamers moved in and out of the narrows. But the best thing, to Chapel's way of thinking, was the complete absence of plowed fields and dusty farmers. However, any illusions he might have harbored about sharping the slickers were soon painfully dispelled.

Young Chapel Lodge was spotted as a raw rube the first moment he surfaced on the waterfront. Two black eyes and a broken hand soon led Chapel to see the errors of blind supposition. So he pondered his predicament and decided that a more forthright means of making a living might just forestall his taking up residence in a pine box in the near future.

The boy needed work and the docks always needed labor,

so Chapel gravitated toward the rugged haunts of stevedores and teamsters. After two days of futile searching and sleeping rough, Chapel fell in with a shifty-eyed bosun's mate named Baily Pryot.

They discovered each other in a dockside rum-dive so disreputable the owner had dispensed with giving it a name. Pryot took Chapel's measure and offered to share his bottle of smuggled Russian vodka. Chapel had never tasted vodka before. He found it reminiscent of tar solvent and so was only mildly surprised that he remembered next to nothing when he awoke many hours later.

Even before he opened his eyes, Chapel Lodge knew he was in a bad way, perhaps dying, maybe worse. He'd never felt so sick.

His body floated left and forward, then right and back. Nausea and profound discomfort greeted every movement. Eventually the fetid pungency and constant throbbing vibration of his surroundings made him wish he were dead. His half-realized world smelled like an oil-slicked harbor at low tide, but somehow far worse by virtue of the odor's clinging proximity.

When Chapel at last opened his crusty eyes he saw very little. He lay on a shabby, thin mattress that smelled of cheap hair grease and aged sweat, and his body continued to move in a most distressing fashion. He tried to sit up, but hit his head on a low metal beam and cried out in pain and anger. A strange voice called out of the gloom. "If your name's Lodge, you'll be wanted on watch at the boilers in ten minutes. . . . I wouldn't miss another watch-call, if I were you, son. Captain Billy Ortega is a thoroughgoing son of a bitch when it comes to strict ship's orders. By the way, welcome aboard, for all it matters to the gulls. There's java in the mess for the weak of heart." With a rude clang of a closed hatch the voice was gone.

It took a while for Chapel Lodge to piece together the events leading to his employment shoveling coal into the boilers of a grain ship bound for Alaska. When at last he located Baily Pryot drinking coffee in the galley, Chapel was ready to eat the man's liver raw. The bosun saw him coming, smiled, and raised his cup in salute.

Weasel-eyed Pryot, amused to the point of coarse laughter, informed young Mr. Lodge that the whole affair had been his own idea. Chapel had even insisted on waking the purser to sign ship's articles at four o'clock in the morning. If there was anybody to blame for his present difficulty, Chapel need only seek out his own wasted reflection in a mirror and rebuke that image instead of his friend.

Pryot swore on his mother's grave that he had tried to dissuade Lodge from such a rash course, but that Chapel had insisted on having his own way at every turn. What was an honest seaman to do? The ship needed a stoker, and Chapel seemingly leapt at the opportunity. "Case closed, mate, signed and fair. Legal under U.S. Maritime law, by God," declared Bosun's Mate Pryot with total conviction.

That was the end of all official discussion on the matter. Chapel soon came to learn that ship's rules and captain's prerogatives were holy writ and should be obeyed above the laws of heaven. Villainous conduct of any description, negligence of duty, or disrespect to officers, carried a variety of very un-attractive penalties far more severe than one would expect on dry land for similar offenses.

Authority was rigid, work was hard, and the days seemed

never ending. This volatile mix of strange and aggressive elements did not bode favorably for Chapel's future in the merchant marine. If prior traditions were to be taken as an indication of probabilities, there was every likelihood that Chapel would visit Alaska in chains and presumably remain there under harsh detention for some years to come.

Many strange and wonderful curiosities abound in this world, and the conversion of Chapel Lodge was not the least of these. One might not be able to put a finger upon the direct cause, but the binding effects of responsibility and discipline upon the boy were remarkable given the context of Chapel's predilections. In fact, Chapel Lodge came to love his life at sea. He soon found he needed and respected this tribe of hard men who patterned and protected his floating world more than he needed life ashore. He slowly discovered pride and purpose in his work because others depended for their lives upon his attention to detail and duty. Being needed and trusted was a novel sensation for young Chapel, and he began to look forward to even the hardest watches to prove himself worthy of that warming confidence.

Chapel began taking a sincere interest in his ship and its workings. Eventually, the stoker's mate and bunker boss commended Chapel to the chief engineer for his spirited attention to duty, a unique quality in a semishanghaied landsman. That simple commendation pleased Chapel more than a mother's kiss, and he worked even harder to garner favorable recognition from his mates and officers. By the time he sailed back into San Francisco Bay five months later, he would not have been recognized in form or fashion by his closest friend—if he'd had one to care either way.

By the time Chapel had spent ten months aboard, he had

been rated an able seaman and received appropriate pay and papers, a truly remarkable accomplishment for a green hand. He had worked hard and wholeheartedly set himself to learn to hand, reef, and steer to achieve that rating. But his first love would always be the great engines and boilers that dwelt in the deepest vaults of his ship. Chapel was fascinated by the scale of power they represented, and the thought of being master of those dynamic forces lured him to study everything he could about those powerful machines.

During the next eight years, Chapel Lodge sailed aboard five good ships and experienced several long, hard passages, but his favorite voyages were always merchant cruises along the coast of California. It was wonderful and strange to see one's homeland from the ocean. The shores defined the edge of everything safe and familiar, yet he never spent any time visiting old haunts. Chapel was more than satisfied with his new home at sea.

He often deliberated upon his life prior to going before the mast as it were, and Chapel had formed the nagging suspicion that perhaps he was just unlucky on land. He'd often heard sailors' gossip reflecting all manner of fo'c'sle myths and superstitions, but the general thread of most tales held that grievous things happened to seamen who went ashore for any long span of liberty, and Chapel was more than willing to accept that axiom on faith.

It was therefore very disconcerting when Chapel found himself beached in San Pedro. Able Seaman Lodge had lost his berth, his home, and his friends. His ship, the steam schooner *Orion*, required new boilers and shafts and would be out of commission for three months at the very least. The thought of being trapped on shore made Chapel extremely anxious. He felt sadly out of place without his ship and messmates and strangely at odds without ship's work to occupy his time. So on his second day ashore Chapel went right out to find a berth on another vessel.

A week went by without success. There were more seamen on the beach than ship's berths out of San Pedro. Chapel had every reason to worry. Many of the men he met at the hiring halls held greater seniority or more practiced skills than he. It looked as though he would have to go begging for a ship, and even that might take weeks of waiting, maybe months of cheap harbor boardinghouses and idle hours waiting for a shorthanded ship to make port.

Chapel made the rounds of every tavern and saloon frequented by ship's officers. Perhaps he would run across someone who could help him find a berth before he ran out of money or sanity. Then one day, while making his futile tour of waterfront dives, Chapel spied a leathered face he knew only too well. It was Bosun's Mate Baily Pryot, and he was deep in conversation with a spotty-faced chandler's apprentice. When Pryot caught sight of Chapel he waved him over and greeted him with sentiments that would have made it seem that they had parted only the day before, when in fact, it had been years since their last meeting. Pryot slapped Chapel on the back and insisted they share a bottle at Galba's Cantina just up the road from the harbor.

Chapel cheerfully accepted the invitation. He hadn't seen a familiar face since he'd been beached, and he longed to pour out his troubles to a comrade of the decks. At first they shared past voyages and ports, but after a couple of glasses of Señora Galba's homemade rat poison, they moved on to present scuttlebutt and rumor, always the seaman's favorite discourse and pleasure. At last Chapel disclosed his sad predicament in terms even Pryot could understand.

"You've got to help me, Baily," Chapel said, "I'm going crazy on the beach. If I don't find a berth soon, God knows what will happen. Probably just get myself in a heap of trouble again. I'm no damn use on land. It's just not lucky for me. If I'd known this when I was a kid, I would have jumped aboard the first ship that came within swimming distance. I've been up and down these docks for days and can't find a berth on a garbage scow. You've always got your finger in the wind, Baily. Tell me what to do or who to see. I'll crew a ship to hell if it will get me off the beach and away from San Pedro. What do you say, mate? Can you do anything for me?"

Baily Pryot swallowed hard and pondered his young friend for a few long moments. After thinking it over he shook his head and pursed his lips in the negative. "I'm sorry, son. I can't think of a thing at the moment. I'm bosun's mate of Pacific Mail's *Columbia*, and I know for a fact we've got more hands than we need. But she's a great little ship for a fact. Brand new. Laid down in Pennsylvania according to her commission plaque. She's fast and sea-kindly, the best of everything and a good feeder. I wish I could get you aboard, old son. You'd like her. And you should see her engine room. Not a fleck of rust; you could eat off the oiler's deck, she's so clean. Just to see her makes you want to move right in and set up housekeeping. Captain Barr sees she's kept as bright as a penny, he's that proud of her."

Suddenly realizing that he was almost gloating over his own good fortune when poor Chapel was in chains against a lee shore, Pryot decided to shut up and drink.

There was a long pause in which neither man knew quite

what to say. Then suddenly Pryot brightened, smiled, and slapped the table. "But wait! Damn me for a tinker, I should have thought of this before. I might just have a barque up my sleeve after all. We crossed wakes with the *Los Angeles* coming out of Newport Beach first dogwatch, Monday evening. We make far better time, you see; that's why we carry the mail," he said proudly. "Anyway, she should be berthing sometime around midnight, and I know the third officer real well. His name is Roger Ryfkogel—strange duck, but a good officer. He owes me a favor or two from the old days. Now, Captain Leland is the devil's own taskmaster by reputation, but fair by all accounts. He works as hard as any man on his crew, and they regard him well for it." The bosun's mate poured out more wine. "I couldn't wish you a better berth, come to think of it. Captain Leland won't abide scrubs or bilge runts, so you'll always find a pretty decent bunch of hands on his decks. He demands a sharp galley too, since the bridge messes on crew's rations. You'd take to the *Los Angeles*; she's a steady ship, like I say, and she pays wages on the spar deck every fourth Sunday like clockwork. That's better than most tubs you can name."

Pryot watched as Chapel's expression turned from one of sad despair to a grin of remarkable proportions. He almost looked boyish in bright expectation. "That's the ticket, Mr. Pryot, you steadfast old jack staff. What a joy you are to see. Shall I go aboard when she docks, or wait till they set first deck watch?"

"I'd do it first thing. You're not the only blue devil stuck on the beach, you know. There'd be good hands salivating at the breakwater if word took hold. These be lean times for poor sea beggars like us. Now listen, the *Columbia* leaves on the morning tide, middle watch. If the *Los Angeles* berths before we sail, I'll go with you and grease the way. If not, I'll write you a note for Mr. Ryfkogel with my compliments and brassbound recommendations. He'll recall that blond music teacher in Oakland I saved him from. That should do the trick. I'd tell you about it, but that wouldn't be on the square. Ryfkogel is a good egg and a Mason like my old man. Bless his bones."

Pryot moved to refill Chapel's glass by way of celebrating a possible solution to his friend's dilemma, but Chapel put his hand over the glass and smiled. "It wouldn't go down well to report to the deck with a load hoisted. Why don't I trade out for the best supper in the house to show my appreciation. I'll even send the bar boy out for cigars later. What do you say?"

Señora Galba took Chapel's money and laid on a remarkable variety of food for the price. The two sailors gorged themselves for hours. Every time a plate was cleaned, it was replaced with another until they could take no more. After their dinner, Chapel and Pryot retired to Señora Galba's little whitewashed veranda overlooking the harbor. From their vantage point on the hill they could see everything that came and went in the maze of docks and piers below. The bar boy brought their cigars and great steaming mugs of coffee laced with sweet, dark rum. The two sailors propped up their feet and enjoyed the shank of the evening in idle gossip and tall tales that passed for fact.

Below in the harbor there was still a great deal of activity. While some ships slept at their moorings, others were alive with bustle and enterprise. Cargo and supplies, mail and passengers came and went under the flickering lights. Their reflection in the water gave the scene a festive air.

It was just about eleven-thirty when Pryot nudged Chapel and pointed with his cigar to the entrance of the harbor. "There she is now. Hard to see, but I know her stacks, lights, and lines. That's the *Los Angeles* all right. She should be berthed across from the coaling wharf in forty minutes or so—plenty of time to finish here and walk down to the docks. What do you say to another mug of this grand Mexican coffee? I swear this stuff could prop up a corpse for bridge watch."

Chapel and Pryot were standing by the wharf in time to see the *Los Angeles* secure her warps and spring lines. She dropped her plank, and a disheveled knot of tired passengers disembarked. Chapel followed Pryot up the gangway when all was clear. He told Chapel to keep silent and let him do all the talking. When they boarded, Pryot asked the officer of the deck to direct him to the third officer, Mr. Ryfkogel. He said he was there on ship's business. The officer told Pryot to wait while a hand was sent to report their presence on board. When he appeared on deck, Mr. Ryfkogel recognized Pryot at once and waved him forward. Pryot told Chapel to stay put and say nothing. Chapel watched expectantly as Ryfkogel led Pryot into the purser's cabin. He tried to pretend that he wasn't apprehensive about the interview, but it didn't work. So as not to fidget he began to pace under the watchful eyes of the deck officer. When Pryot emerged ten minutes later, Chapel was almost biting his thumbs.

The bosun approached with a big grin on his weathered face. "You're in luck, son, though it goes hard for the poor bastard you're replacing. The engineer's mate smashed up both his ankles in an accident. A deck hatch slammed down on his pins before he was clear. Mr. Ryfkogel says that if the chief engineer passes on your ticket, you can sign on with the purser first thing in the morning. Do you have your ticket on you? Well, never mind; you can wave it at the purser when you report aboard. The chief engineer's name is Mr. Gladis. You had better go below before he turns in for the night."

This time it was Pryot's turn to wait on deck. He passed the while trading lies with a chief petty officer of the Revenue Service, who punctuated his colorless fables by spitting tobacco juice into the bay. Pryot could muster only marginal interest. It was time he should think of rejoining his own ship. He could see her loading coal across the way. When done, she would depart on the morning tide.

MR. GLADIS WAS A JOVIAL, RUBICUND OFFICER with a propensity for weaving bad puns into the conversation, but he was a thorough examiner for all that. Chapel could see by the condition of the engine room that Mr. Gladis was a stickler for order and Dutch polish. Chapel waited pensively for the chief engineer to make a decision, but Mr. Gladis seemed in no hurry to make up his mind.

It was half-past midnight when Chapel reappeared on deck. He wore a broad grin. Pryot slapped him on the back, laughed, and led him down the gangway arm in arm. He suggested they find a hot rum to celebrate. Chapel was amenable, so off they went.

As they walked up the dock, Chapel laughed to himself. "You know, Baily, I thought tomorrow would be a special day for me."

"Why, mate? What's so special about April nineteenth other than it's still 1894?"

Chapel looked a little shy about his answer. "It's my . . .

That is . . . I mean, April nineteenth is . . . it's my birthday. I never really celebrated my birthday before, because nothing decent ever happened to me on my birthday. But thanks to you, Baily, I have something to rejoice in. The mug is on me, sir. It's the least I can do for a man who pulled my keel off the mudflats."

Chapel was as good as his word. He walked Pryot back to his ship in time for sailing. He stood and waved farewell as the *Columbia* shipped her hawsers and floated free from the pier. Pryot waved back and then went below to his duty station.

Chapel, excited and with little need of sleep, walked back to his shabby boardinghouse to pack his gear and secure his papers. Like most sailors, Chapel had been expected to pay every week in advance for his lodgings, such as they were. He would sail with two days owed to him. He left his landlady a note with a reminder to that effect and his thanks, and said he looked forward to his return. Of course, the last thing he ever wanted to do was to stay in a boardinghouse again, but he thought it politic to leave behind a good impression just in case, God forbid, her services were ever called for again. With his accounts cleared, Chapel threw his worn seabag over his shoulder and made his way back to his new ship, his new home, through dawn's mist-shrouded glow.

Relieved and happy, he whistled little snatches of songs as he walked along. San Pedro, like most big ports, stayed awake and attended to business at all hours. Ship chandlers, victualers, rope yards, coal merchants, saloons, brothels, and jails all kept the same schedules. Chapel watched as bumboats and hoys plied their way back and forth to the vessels moored in the roadstead.

Chapel reported to the purser of the *Los Angeles* as soon as he came aboard. He showed the officer his seaman's papers and told him that he had already been approved by the chief engineer the previous evening. The purser disappeared for a moment to confirm Chapel's statements and then returned with the ship's register.

Chapel signed the book, was allocated a berth and told to report to Mr. Gladis as soon as possible after stowing his kit. The ship was due for departure as soon as the last of the cargo and passengers came aboard. Chapel would be needed at once.

After securing his gear, Chapel reported to Mr. Gladis and was put to work immediately back-flushing the boiler's lines. He also helped the stokers rake down the ash boxes and feed the boiler fires. It took only forty-five minutes to bring the steam gauges back to full working pressure and ready for sea. All was in order for departure as soon as the bridge telegraph signaled orders.

Mr. Gladis was an amiable enough officer as long as every detail of an assignment was accomplished to his satisfaction. But one of the stokers warned Chapel that Mr. Gladis could easily turn and rattle if his orders weren't attended to with instant dispatch. This didn't particularly disturb Chapel. He was a solid hand and attentive to his duty. No officer had ever found him wanting in diligence, so it was no surprise that Chapel got on well with Mr. Gladis.

He found the spirited chief engineer both gregarious and sharp-tongued in a fashion only the Irish could balance with grace. A good-humored man in the main, Mr. Gladis appeared more than willing to help an earnest seaman master new skills, but only if he thought the pupil worth a tinker's damn.

The *Los Angeles* was steaming out of harbor by seven-thirty in the morning watch. The bell sounded the beginning of the forenoon at eight while Chapel stood noting down steam pressure, condenser temperature, shaft revolutions, and the like. He wrote down the appropriate numbers in their respective columns on the engine-room log and noted the time of each reading. This was normally done every half hour of the watch. If the ship was maneuvering in contrary seas, restrictive channels, or in an emergency situation where the engine's speed and direction were of constant importance, then the readings and times would be logged more frequently. The Pacific Steamship Company took pride in demanding detailed logs from her ship's captains. In turn, Captain Leland demanded the same from his bridge, engineering, and cargo officers.

Mr. Gladis was in the midst of explaining that the condenser-coil temperature gauges were only marginally reliable and that allowances of ten to fifteen degrees would be required on certain occasions when the watch bell rang out. Chapel made no move to leave his station, but continued to listen attentively to Mr. Gladis' explanations. Chapel had no intention of leaving his post until the chief engineer dismissed him, regardless of the watch bell.

Mr. Gladis well appreciated the reality 'tween the decks. All seamen, merchant hands especially, were constantly in want of decent rations and sleep. They rarely volunteered to surrender the opportunity to acquire either unless a threatening ship's emergency called them to their duty. Chapel's reluctance to leave the engine room without proper dismissal impressed Mr. Gladis, and after he had signed off on the logs, he told Chapel to take the fuel-consumption records to the purser's cabin. He was then given leave to stand down for breakfast and some sleep.

In fact, for reasons that eluded him, Chapel didn't really feel the need for sleep. He had taken no rest the night before while keeping company with Baily Pryot, but the joy of being back at sea in a sound ship lifted his spirits beyond all fatigue.

At the purser's cabin the steward told Chapel that the officer in question was presently in the company of Captain Leland on the bridge. Chapel made his way to the bridge, where he found the captain, Mr. Ryfkogel, and the purser deep in deliberation on matters of impending foul weather and the viability of their next port of call. Chapel made himself inconspicuous next to the chart table and waited to be recognized. While he listened, Chapel learned many things he had been curious about. He had wanted to ask Mr. Gladis several questions about the voyage, but he knew from experience that most officers didn't appreciate inquisitive seamen. He had let the matter pass. The destination really mattered very little to Chapel. It was the course that interested him most, and the kinds of seas they would encounter on their way.

The purser informed Captain Leland that the passenger list numbered forty-nine rather than the expected fifty-one. Two passengers had obviously missed the sailing. They were a cheerful bunch, he said. Most were on their way to the glittering Midwinter Fair in San Francisco. The purser noted that several passengers had started celebrating a little early. Mr. Ryfkogel laughed and speculated that they would regret their imprudence if the ship encountered spotty weather.

The purser went on to sum up the cargo manifest and submit the sheets for the captain's signature. The *Los Angeles'* cargo at present consisted of fresh butter, dressed veal carcasses,

Swiss cheese, grapefruit, oranges, lemons, pepper, and chrome. The vessel was scheduled to make a routine stop at San Simeon, where eighty tons of wool were to be taken on board, and that would complete her manifest for San Francisco.

Chapel watched quietly as Captain Leland signed the manifest. Mr. Ryfkogel looked over and noticed the young crewman standing quietly and holding the chief engineer's log, also awaiting the captain's signature. The third officer waved Chapel over and inspected the appropriate sheets. He then handed the log to the captain, who inspected, signed, and returned the log to Chapel with permission to proceed with his duties.

Chapel restored the volume to its assigned compartment in the engine room and made his way to the crew galley for hot coffee, cook's two-pound sinkers, and a greasy fried-egg-and-bacon sandwich.

Before bunking down for a brief sleep, Chapel took a turn about the fo'c'sle rail. The ship had quickly cleared the tepid, oily mists of San Pedro, and the morning sun and swift on-shore breezes had scoured the sky to a bright lapis blue. All of life's important keys surfaced in place at that moment. Chapel's course looked fair and full of modest assurances. A smooth passage north on bright seas was all the medicine he needed to purge memories of his recent, desperate beaching.

At last Chapel went below, found his berth, pulled off his boots, and hoisted himself into his bunk in one flowing movement. His eyes lazily followed the familiar dancing patterns of reflected sea light on the overhead for ten seconds, and then he sounded like a whale into the deepest waters of sleep.

When Chapel reflected upon the subject later, the dream he had must have begun the very moment he fell asleep, and it didn't cease in its intensity, detail, or exotic lucidity until he was called for the afternoon watch. Like many people, Chapel had experienced dreams of flight. There hadn't been many, three or four in a lifetime, but he had cherished every fraction of those dreams and could recall them for comfort at any unhappy moment. He had also experienced several dreams that found him underwater without the necessity of breathing, a slow-motion sensation of gliding through emerald shafts of light piercing deep into the sea. He had enjoyed those dreams and always hoped for further visitations. But this particular dream, though seemingly a combination of both original elements, was, in its expression, totally different.

In his dream Chapel stood near the toe of a freshly built pier. He could even smell the fresh-hewn timbers. The pier showed not the least-soiled hint that ship or gull had ever visited the site. The fresh construction jutted out into an empty and tranquil bay. When he looked over the edge into the depths, Chapel could see all the way to the sandy bottom. The fish winged through the clear waters like darting birds. Then suddenly Chapel felt a broad, irresistible pressure thrusting him forward. He had no course but to allow himself to be propelled off the end of the pier and into the bay. There he bobbed for a few moments like a buoy, never sinking below his waist or touching bottom.

Then the invisible source of pressure reinstated its will and began to drive Chapel forward, at first slowly, then gaining speed. With the lower half of his body submerged and the upper half slicing through the waves, Chapel moved forward through the breakwater out into the wide, green ocean.

He moved effortlessly through rolling swells. One moment he was abreast of the surge and the next, rising so high that he looked down on the bottlenose dolphins gamboling in the bow wave his body created. But no matter how he strained to see what propelled his motion forward, Chapel's field of vision was limited to what lay ahead or aside. It might have been the broad head of a sperm whale for all he knew. This was not to say that Chapel didn't find the whole sensation exhilarating, because he did. In fact, Chapel couldn't remember having had so much fun in his whole life.

After a short while he totally immersed himself in the exotic sensation. He felt like a winged statue he had once seen in a park, arms swept back, the cresting froth of seafoam dashing against his frame as he cut through the swells.

In this manner Chapel's dream conducted him through many oceans and alien ports. But in every case, no matter how fascinating or wondrous, Chapel fled from the busy harbors to the safety of the open sea. There he felt kin to important natural forces like tides, currents, and the vast swarms of ocean life dashing all about beneath him. Only when he was free from the bondage of the shore did the flying fish and dolphins delight in his company.

In this guise Chapel sailed on until he became aware that he viewed the world from the perspective of a ship's figurehead. Indeed, he felt as though he had become a ship himself, and this wonderful realization pleased him immeasurably.

It all made perfect sense in his dream, and Chapel basked in the simple magic of the answer. He saw that some men were born to the plow or the anvil and some to the loom, but it was destiny's resolve that Chapel Lodge should find his mission as a great ship. Nothing could have been more logical, to Chapel's way of thinking.

The dream ended abruptly when a sooty Filipino stoker

named Cricket gently shook his arm and indicated a change of watch was at hand.

Chapel pulled on his boots and grabbed a mug of thick coffee from the galley on his way to the engine room. Mr. Page, the second engineering officer, was still on duty awaiting Mr. Gladis to relieve him. Chapel took his counterpart's place with Mr. Page's permission and perused the engine-room logs from the last watch.

Seaman Chapel followed his normal routine with best efforts, and certainly no one on his watch would have guessed he was acutely distracted by a dream. Yet he was fearful of letting any detail escape, fearful the dream might disappear, like most important revelations. Rarely shared or heeded, dreams of keen personal consequence live for the life of the dreamer only. Chapel knew instinctively that the key to his nature lay within the folds of this dream, and he believed that every particular had to be memorized before it faded back into the twilight.

Mr. Gladis finally appeared. Cheerful and animated as was his custom, he vocalized in a semishout over the din of the engines. The chief engineer was loudly explaining about having served as second engineer aboard the *Wyanda*. It took a few moments for Chapel to understand that the *Los Angeles* was a decommissioned revenue cutter and that her launching plaque read *Wyanda*. Chapel found it difficult to gather the traces of the chief engineer's narrative, and though he would have bet good money that this was not to be the last time he would hear this story, Chapel thought it best to pay attention, if only for the sake of his amicable relationship with Mr. Gladis.

Chapel tried his best to follow the point of the story, but

the memories of his dream blossomed again and he lost all track of the rousing tale Mr. Gladis was attempting to spin. Though his work showed little sign of preoccupation, Chapel was nonetheless haunted by the tantalizing recollections of his dream for the rest of the day.

When he was eventually relieved from his watch, Chapel made his way to the galley. He had found his appetite again with the power of the dream, and he felt equal to anything the Chinese cook might threaten him with. He was pleasantly surprised to be served a heaping bowl of rich lamb stew with plenty of turnips, onions, carrots, and small potatoes.

The cook's mate handed out half loaves of hot bread and little paper cups of pale butter. Chapel chewed, smiled, and thought the stars of fortune might just be settling in his modest corner of the sky. Supper proved all he could have wished. His messmates seemed honest, soft-spoken, and congenial coves that made no attempt to disturb him from his ruminations. For that and other blessings, he was truly grateful.

Chapel's dream surfaced once again through the smoke of his afternoon pipe as he watched the coast of San Simeon come ever closer. He looked aft toward the bridge and saw Captain Leland on the port wing of the bridge with his binoculars. It appeared that the captain never left his station. Every time Chapel looked up from the fo'c'sle, every time Mr. Gladis had called up from the engine room, there was Captain Leland, high above and holding dominion over all save Providence.

Chapel confidently returned to his pipe and his daydreams. Moments later he almost jumped out of his skin when the chief engineer tapped him on the shoulder. Mr. Gladis gave Chapel a broad grin and shook his head.

"Where you been, boy? I tried to hail you from the companionway three times, but your head was in the haze. Some sweet dolly's parting words clotting your ears, son? Well, you never mind all that, boyo. The dear little things will sink their gaffs in you soon enough, to my way of thinking. It's not as though we're off to India, you know. By the way, I need you to run an errand for me when we dock. We're taking on eighty-odd ton o' wool, so we should be loaded, hatched, and ready to clear in two and a half hours, give or take a tick."

Mr. Gladis took a moment to light his own pipe from a rope match, pointed to the small bay, and then continued. "At the top of the hill over there to your left is Que Chew's Emporium, right next door to old Billy Doonen's Cafe."

Mr. Gladis pressed some money into Chapel's hand and winked. "You tell old Chew Mr. Gladis is in need of a half pound of his best Turkish shag tobacco and two bottles of my special Chinese medicine. He'll know what you mean. I also would be obliged if you would give him this letter to post. I have included the cost."

Mr. Gladis handed Chapel a long manila envelope and, as an afterthought, dropped a few more coins into Chapel's palm. "Get something for yourself at Billy Doonen's, son. I swear he's got the best German suds around. A little something for the black gang wouldn't go amiss either, if you take my meaning." With a wink, Mr. Gladis produced a shiny galvanized beer bucket like a rabbit from a hat.

Chapel looked at Mr. Gladis, smiled, and then cast his eyes to Captain Leland on the wing of the bridge. Mr. Gladis guessed the question. "I've already sounded that quarter, Mr. Lodge. Half the Turkish shag is for Captain Leland, and the suds are his present to the Filipino boys. He brags of having the best black gang in the company's fleet. It pleases him to pay them special tribute now and then. And there isn't one of them coves that wouldn't take a bullet for their Señor Capitano. Just see to it you get your carcass back on board in time. You'll hear the ship's whistle blast the last half and quarter hour and, trust me, Captain Leland won't wait for you, son. So make it sharp and timely, and spare us all his temper."

A strange sensation overcame Chapel as he made his way down the gangway to the long pier at San Simeon. He felt a sense of cold foreboding about leaving the ship. He kept looking over his shoulder as he made his way up the road. It was as though he expected his ship to disappear at any moment, leaving him beached and homeless again.

Old Mr. Que Chew bowed at the mention of Mr. Gladis. He was most happy to assemble Chapel's order, with special compliments to Mr. Gladis, of course. He had seen the *Los Angeles* come in and was only waiting for his old friend to make an appearance. The old Chinaman said he was sorry not to have the honor to wait on the chief engineer personally, but he understood the constraints of duty. Bowing once more, Mr. Chew asked that his best compliments be forwarded to Mr. Gladis.

Before he left, and using his own funds, Chapel purchased a three-pound bag of homemade, peppermint-stick candy, and the same weight of licorice taffy. He knew the Filipino stokers were more than a little fond of both. Peppermint, according to black gang mythology, helped stokers bear the incessant heat of the fireboxes and boilers. Licorice helped relieve the effects of coal dust in the lungs.

As suggested, Chapel stopped off at Doonen's Cafe for a beer and to fill the suds bucket, but he kept walking out to the front porch to make sure that the *Los Angeles* hadn't secretly slipped her cables and deserted him. He knew these sensations were absurd on the face of it, but Chapel could not fend off the apprehension and anxiety that he might be deserted and left to his own unlucky, landlocked devices.

He made his way back down the road to the pier long before he was expected. Numerous wagons had disgorged their loads of wool bales before heading back up the hill. Chapel stood next to an old, crippled sailor watching the ship's derricks neatly lift and stow the huge bales in her holds. The old sailor had lost a leg and used a crutch cut down from a small oar. He leaned against a piling with an inescapable gaze of longing and sadness in his eyes.

Chapel knew instantly the specific yearning that gnawed away at the old man's heart. He would have worn a similar expression if his secret dread had been fulfilled by his worst expectations. To stand ashore while life and home departed on the evening tide without a token of regret seemed the worst of all possible fates to Chapel. It had been known to break a poor sailor's spirit.

The two seamen watched the ship load cargo in silence. Their bond was obvious and unspoken. Without taking his eyes from the aerial ballet of wool bales, Chapel proffered the bag of peppermint sticks as an open invitation. The old man's dismal countenance brightened appreciably as he helped himself to a red-and-white-striped glory with the reverence usually afforded a two-dollar, thigh-rolled, Havana cigar. The old man thanked the young sailor, but the sound of the steam derricks and the shouting of orders drowned him out. Chapel didn't notice. His eyes were for the ship alone. The cargo holds inhaled wool bales by the ton without pause. Captain Leland still maintained the bridge, but supervised the loading through his cargo and deck officers.

Noticing the young sailor's preoccupation, the old man repeated himself. "Thanks. Don't mind if I do on a day such as this. Peppermint's good for just about anything, they say."

The old seaman sucked on the stick for a moment and then looked Chapel up and down as though appraising a split mast. "You a stoker, mate? It's a stoker that's got a real tooth for peppermint. It's the air down in the belly of the beast, you understand. The stink and heat be more than any but the condemned should have to bear."

The old man pulled the candy from his mouth and admired the spiral design at arm's length. "I was captain of the foretop years past. Still miss the sweet air high in the trees. A body could almost see all the way to Java on a sharp day. That's what we used to tell the new fish when they balked at the climb. Nowadays most swabs would rather cut their own throats than work the yards. Don't blame 'em much, come to judge. Lost my leg up in the trees. Still dream about it sometimes. Got to be born crazy to do stuff like that. You crazy, mate? Hope so. Crazy is the only way to live, and it's the only sensible way to die."

Mr. Gladis was on deck talking to Mr. Ryfkogel when Chapel came back aboard. The chief engineer noted that his mate sported the look of a poor, lost hound newly found by the pack. Chapel almost shivered like a puppy with the joy of being safe aboard and among friends again.

He handed Mr. Gladis the full beer bucket, shag tobacco, and medicine and, as an afterthought, pulled the bags of peppermint and licorice from his coat pockets and handed them over too.

Mr. Gladis smelled the bags and grinned. "The black gang will love you like a brother for this, Mr. Lodge. They've a real appetite for this stuff down there. I hope you're not bucking for my rating, Mister Lodge. I've got four daughters to feed, and if I didn't go to sea, I not only couldn't feed the little cows, but I'd never get the head to myself again." This observation seemed to amuse and divert both officers long enough to allow Chapel to retreat to the galley without giving offense.

After a greasy meal of biscuits, ham, and gravy, Chapel retreated to his bunk to sleep before taking the second dogwatch with Mr. Page. Chapel closed his eyes with the sincere hope that some part of his previous dream would return to delight his slumber. Though the images eluded him, Chapel did have one glimpse of the familiar, but it wasn't one he particularly relished.

He dreamed he rested gently at anchor in a broad bay surrounded by dusky mountains. Then, without the usual telltale indications to mark such events, the weather changed abruptly for the worse. With wind and waves operating in direct opposition, he began to swing and pitch erratically on his taut anchor chains, his bow angrily tossing up and down like a stallion's head resisting the halter rope.

Chapel awoke in some confusion. He knew where he was, but the residual sensation of the chopping seas, deep swells, and coarse winds remained with him. He could feel the adverse struggle of elements even as he lay awake in his bunk. Then it struck him like a mallet that this was no clinging dream, but the real sea conditions as they stood at present.

Chapel quickly pulled on his seaboots, grabbed his oilskin,

and made for the spar deck, but this told him little of value other than the weather had turned dirty with an onshore gale in the wings. It was far too dark to see anything but the familiar glow from the ship's lights. Chapel squinted against the rain and noticed that Captain Leland no longer held his place. Third Officer Ryfkogel was standing the bridge watch instead. His dark, chiseled features were recognizable even in the soft illumination afforded by the binnacle lights. The master's mate could be seen working the helm with more-than-usual vigor.

Sometimes the ship would feel as if it were making good way when, in reality, the winds and the tides saw to it that the vessel traveled nowhere at all. If the ship's engines went soft at a time like this, with a fast incoming tide, the situation would certainly prove catastrophic. It was every coasting captain's nightmare to run out of power, leeway, and ideas all at the same time.

Wearying of the deck's discomfort, Chapel made his way to the galley for a mug of "muscle" and some of cook's sweet Indian fry bread. Just as Chapel took his first dunk in the thick, sweet coffee, Mr. Gladis came through the companionway, bracing against the rolling and pitching of the ship. Conditions had become noticeably worse in the last few minutes, but the chief engineer took the weather in stride as he grabbed a mug of coffee from the cook's mate and sat down across from Chapel.

Mr. Gladis looked introspective and fatigued, but he surfaced from his thoughts with a smile. "Glad I found you, Mr. Lodge. I have a disagreeable request that I would prefer not to make an order, if you get my drift. Poor young Samoza broke some ribs in a fall from the catwalk. I've been robbing Peter to pay Paul on the watch list all evening. I need you to double up with the black gang for half your watch so I can catch up. The bunkers need balancing. We're eating fifty-five scuttles an hour, but someone has misplaced the bunker charts, and I suspect too much coal has been shunted out of number two, starboard bunker. I'll send someone to replace you at nine-thirty. Then you'll have plenty of time to help me replace the grease-dog ring on number three cylinder."

Chapel nodded, sipped his coffee, and eyed the galley clock. He had eight minutes to wolf down a meal before immersing himself in a cloud of coal dust. He saw little purpose in discussing the unalterable when it was food he needed to shovel coal. Mr. Gladis didn't actually wait for a reply; he swallowed his steaming brew at one go and made his way off to other duties.

With the filth of the coal bunkers in mind, Chapel quickly changed into his bilge slops before reporting to the engine room. The boys on the black gang were pleased to see Chapel and slapped him on the shoulder with many thanks for his gift.

Chapel knew from firsthand experience that theirs was a type of labor that required both studied endurance and a strong back. The ship's safety and speed required that a predetermined workload be sustained in a timely fashion twenty-four hours a day, regardless of adverse circumstances or crew shortages.

Chapel liked the stokers for their sense of cheerful cooperation and gentle humor in the face of hardships no deck officer could ever know. The sturdy Filipinos worked their broad shovels from bunker to coal chute to firebox in a kind of congruous ballet that required meticulous timing and balance. All the while they would chatter away like jungle birds. Whether they spoke Spanish, English, or one of their own dialects, they trolled out comments on any subject that pleased them at the moment. The theme didn't matter as long as a cheerful round-robin of clever interjections and humorous commentary was kept buoyant.

The black gang's cultural bonds and familial support seemed to produce an anesthetic that subdued the chronic pain and stress their dark and perilous routine engendered. Whatever the root source, their courage and jovial dispositions made dangerous and unpleasant labors bearable, even for Chapel.

The hardest and most dangerous task allotted the black gang was accomplished deep inside the coal bunkers on either side of the ship. Little or no light was allowed to enter these narrow cells, as an open flame or electrical spark might ignite the coal dust and literally blow the ship out of the water. The measured use of fuel from all six bunkers was required for the ship to maintain its equilibrium.

Depending on the location and stability of heavy cargo, coal might be reshipped from one bunker to another to trim the vessel by the bow or stern, whichever applied to the prevailing requirements. This was arduously accomplished one shovelful at a time, hour after hour, day after day, and night after night. Chapel judged ship's boiler decks and coal bunkers to be any Christian's vision of hell. He was therefore fascinated by the ease with which the Filipino stokers, a very orthodox clan, cheerfully managed to disregard their surroundings altogether. They simply immersed themselves in reinforced memories of home and family. The significance of their sacrifice held the stokers in a common bond of mutual support. Every man's children would have a better life than their fathers, even if it meant they spent years slowly expiring in the belching black guts of a stinking Yankee freighter.

Chapel thought it interesting that most of the black gangs he had ever come across were always akin in some fashion. There were exceptions to the rule to be sure, but he had noticed how many stokers on any given ship were all Portuguese or Cubans, Irish or Chinese or, in this case, Filipino.

He surmised that the burdens of the black gang being what they were, it would represent greater safety and fellowship if the stokers were all of the same tribe. He had known of ships whose owners had taken on the strangest mix of crews. There was the *Prince William* out of Sydney, for instance. That vessel registered Peruvian owners, but her captain was Dutch–South African, her deck officers Italian, her able seamen all Danes, her engineers German, and her black gang, appropriately enough, Welsh coal miners. Chapel often wondered how many translations an order would require to make it from the bridge to the bunkers on the old *Prince Willy*.

While Chapel and the black gang shoveled coal, the *Los Angeles* began experiencing a particularly bad turn. The wind, tide, and waves caused the ship to pitch and shudder with ever-increasing ferocity. It made work in the dim bunkers hazardous at best.

Tino Bracas and Chapel were moving coal toward a bunker chute that fed the open scuttles in the boiler room, but the coarse motion of the ship obliged them to halt their work and brace themselves upon their shovels on every downward pitch of the bows.

Chapel heard the distant clangs of the engine-room telegraph over the pounding of the great steam pistons. It was obvious from the repeated code that the ship was changing course and speed, possibly to address the prevailing seas from another quarter. It was curious how well one could know everything about a vessel's movements from the blind depths of her bunkers or engine room. Chapel was reflecting in this manner when suddenly the whole ship trembled and shuddered with such violent force that both he and Tino were thrown off their feet.

In that same instant a great granite claw came gouging through the chine of the hull, ripping the iron plates like paper as it traveled toward them from bow to stern. The seas immediately flooded in behind the advancing claw, and in seconds Chapel and Tino were up to their waists in freezing black water. Both men scrambled up and out of the bunker just in time to warn the rest of the black gang to close the firebox doors and get the hell out of there. Chapel herded his charges out of the boiler room like a barking terrier, and as the last man out he closed and secured the boiler-room hatch. Even as he did so Chapel could see broad channels of black water cascading over the top of the bunker they had just occupied.

Chapel immediately looked about for Mr. Gladis, but could not spot him in all the confusion of frightened seamen desperately clambering to the relative safety of the upper decks. Then the slumped figure of Mr. Gladis slowly crawled from between the rotator blocks where he had been thrown when the ship struck. Chapel rushed to help him to his feet. The chief engineer didn't seem badly hurt, though he was somewhat dazed from a sharp blow to the head. Mr. Gladis had been confirming a signal from the bridge when the ship struck, and he still clutched the handle of the telegraph, which had come away in his strong grasp when he was catapulted off his feet and across the grating.

Chapel was stunned to hear Mr. Gladis scream in pain when grasped about the chest. Chapel knew at once that Mr. Gladis' injuries probably included several cracked or broken ribs or worse.

Once ensconced in a place of relative safety, Mr. Gladis gasped instructions for Chapel to go on deck at once and seek orders from the first officer, or "whoever looks like he knows what the hell he's doing." Chapel hesitated and suggested that now was the best time for both men to make their way up, but Mr. Gladis was insistent that his injuries made it impossible to return to his station in time to effect the orders. He tried to push Chapel toward the ladder, but the pain prevented the gesture, so he pointed and ordered Chapel to go at once.

No one could have been prepared for the scene that presented itself on deck. The storm-launched waves and howling winds combined with the increasing list of the crippled ship had caused pandemonium and panic, but Chapel was truly distressed to see the crew in no better command of their wits than the terror-stricken passengers.

Mr. Ryfkogel was standing on the starboard wing of the bridge screaming coarse obscenities through a megaphone at a commandeered lifeboat that had left the ship without permission. Captain Leland suddenly emerged from the bridge house and took the megaphone from his enraged third officer.

As he struggled to climb to the bridge, Chapel tried to hear what the captain was yelling at Mr. Ryfkogel, but the death screams of emergency whistles and the despairing clang of bells owned the night. He looked over the side toward the object of Mr. Ryfkogel's thunderous denunciation in time to see Captain Leland's prize black gang slowly disappear toward the rotating Cyclops of the Point Sur Light in a half-filled lifeboat.

Chapel watched as his mates rowed off with "the devil in

the stern sheets." He spat out a short curse of his own and continued up to the bridge.

Captain Leland was emphatic and brusque. The engine room was to be abandoned at once. The seas would quench all fear of fire, though explosions were still very possible. He said there was no duty left but to save as many lives as Providence would permit. With that, Captain Leland put the megaphone to his mouth and began to sort out the plight of the frantic passengers and crew still left on deck. In moments the captain's thundering voice and force of will restored the frenzied passengers and crew to a fair degree of self-possession and good order.

Chapel prepared to charge down to the engine room to report to Mr. Gladis. He physically induced the gaunt and terrified bosun's mate, Mr. Roody, to follow below directly and bare a hand hoisting the injured chief engineer up on deck. The captain's express orders and Chapel's clenched fist proved ample persuasion for the fainthearted Mr. Roody.

Mr. Page, having just emerged from the rope locker with a coil of stout line, offered to return below and assist with the rescue. He warned that the ship was torn through the bowels from stem to stern. There was eight feet of water in the holds and no working pumps to speak of. The necessity for dash was explicit if they were to return to the deck alive.

Chapel led the way down the companionway ladder to find Mr. Gladis resting uncomfortably where he had left him. The man was certainly conscious, but suffered in the darkest manner from spurs of unbearable pain. The extent of his distress registered in the livid color of his complexion and the contortion of his features when subjected to the slightest movement.

While Mr. Page fabricated a bosun's harness, Chapel and

Mr. Roody fished the engine room's block-and-chain hoist to an overhead beam. It was in this way that they hoped to elevate Mr. Gladis to the upper catwalk and then onto the deck. Their efforts were so concentrated that no one seemed to notice that the frigid seawater had rapidly risen to the height of their hips. All the reeking filth and scum that had rested for years in the rusting bilges now floated on that rising water like lumpy crude oil.

Just as Mr. Roody secured the hoist, the ship, still impaled on its granite claw, gave a violent shudder and heeled ten degrees to starboard. The block and chain, which was not yet secured, slid off the catwalk before Mr. Roody could grab for it. The twenty-pound block plummeted down in a riotous tangle of chain that swung directly toward Chapel's head. The bosun's mate shouted a warning, but Chapel was still trying to regain his footing from the lurch of the ship. With the timely alarm, however, he did manage to avoid a direct blow as the lethal mass crashed into the steam return valve. The valve joint ruptured on impact, releasing a blast of scalding steam that caught Chapel square in the face six feet away. Ke Hop, the ship's second cook, said later that he could hear Chapel's scream all the way up on the galley deck. He said it froze the blood in his veins because it sounded so much like the dying ship's whistle.

Chapel was now blind and in excruciating pain. The how and when of his escape from the flooding engine room seemed more a matter of raw torture than deliverance. Every movement brought gasps of unbearable suffering from Mr. Gladis, while Chapel's agony peaked higher with every moment. His only balm was the chilled fetid water swirling about his stomach. With this he bathed his scalded face as the pain increased.

Mr. Page and the bosun's mate deposited their charges near the bridge, where they could be seen to by others and eventually helped into the boats if their luck held out. But luck, by its definition, is usually in very short supply upon the warping decks of a fast-sinking ship.

Chapel's panic subsided with the knowledge that he would not at least be trapped below when the *Los Angeles* settled to the bottom. His world was now closed to all vision, so he began to piece together the frenetic activity on deck with the evidence of sound alone. He could hear Captain Leland close by thundering orders to the lifeboat crews.

When the black gang had absconded with the first lifeboat, it left the ship with only two remaining cutters and the motor launch. Captain Leland had ordered that the launch tow the cutters back and forth to shore until most of his eighty-five charges had made it to the safety of the beach below Point Sur. Chapel, Mr. Gladis, Mr. Page, Captain Leland, and three slightly injured passengers waited for the motor launch to take them aboard. They would be the last survivors to go ashore.

The night winds had grown in force, and the sea formed into hammerlike breakers that crashed against the port beam with deafening regularity. The surf to starboard, facing the beach, had taken on a hazardous chop. The shore breakers could be heard but not seen. They waited, but the launch did not return. Mr. Page came to Chapel with life jackets and bid him to put one on immediately. These were cumbersome, vestlike affairs that contained large blocks of cork front and back.

It was difficult enough getting a blind man into one of these contraptions, but poor Mr. Gladis was another and certainly more painful challenge.

Chapel helped as best he could, but without sight he

was less than useful. Sadly he was obliged to sit and voice hollow assurances while Mr. Gladis moaned in pain. At last the two men were fitted up, and as added insurance, Mr. Page lashed the two men together with a length of line. Mr. Page apologized for the "crippled leading the blind" arrangement, but he thought it safer to handle one rope rather than two in the dark.

Mr. Gladis gasped out the observation that the rigid life vest, tightly lashed about his torso as it was, actually provided considerable relief to his tortured ribs. He felt a little more confident about the situation and told Captain Leland that he would look after Mr. Chapel should the need arise.

That very necessity arose thirty seconds later as the *Los Angeles* began to settle to the bottom of the ocean, seven hundred yards from shore off Point Sur.

Within moments the sea had taken possession of the decks and Captain Leland was forced to herd his charges toward the rigging of the ship's vestigial mast. As the broken ship was sucked from beneath them, the hapless survivors climbed and clung to the ratlines and stays. Captain Leland shouted that the bottom off Point Sur was relatively shallow, and this fact was immediately confirmed when the mast ceased to sink and temporary refuge was afforded just below the flag yard. The company standard still flew from the top of the mast.

It wasn't much of a hedge against immediate death, but Mr. Gladis observed that it was a damn sight better than nothing at all. In fact, Mr. Gladis was feeling somewhat better about everything. Since floating, even in the angry chop, took the pressure of gravity off his injured ribs, Mr. Gladis was allowed the privilege of breathing without incessant pain.

Chapel, on the other hand, could do little to influence his

destiny except hold on tight and avoid drowning as best he could. Their biggest worry at present, besides the obvious absence of boats to carry them ashore, was the frigid temperature of the water. Captain Leland worried that cold hands would lose their grip, and he encouraged everyone to cling to each other as well as to the rigging.

In all, Chapel, like Mr. Gladis, was feeling his injuries less. The cold salt water bathed his scalded face to a point of tolerance, and though deeply worried about his eyes, Chapel felt that he had at least a fighting chance of survival. Now that he was embraced in the arms of the sea, he felt safe. He could swim, blind or not, and that was more than could be said for the poor *Los Angeles* now resting on the rocks beneath them.

If all else failed, Chapel felt he could always swim to the sound of the surf in the hope that God loved fools enough to bring him to the shore safely.

From out of the storm a large ocean swell transformed itself into a rogue breaker that crashed over the ship's mast, engulfing the survivors clinging desperately to the rigging. When the wave passed, Captain Leland's worst fears were realized. The two injured passengers, who had timidly held on with the others when the ship went down, were gone.

The couple's cork vests would have doubtlessly brought them to the surface again, but the starless sheet of night hid everything beyond the next wave, and finding the couple would prove little more than an exercise in futility without a boat. Captain Leland, a good Catholic, crossed himself with pragmatic reverence.

The captain kept his few remaining men close about him for fear of losing another soul to the waves. Though his own strength ebbed slowly into the frigid waters, Captain Leland pestered and prodded his half-drowned crew to hang on for their lives. Where he found the will to be optimistic about their future was a mystery to one and all, but they were obliged for his strength of character. They had been clinging to the mast's tattered rigging for close to an hour by Mr. Page's calculation, and there hadn't appeared so much as a ghost of possible rescue. Where were the damn boats? Why hadn't the motor launch returned as ordered?

Chapel, isolated within his blindness, was perforce required to interpret everything from the inside out, and it was one of these intuitive themes that peacefully indicated to him that his suffering would soon come to an end.

His limbs were no longer governed by the rigid cold. In fact, he felt new warmth rise within his bones. It beckoned him to release his grasp on fear and sleep untroubled on the cresting foam. To sleep was to surrender oneself into the hands of creation. All he had to do was let go and drift away on the waves. Luckily he was still lashed to Mr. Gladis, who in turn was secured by a strong line to Mr. Page.

Abruptly, and from the bleak void beyond his last dreams, there exploded an intrusive bubble of shouting and banging. Unexpectedly, Chapel slowly became aware of being discourteously hauled into the air like an exhausted tuna and then lifted down over the gunwales of a boat.

In his disjointed confusion, Chapel thought he heard the earnest chirping voices of his black gang, and he called out Tino's name. In response, he heard Tino's voice tell him that all was well. Then he glided into a relaxed dream of his own death. He wondered what his mother would say, and laughed.

Chapel had become reconciled to the thought of passing on and subsequently resented the wrenching summons to

return to life. It was his last thought before passing out in the
bottom of the Point Sur lifeboat.

IT WAS HOURS BEFORE CHAPEL COULD RELIABLY DECIPHER the
credible difference between dreams and reality. He had heard
people talking from beyond the uncertain veil of consciousness. The voices mixed with his dreams, and he was surprised
to hear Mr. Page's voice emanate from his mother's mouth,
while his old dog, Grover, moaned and swore blue lightning
just like Mr. Gladis.

While slowly coming to the surface of authentic comprehension, Chapel became aware that he still experienced the
same angry frustration and annoyance that had marked his
reluctant extraction from the safe, warm eternity of the sea.
For Chapel, it almost felt akin to being forcefully dragged from
his home.

His first waking sensation was one of extreme discomfort.
Chapel remembered that his face had been soundly cooked, but
he now experienced a burning sensation all over his body.
When he tried to move, Chapel found himself completely
sheathed and swaddled in a heavy cocoon of considerable thick-
ness and strength. He couldn't even move his arms.

Chapel knew it was still dark and that he lay upon the
beach, the first because he could still smell the salty night fog
and the second because he felt the pounding of the surf through
the sand. He knew he was sheltered under a tent, because
he could smell mildewed canvas, but the exact purpose of his
heavy shroud disturbed his thoughts considerably. He imagined he had already been wrapped in old ship's canvas, ready
for burial. He longed to tell somebody he wasn't dead. At least

he didn't think he was dead. After several moments of fruitless struggle against confinement, Chapel cried out for release. He swore his whole body was a bed of coals and begged for his liberty before he went mad with the torment.

A familiar and restoring brogue came out of the dark in short, emphatic gasps. It was Mr. Gladis. "Go a mite easy there, Mr. Lodge. You're safe now, old son. A doctor has already gauged your timbers. You'll float again. He said you suffered something evil from the cold. Battened you down for warmth, he did. Mr. Page here has a bottle of medicine for you. See to his needs, Mr. Page. Just breathing plays raw havoc on my ribs just now."

Chapel felt Mr. Page kneel and slide his arm under his neck and shoulders. Page lifted the helpless bundle a few degrees, placed the spout of a small bottle between Chapel's lips, and coaxed him to drink it all. "The doctor says you are to swallow it all, Mr. Lodge. He warranted it would make you as comfortable as conditions allowed. He also said your burns weren't to give you cause for undue distress. He said that once the swelling went down you would get your sight back."

Abruptly Chapel began to violently cough and sputter. The bitter flavor of the syruplike concoction had suddenly met resistance. Chapel begged for water. Mr. Page obliged and at last managed to muster the last of the medicine down Chapel's gullet with additional water to help the tonic pass.

Mr. Page spoke words of reassurance all the while. "That there doctor is a genuine piece of work if ever I saw one. He's as tough as a bosun's boot, and that's no mistake. When he heard our poor ship was stove in on the rocks, he borrowed a stallion and galloped all night to get to us. You can show your gratitude with patience, Mr. Lodge. Rest easy. The doctor said he would return. You just sleep while you can."

The cumulative dosage of reassurance and remedy had their effect. Slowly Chapel could feel all previous discomforts and trepidation slip away to be replaced by a warm, drifting sense of well-being that excluded all reference to the terrifying experiences of the last few hours. Within a few minutes he was adrift in a sleep impervious to the assault of dreams, but he looked like a dead walrus.

Mr. Page commented on the eerie similarity to Mr. Gladis. The chief engineer laughed, which caused him to wince convulsively in pain. He sputtered out orders as though still aboard ship. "Now, stuff that nonsense, Mr. Page, and make yourself useful. Rummage up some dry tobacco and a dram of something besides water. Black rum would be much appreciated, if there be such about. I'm like to blow out my valves with the pain in me staves, so put your soul into it, if you please."

WHEN CHAPEL AT LAST AWOKE from a dreamless pit of drugged sleep, it was to find he was in another setting altogether. Though his eyes were still well bandaged, he could sense that he now lay on a narrow metal bed between clean sheets. He had been washed and dressed in a long flannel nightshirt.

He lay quietly, enjoying long-forgotten sensations of peace and warmth. After a while he began to wonder if Mr. Gladis and Mr. Page were savoring similar joys, so he called out their names in a rusty unused voice that reflected his weakened condition. There was no answer but the echo of his voice in an empty room. He called again and, in response, he heard a door open and footsteps approach his bed. Sadly the voice of his visitor was unknown to him.

"How fare you, sailor? I'm Willard Copes, assistant light-keeper, Point Sur Station. We were beginning to wonder how long you would sleep. You've been kissing feathers for two days now. Dr. Roberts said you would sleep a while, but we didn't think you'd be out this long. He gave you a draught to that purpose, I know, but we worried he might have overdone it. If you're fit enough to eat, I'll have some food sent up to you. Doc said to keep it simple at first, but you should regain your gut in a day or two. He left some ointment for your face too. He was confident we could take off your bandages in a few days. He couldn't say for certain, of course, but he's of the opinion that your eyes will take care of themselves if you're careful with the burns."

Chapel asked after Captain Leland, Mr. Gladis, and the others. Mr. Copes said that the coastal freighter *Eureka* arrived off the point shortly after the accident. The storm had moved on east by then. She had taken on those survivors who had regained their composure enough to step aboard another ship and had transported them north to Monterey.

Those who had seen the hand of the Almighty imprinted upon the disaster chose to be carted north in wagons rather than face another voyage. Under the circumstances, it was probably a sound decision, according to Mr. Copes.

The last survivors had departed the previous day. Mr. Gladis was transported with the help of a mule litter fashioned by Mr. Page. The remaining survivors were anxious to get as far away from the site of the wreck as possible. The others, like Mr. Gladis, needed further medical attention in Monterey. The coast road couldn't have proven a comfortable journey at that time of the year. The road was badly rutted by the winter rains, and rumor had it there had been landslides just south of Yankee Point.

Noting Chapel's melancholy silence, Mr. Copes said that officials from the Pacific Steamship Company would arrive in a couple of days to inspect the site of the wreck. Chapel could, no doubt, make arrangements for return transport and back wages with them. Until then, Doc Roberts had ordered rest, hot food, and perhaps a whisper of medicinal whiskey after dinner to abet a sound sleep.

With that pleasant promise, Mr. Copes bid Chapel a peaceful recovery and departed with a light step. Chapel turned his anguished face to the warmth of the afternoon sun as it came through the window. He was consoled by the sensation that he could see as well as feel the light through his bandages.

That night Mr. Copes was as good as his word. After a delicious dinner consisting of creamed chowder of abalone and clams and a half loaf of hot fresh bread, Chapel was presented with a generous tumbler of peat-flavored whiskey. Mr. Copes stayed for a while to keep him company. He expressed a very natural curiosity about the disaster, but his questions were professionally pointed and almost crossed the hedge into language similar to that of an official inquiry.

After a few minutes, Mr. Copes apologized by saying that he had been a lighthouse hand all his life. It was his nature to take a veteran's interest in such particulars.

Chapel spoke freely of what he knew, but stated for the record that it wasn't very much. Only those on the bridge could know the truth of the matter, and the bridge officers alone would be consulted by any official board inquiry. "The engine-room black gang certainly knew when the ship was bound for the bottom, because we were the first bastards to get wet. Un-fortunately, we knew little else save bilge gas and blind panic. If the *Los Angeles* died from negligence, sir, we would be hind-most in line with knowledge of it, or blame for it."

Chapel was relieved to hear that Mr. Copes was called to agree. He said he had known many a shipwrecked seaman in his time and well understood the guarded prerogatives of rank. The truth was whatever an officer said it was, and no argument was tolerated. Mr. Copes at last took Chapel's empty glass and, after changing his medicated bandages, wished his patient a good night.

It was as still a night as that part of the coast might experi-ence, but it did not remain that way for long. As Chapel lay upon his bed he could distinguish every variation in the inten-sity and direction of the rising wind. His hearing had become acute in the few days he had been denied his sight. He knew that the winter tides were exceptional in this phase of the moon. If the offshore winds continued to rise to meet the in-coming tides there would be little of the poor *Los Angeles* left for the Pacific Steamship Company representatives to inspect when they did arrive.

Sad little indeed, save beached hatches, spars, and general flotsam. The rest, the sea-torn bones of a dead ship, lay washed beneath the waves off Point Sur. These sorrowful reflections gathered momentum as Chapel regarded his own future. He was disheartened at the thought of finding himself beached once more after so short a voyage. He was no better than the flotsam now strewn upon the coast. Even as human salvage, Chapel was worth far less than the lost chrome and wool in the ship's hold, and that knowledge secretly angered him.

Like most seamen, Chapel had a tendency to awake

automatically at every change of the watch whether he was aboard ship or not. This night was no different, but each time he awoke, his resentment surfaced afresh to plague his soul.

Prior to waking for the last time, Chapel suffered a nightmare of jolting reality. Though woven within an array of images he didn't really comprehend, Chapel unquestionably saw himself as old, bent, bat-blind, and wallowing among the iron-sick hulks of beached derelicts like himself. His end would come without dignity, without grace, begging for pennies and praying for death. He had seen such images numerous times in his travels and feared that fate above all others.

When he awoke from the dream, Chapel found himself caught on a thorn of envy and resentment. He begrudged every man who possessed his freehold outright. Every owner of his own ship, every master of his own land, was a king compared to Chapel. His life and future were conceded to the whims of authority or the ravages of nature. Nothing was truly his own.

Chapel immediately decided it was time to face several realities of an unpleasant nature. The first step would be the hardest. Everything depended on what he discovered in the next few minutes.

Chapel knew the approximate time. He could hear the first stirring of men as they coughed and hacked their way from the grasp of sleep. He sat up on the edge of the narrow bed and began to unwind the medicated bandage that covered the upper half of his face. The layers of bandage seemed unending, and with every loosened wrap, Chapel balanced between dread and steely resolve to know the truth. At last the cotton pads over his eyelids came away with the end of the gauze.

Slowly he reached up to gently touch his scalded face.

Though it seemed swollen and tender, the pain was no worse than a common sunburn. Next he touched his eyelids—they too were swollen and raw. When he tried to open them, nothing happened. The muscles were willing, but the eyelids refused to rise. With a gentle touch, Chapel determined that his eyes were sealed with a crust of dried tears. He rose and felt his way to the washstand. He had heard Mr. Copes use it and knew its approximate location. Gingerly, Chapel poured cool water from the pitcher into the basin, found a cloth, and began to bathe his eyes until the dried tears dissolved and allowed his tender lids to open.

Chapel was lucky that he had not removed his bandage in the full light of day. As it was, even in the quarter-light of dawn, with the sun still east behind the mountains, Chapel was almost thrown off his weakened legs by the intensity of light. But light there was and shadow too. Though blurred, every detail at hand registered. The particulars of his environment fell into place, and a sense of relief and tranquility warmed even his frigid bare feet.

When Mr. Copes found him twenty minutes later, Chapel was standing by the window in his nightshirt watching the sea-reflected sunlight rush toward the shore as the sun rose in the east behind the Big Sur range.

It was a remarkable view perched high above the Pacific on Point Sur Rock. Chapel was entranced. He couldn't even look aside when Mr. Copes greeted his patient with a great, steaming breakfast on a tray. The smell of sausages, flapjacks, and coffee would have driven an innocent prisoner to confess anything. Still Chapel did not move from the vision before him.

Mr. Copes appeared surprised to find his castaway up and recovered to such a remarkable degree. As a gentleman burdened with a substantial pair of glasses himself, Mr. Copes had deeply sympathized with Chapel's injury. He was gratified to discover that Chapel's blindness would not be a subject of discussion anytime in the near future.

Mr. Copes at last settled Chapel into his breakfast with a promise of a short walk about the lighthouse rock in the afternoon. While Chapel ravenously devoured his food, Mr. Copes shared the most recent scuttlebutt concerning the wreck of the *Los Angeles.*

Placing a finger to the side of his nose with a wink, Mr. Copes indicated that there was much to tell of a surprising and unhappy nature. He also suggested that what passed between them should be considered confidential until after Chapel's interview with the officials of the Pacific Steamship Company.

According to Mr. Copes' representation, word had already come down from Monterey. There were any number of strange tales circulating. That was to be expected, of course, but most wrecks could always be placed at the door of human error. Sadly, the *Los Angeles* could now be mustered on the rolls of the latter. Chapel stopped eating at once and looked up. He had lost all interest in food with the mention of his dead ship. "What was it? What drove her down onto the rocks, Mr. Copes?"

Mr. Copes was somewhat taken aback by the vehemence of Chapel's response, so he searched carefully for an appropriate place to begin the tale. His disclaimers concerning the final authority for the news only agitated Chapel further, so he just began. "Well, according to our Mr. Keely, who accompanied the ship's officers to Monterey, the blame pretty much rests with your enterprising third officer, Mr. Ryfkogel. Though to be fair, Captain Leland has taken all responsibility for the disaster. After your port call in San Simeon, Captain Leland stayed on deck until the bridge marked Piedras Blancas Point, approximately seven-thirty P.M. He'd held the watch since seven-thirty that morning. He ordered a compass course calculated to keep the ship well in the offing of our jaws and even went so far as to leave orders to be called when Cooper's Point came abeam. Cooper's Point is about five miles southeast of us. As you must remember yourself, the *Los Angeles* made her way north with a southwest gale off her stern quarter and bull squalls nipping at her heels all the way. Some very thick rain, as I remember, came down by the barrel for three hours—drowned Mr. Maynard's prize pig, the one he was saving for our New Year's feast. Do you like roast pig, Mr. Chapel? I can almost smell cook basting a leg of pork right now."

Chapel's look of impatient indifference on the subject of pork at last impressed Mr. Copes, and he went on with his story. "I'm sorry, Mr. Lodge. I was forgetting your ship, your pardon. Well, to put a tail on the dog, Mr. Ryfkogel didn't mark Cooper's Point. Maybe he didn't see it at all in those squalls. He thought he still possessed enough sea room to mortgage off the lee shore, so he altered course to cut inshore of the kelp beds off Cooper's Point to gain the advantage of more amenable conditions—wrong place, wrong time, sad to say. Your third officer shouldn't have changed course without consulting Captain Leland first. All proper procedure aside, Captain Leland is one of the finest coasting pilots that ever was. In that weather, I wouldn't have altered Captain Leland's set course without firm orders for love or money. If you're that witless, you might just as well jump over the side. Your end would come up craps either way."

Mr. Copes shook his head sadly, took off his spectacles, and wiped his face with a large blue bandanna. When he looked up he spoke softly. "I'm not all that sure how he did it, but your Mr. Ryfkogel found the meanest granite spike for a hundred miles, just about seven hundred and fifty yards off the Point there. He skewered your poor ship on her like a pike on a pole. That makes the second corpse for that bloody rock since I've been here. Oh, you can't see it, of course, but that bloody tooth will bite the keel out of any vessel that even dares come near it. We used to have a dog like that, as dangerous as a drunk judge. Shot the fool dog. Can't do a damn thing about that cursed rock."

Chapel's expression of concern encouraged Mr. Copes to continue his point. "Didn't I mention it before? I'm so sorry. It's been such a point of discussion around here that I thought I had remarked upon the oddity of it. Nineteen years ago the *Ventura* met her end on that very same villain. I was just a new fish then, but I remember it was far worse to my way of thinking. The *Ventura*'s captain lost all control of his men. It was . . ."

Chapel waved his hand before his face as though he were denying another morsel of food before choking. Mr. Copes was pained to find his news so distressing and begged Mr. Chapel not to anguish so. All was as well as could be expected. Only six people had lost their lives—a credulous bargain when one considered the alternatives.

Again Chapel gestured for Mr. Copes to cease. He looked almost ill. Mr. Copes went silent. After a moment he rose to leave, not wishing to trouble the unhappy seaman further.

Chapel recovered himself and apologized. To change the subject he asked for his clothes and the loan of a warm coat. Chapel said he would take Mr. Copes up on his offer of a walk. He complained that he was coming on rather stiff without his normal exercise. Staying abed made him jittery. He needed to get about to feel better and requested a tour of the lighthouse when Mr. Copes could find the time.

Mr. Copes said he would be happy to show Mr. Lodge around and indeed returned ten minutes later with his clothes, now dry and relatively clean. His leather seaboots were somewhat worse for wear due to their long immersion in salt water, but a little mink oil and tallow might bring them back.

Kindly Mr. Copes also brought a sturdy waxed-canvas deck coat, which must have belonged to a ship's officer at one time. He also proffered another gift. He had noticed how Mr. Lodge squinted when the full light of the sun came up from behind the mountains and thought he might be of some service in that regard. He handed Chapel a pair of steel-framed dark glasses with round beetle-green lenses.

Chapel had seen Captain Leland wear similar glasses to cut the glare off the ocean. Chapel accepted the gift with gratitude and immediately put them on. He expressed satisfaction with the improvement. He confessed that strong light still caused him slight discomfort. He was tired of squinting, he said, as it caused his scalded eyelids some pain to do so.

Ten minutes later Chapel stood at the rail of the light tower while Mr. Copes pointed out the *Los Angeles*' last resting place. Chapel could just make out the flag yard with its tattered Pacific Steamship Company pennant flapping stubbornly above the waves. The signal mast and rigging had been his last refuge before rescue. He found it difficult to take his eyes from the scene.

Mr. Copes then pointed out the area where the survivors had been brought ashore. There Chapel saw the broken line of debris running up the beach. He also saw the *Los Angeles'* lifeboats and motor launch pulled up just above the high-water mark. One of the lifeboats had already suffered from the sharp winter tides. She lay on her beam-ends, half filled with sand and storm-shredded kelp; her stern received the pounding waves and would not long remain in one piece. The motor launch, because it was larger and more difficult to haul out, would soon suffer the same fate if she was not tended to, but Chapel said nothing of this.

Mr. Copes remarked that most everything salvageable had already been gathered up by the locals, which was their right. He related that when Dr. Roberts first saw the dressed veal carcasses from the ship's cargo tossing about in the surf, he thought they were mutilated human casualties of the disaster. He was much relieved to discover his error.

What meat could be retrieved was hauled away; the rest made up a sizable honorarium for the sharks. They had become quite numerous after the wreck. Mr. Copes even gestured to three large whites patrolling the shore just beyond the breakers. Doubtless they were awaiting further tribute to wash from the wreck as she slowly broke up on the submerged rocks off Point Sur.

"Of course," said Mr. Copes, "we might not have known you were out there in the first place. The night was that thick and blind. We couldn't hear your signals over the gale, either. The light only moved out six hundred feet and then came home with its tail between its legs. You must have seen us, but I'll be damned if we could see you. If it hadn't been for those Filipino boys in your black gang, we might not have known about the wreck at all. One of them climbed hand over hand up the seaward slope to get us to man our surfboats. Against all our appeals the black gang attempted to launch back to the ship, but the surf capsized their lifeboat and knocked them about something fierce. The little beggars were going to try it again, but Mr. Keely insisted that they stay ashore. They would have been killed, sure as God made fools and politicians. It takes long practice and skill to launch a thirty-foot boat into a twenty-foot surf. Not just any able hand with an oar can do it. Those boys were spent. Never would have made it a second time, but you can't fault their pluck. Six little gobs in a thirty-footer? The sweeps were three times taller than they were, but as faithful as wolfhounds and twice as tough. Four of those boys joined our surfboat crews and went out to bring you and Captain Leland in."

Chapel felt a sharp, rushing glow sweep over his entire frame. It flushed his face and sent cold shivers up his spine. He began to tremble, and through it all, he nursed a spike of guilt for believing the worst. The black gang's desertion had disturbed him deeply. He knew those men to be anything but cowards, yet it had seemed to all that they had abandoned their friends.

It was comforting to learn that the black gang, in fact, had shown more common sense than Mr. Ryfkogel would ever testify to. It would make no difference to the official version of the truth. Most ships' officers were a breed apart when it came to intelligence. It was not healthy to put your life in their hands when better alternatives showed themselves.

Chapel could easily fathom the black gang's reasoning. He only wished that they had called out their purpose on that night. It would have set the lie in the third officer's teeth and forced him to swallow his curses. How Mr. Ryfkogel could explain missing one of the most prominent lighthouses on the coast would have to be defined to somebody in authority, but Chapel was confident no one would ever hear an answer worth a damn. The truth, or its facsimile, would be disguised in a formal court jargon specifically designed to keep swabs like him in the dark. So be it. They were a breed apart, for sure.

"Was Captain Leland informed of all this?" asked Chapel.

Mr. Copes assured him that the captain knew all. Mr. Keely had even enlightened Captain Leland about the courageous conduct of his black gang. The captain seemed relieved and gratified. He in turn had seen to it that the Filipinos received every consideration and care, insisting they be taken north with the other survivors.

Tino, Chapel remembered, had told him he had relatives working in Salinas. Lots of Filipinos in Salinas, Tino had said. At least the boys would be close to family and friends. Chapel hoped he would get the opportunity to see them again. He wanted to thank them for saving their hides in spite of Mr. Ryfkogel's foul curses.

All of a sudden Chapel felt bone-weary. The sensation of complete exhaustion came over him in chilling, clammy folds. He found himself forced to sit down until the spell passed.

Mr. Copes suggested that maybe he should escort his charge back to his room. Perhaps Mr. Lodge should call it quits for a while. He could not expect to feel his old self on his first day up and about. "Besides," said Mr. Copes with a chuckle, "Mr. Beauvell, our esteemed cook and surfboat coxswain, has promised a glorious leg of veal, roasted to perfection with apples, oysters, onions, and black currants. He named the dish in honor of the founder of the feast. He calls it Ternera de *Los Angeles*. He saved two whole veal sides from the surf. Today, if you like, you can mess down with us, meet everyone, feel more on deck, less cumbersome than eating in bed. But perhaps you should bunk down for a while. Let me hoist you up. We'll get you out of this damp wind first thing."

The supper was everything Mr. Copes had promised, but Chapel found himself beset with a quandary that prevented anything like a real appreciation of Mr. Beauvell's talents. Chapel appeared preoccupied, and the lighthouse crew, though a jovial set at mealtimes, were inclined to let Chapel brood without comment.

Coming so dangerously close to death at sea often put survivors off their feed. Sometimes the consequences were far worse. There had been that young woman from San Diego. She had survived the wreck of the *Ventura* only to go mad with grief and throw herself off a cliff near Notley's Landing when they were taking the survivors north to Monterey. She had lost her young husband in the disaster and chose to join him in death rather than go on.

The human soul could tolerate only so much anguish before failing like a cracked eggshell. Chapel recalled an old carpenter's mate who had once confided that life didn't make you stronger with time. Just the opposite—it made you more fragile with each passing year. Things like misery, affliction, and torment just sped the progress toward the "shroud eternal."

That night, in spite of his weariness, Chapel found it next to impossible to sleep. Even the fine, dark rum Mr. Copes shared with him after supper encouraged wakefulness rather than sleep.

He tossed about to make himself comfortable, but his restless self-questioning found lumps at every turn. Again and again he mulled over future prospects. Each possibility seemed blunted by the fact that his life was not in his own keeping.

Chapel was also keenly aware that sailors who did survive an unlucky wreck were themselves seen as ill-starred and were often unwelcome Jonahs aboard their next vessel, as though they themselves were the responsible agents of the ship's destruction.

He had met seamen who had spent many months beached because their fellows, an infinitely superstitious lot, would not tolerate even a hint of bad luck near their ships.

Chapel was not resentful. He readily understood the power of a seaman's affinity for his ship. He harbored the same feelings. He too would be wary of a star-crossed hand who had ships die beneath him or who constantly found himself beached by ill fortune.

At last Chapel slept, but the crossover between the cares of his waking state and those of his dreams was marginal at best. He dreamed of being taken aboard the power launch after the wreck, but when he opened his eyes in the dream he was alone. There remained no evidence of the men who had pulled him from the frigid waters.

Instead, he found himself adrift on a glass-smooth sea, floating gently upon swells of translucent, green water. When he looked down he found himself gripping a hand line and bobbin. He was fishing and, from what he could remember from the dream, enjoying himself immensely; in fact, the feeling of well-being stayed with him for quite some time.

AFTER DRESSING AND TAKING BREAKFAST with his hosts the next morning, Chapel determined to walk down the steep road from the lighthouse and across the broad isthmus that led to the coast road. He needed the exercise, and though heartened by Mr. Copes and his attentive friends, Chapel resolved to spend as much time alone as possible. He had much to mull over, and the distractions of even friendly conversation set him at odds with his thoughts.

As he made his way down the winding road from the lighthouse complex, Chapel passed two of the lighthouse attendants on their way up. The men were deep in discussion and almost missed Chapel's greeting. He heard them speak of the remaining lifeboats. The first man said he feared the high tides would either destroy or refloat the boats by tomorrow if left unattended.

They were expecting Stew Paterson, from the logging company, to bring down a long team of mules to help draw the boats farther up on the beach until Pacific Steamship decided what to do with them. But just when they could expect the team to arrive was anybody's guess.

The second man piped in with the opinion that it was all a great waste of time. The boats were a write-off for the company. In all likelihood they would never hear another word about it. "Those boats are as good as kindling right now," said the second keeper. "No good will come of the effort. Mark me, kindling by the fourth tide, or I'm a Welsh mine pony."

Chapel decided to go have a look at the boats for himself. They were all that was left of his ship, and he determined to bid them a friendly farewell before the surf and tides reduced them to painted bones among the spindrift and beached kelp.

It was a long walk down to the shore, but Chapel felt all the better for the excursion. He made his way out to the beach and the wet, hard-packed sand just below the tide line. Scattered debris from the *Los Angeles* still littered the beach. There seemed little left of value except to the crabs and gulls. Everything of even marginal utility had been carted away by the local inhabitants.

Higher on the shore, Chapel could still make out the tracks of the wagons that had come down to the beach for that purpose. He supposed that it had been one of those conveyances that had hauled his unconscious and waterlogged body up the hill.

As he approached the boats, Chapel saw for himself that what the two lightkeepers had said was true. As he had seen from the lighthouse, the lifeboat used by the black gang was now banked and half buried in wet sand above the low-tide mark, and the other, though seemingly intact, had a part of her port stern stove in by a spar that had crashed through her strakes on the crest of a wave.

The motor launch, though larger than the other two boats and in relatively the same position on the beach, seemed to have survived unscathed. It was obvious that her stern had been washed repeatedly by the tides. The waves had undercut the sand beneath the aft portion of the launch, and it was a sure bet that the next few tides would either tear up her stern or continue the erosion under her keel until she either broached to an incoming wave and swamped or floated away on the foam to return to shore as painted driftwood in a few weeks.

Chapel indulged the sailor's instinct to climb aboard and inspect the extent of damage, or in this case, salvage—an immemorial tradition following the death of ships. He was naturally surprised to discover everything in place. The double-ended motor launch had only recently been converted from an oar- and sail-driven thirty-foot cutter. She was powered by a cranky two-cylinder Union gas engine that could brag only minimal practicality in anything but harbor conditions.

For this reason her masts, yards, and lugsails were still soundly lashed to the thwarts, and her oarlocks and tholepins were stowed in their proper places. Her long sweeps had been replaced with box oars, but aside from that, everything Chapel expected to find on a motor launch cum lifeboat was there.

An afterthought brought Chapel to inspect the fuel tank. He found it more than two-thirds full, approximately twenty gallons. The water casks were sealed and full and the soldered, tin boxes of emergency rations were still securely stowed in the appropriate lockers beneath the stern sheets.

Hand lines, fish tackle, sea anchor, and spare stores remained in place under the bow locker. Chapel supposed that the local ranchers had little use for oars, sails, or the like. It was sad to imagine this motherless child as so much driftwood, but it was already too late to save her.

The worst of the winter tides were due in the next forty-eight hours. He had heard the lighthouse keepers speaking of it. It seemed most unlikely that the Pacific Steamship Company would send a vessel to retrieve three storm-battered boats. The tides would steal their property from under their noses, and no one would really care. Already the southwest winds were adding to the momentum of the swells. If the surf cut up rough, the next few tides would see the last token of the *Los Angeles* above the waves. Her signal yard and company pennant would be drawn back into the sea. As for the boats, when the mule teamsters finally did arrive, they would be looking at an empty beach.

Chapel shook his head and jumped off the boat onto the wet sand. Little puddles of seawater instantly appeared in his footprints. He looked up to the lighthouse and experienced a spontaneous shiver.

Great ribbons of drifting fog had appeared without Chapel's notice. They wrapped themselves about the great rock like giant fingers. The light flashed out across the misty waters, and the sonorous bellow of the foghorn began to reverberate over everything.

As he walked toward the road that climbed up through the advancing mists to the lighthouse, Chapel turned one last time to look down at the shore. Within moments everything became one with the fog and all detail melted away.

Chapel began to reflect upon questions that were only now finding resolve and purpose. He faced a world of diminishing prospects, and only determination and ingenuity could lead him out of his pit of aching uncertainty. But one thing became certain with time. If the dream was a true reflection of Chapel's soul, then he was free to be his own vessel and his own master. All he needed to do was chart the course and leave the rest to faith and the dream.

MR. COPES WAS DISAPPOINTED not to find Chapel at supper. He was also disappointed in his search after the meal. He discovered after asking others that Mr. Lodge was nowhere on the premises. So without company, Mr. Copes enjoyed the dark Jamaican rum all by himself and went to bed. He would rise to tend the light by three—plenty of time to look in on the castaway then.

When Chapel proved still absent at three in the morning, Mr. Copes became alarmed. He informed the others of his discovery, and a small search was mustered out at first light.

The fog had advanced in heavy damp waves of ever-increasing density throughout the night. Even with a storm lamp set bright, it was difficult to know where to set foot, much less carry out a competent search over acres of hillside and shore.

The men returned after an hour of calling Chapel's name into the foggy void. Lamentable though it was, the lighthouse crew were forced to surmise that unfortunate circumstances might have led to an accident. It was a long fall off Point Sur, and the fog would have disguised every track up the hill save the main road, and that was none too safe under certain conditions.

Whatever the truth behind the disappearance of Mr. Lodge, nothing could possibly be accomplished before the fog lifted. As it stood, the lighthouse crew had their hands full with other duties. Mr. Lodge was in God's hands until something like a real search could be fielded.

It seemed markedly unusual to everybody's way of thinking, but the impenetrable coastal fog lasted four days and nights without breaking. The warning horn on Point Sur almost set everyone within earshot at one another's throats before the gray wall lifted. A serious search for Chapel was initiated for part of each day, but nothing of substance was ever discovered. The tidal surge had predictably made a mess of the lifeboats, but that had been expected.

The capsized lifeboat was buried even deeper in the sand, and the waves had torn off the rudder and rudderpost and cast it up on the beach like a bone. The second boat barely floated sixty yards offshore, suspended between heaven and hell by her airtight lockers, a sad purgatory that would not last for long. The motor launch, however, was gone, but it was not re-marked as anything unusual. Everyone had seen how precari-ous her beaching had been. The boat would no doubt be found dashed against the rocks or swamped upside down somewhere.

The loss of company property, of course, meant little when set against the disappearance of one of the survivors. But in the end Mr. Chapel Lodge, ordinary seaman, late of the wrecked *Los Angeles*, was to become just another unhappy footnote in a long report to the Lighthouse Service.

It might be equitable to say that Mr. Copes, and perhaps others, remembered the poor lost sailor in their prayers for a while, but no other observances were ever seen as necessary or appropriate.

Twelve years had passed since the *Los Angeles* disaster, and few but coastal residents and seamen bothered to recall the incident. The tale was trotted out for curious tourists now and then, but most of the time people preferred not to speak of the episode. Then one day a well-dressed gentleman with snow-white hair and a handsomely manicured beard made his way down the Monterey wharf with a lovely young woman hanging happily upon his arm.

The gentleman wore a light-blue, linen suit and a dashing straw boater worn at a rakish angle. He carried a walking stick to address a limp of the left leg, but the impairment didn't seem to hamper his movements to any great degree.

The young woman, the gentleman's granddaughter by all appearances, insisted that they descend to the lower level of the wharf where the fishing boats unloaded as they came in. She maintained that the freshest salmon could only be purchased right off the boat.

The old gentleman smiled, acquiesced indulgently, stroked his goatee, and followed with a wave of his stick. Once below in the cool shadows beneath the main wharf, the stench of the fishing trade became more pronounced, but the old gentleman reveled in the aroma. When the young woman dashed off to inspect a promising catch being unloaded, the gentleman settled back to watch the approaching boats come off the bay.

One boat in particular caught his attention. The small craft was unusual for a Monterey fishing vessel. It sported an odd little pilothouse well astern that was obviously not part of the original design of the vessel. With its diminutive mizzenmast and staysail, the boat had the look of a small Norwegian trawler without the normal net booms.

Instead, she carried three large tackle reels port and starboard. The gentleman estimated that each reel must have carried at least two thousand feet of sturdy linen line. No other standard fishing gear was visible. Something about the boat's design caught the old gentleman's eye. He couldn't quite place where he'd seen those lines before, but he would remember.

As luck would have it, the boat in question made points to land near the very spot where the man was standing. As he watched, a handsome Mexican boy with shaggy hair came forward from the pilothouse to prepare the spring lines for docking. The gentleman noticed that the vessel wasn't a company boat because she carried no fleet number on her beams, but he did mark the name hand-painted in red letters on the bows. She was called *Trabar Fortuna*.

As the fishing boat coasted toward the landing, the Mexican boy prefashioned a full hitch in the bowline and then cast it deftly over the appropriate piling. Before the bowline had even gone taut, the boy had accomplished the same with the stern. The vessel came gently to rest against the pilings without even a squeak. The white-haired gentleman nodded his head and smiled in admiration. But he couldn't shake the feeling that there was still something odd about the little vessel. He couldn't quite put his finger on the incongruity, but it was there somewhere.

The gentleman's curiosity had been piqued. He made his way to the edge of the dock, exchanged a smile with the cheerful Mexican boy, and looked into the open fish holds. He was surprised to find not fish, but sharks. Small, exotic sharks with dark skins and eyes like precious emeralds. Albino sharks two feet long with eyes like burning rubies and fins tipped in mother-of-pearl.

There were sharks only eighteen inches long that sported camouflage akin to jungle cats and possessed eyes like large, jet-black pearls. As his well-schooled gaze ran over the boat, the gentleman's eye was caught by a stamped commissioning plaque attached to what had been the foremast step. It had been painted over many times, but he could still make out the letters even at that distance. *USS WYANDA*. He smiled and nodded to himself again.

The captain of the fishing boat emerged from the little pilothouse. He was weathered beyond any judgment of age. He could have been thirty, or he might have been forty-five or fifty. It was impossible to tell. He wore a Portuguese knit cap and a hooded sea coat. He walked toward the holds and stared up at the dapper older gentleman through archaic beetle-green dark glasses.

The stranger touched his hat in an offhand military fashion and began to inquire about the oddity of the catch. "Where do you hunt these strange specimens, sir? I have never seen anything quite like them."

The fisherman touched his cap to return the salute. "I take

them deep, sir, very deep. There's a mighty great valley that cuts across the bay out there, an almighty trench. No bottom at all sometimes. These wonderful critters live thousands of feet down, sir. Takes hard work to set and draw trawl lines that deep, but it's well worth the effort, sir. The wee beasties are worth their weight in gold."

The fisherman laughed at the look of incredulous skepticism on the elegant stranger's face. The fisherman winked at the Mexican boy as though they shared a private joke.

The old man smiled and asked, "So she's a lucrative little venture, is she? She looks like a craft worthy of her heritage."

The fisherman grinned with pleasure. "Well yes, sir, when the luck is with us, but beyond that, it gives a man great pleasure to be master of his own craft, so to speak." The fisherman seemed to enjoy his own pun, but continued when he found his audience had taken no notice. "I take little pleasure in anything but my boat and my skill. But you know how it is, sir."

The man stroked his goatee and nodded. "But to who do you sell these unusual creatures? I've never seen one on a plate, and I've messed down on my share of fish, I can tell you."

The fisherman smiled and began sorting the varieties of catch into separate baskets fetched from a dock shed by the Mexican boy. "Why, sir, I sell them to the gentlemen standing just behind you, and a very generous lot they are when they get what they want. They never fail to clear out my whole catch, and for that my little ship and I are deeply grateful."

The man slowly turned about and noticed six well-dressed Chinese patiently waiting politely for an opportunity to speak to the fisherman. They smiled self-consciously, bowed slightly, but said nothing. The white-haired gentleman faltered a graceful apology for the interruption of business, tipped his boater, began to withdraw, and then stopped.

"How did you come by your unusual vessel, sir, if I might ask? Just a matter of idle curiosity, I assure you."

"You're by no means the first to ask, and the answer is always the same. Blind luck, sir, and that's the God's honest. Take it from a ship's brat what knows, as they say. It's always a matter of blind luck for men like us. As long as God loves fools and the fishing is good we go on. As for my boat, it would be fair and honest to say we found each other, but isn't that always the way of it, sir? Like true love, every now and then a fellow gets lucky, don't you know."

A young woman's voice called out from a distance, almost lost over the noisy commotion of the wharf. The old man turned to the sound. The girl called out again.

"Grandpa! Grandpa, come here at once. I've found the king of all salmons. It will make the wedding supper supreme. Where are you, Grandpa? Come give this man his price before it's gone! Captain Leland! Are you there? Captain Leland? Show yourself, Grandpa. This beauty isn't getting any fresher."

When the fisherman heard the gentleman's name called out he looked up in surprise. He would have said something to his old captain, but the gentleman had disappeared, leaving a file of eager, bowing Chinese to take his place.

At once the bargaining began in earnest. The smiling Mexican boy translated bids and counteroffers at a mile a minute. The Chinese spoke near-perfect Spanish, but little English. This paradox always amused most people. These important Chinese customers were appraised as fine doctors among their own society, though the fisherman suspected more magic than medicine to their arts.

In the end it hardly mattered. The Chinese always paid top prices, bowed politely, thanked Captain Lodge for his efforts, and never made a fuss. Lodge seized on these unadorned courtesies as high praise for a plainspoken fisherman with no home save his boat.

Plain he may have been, but Chapel Lodge lived a long, enterprising, and cheerful life. He died in his sleep aboard his last boat, the *Dulce Fortuna*, at the venerable age of eighty-six; his faithful old bilge cat, Mr. Pepper, stayed with him until the end. It was agreed by all that Captain Lodge passed away gracefully at home and in the very best of company.

An Unbecoming Grace

⁓

Doc Roberts was a respected medical man and good friend to almost everybody on the Monterey coast. In one sense it might even have been said that he was indispensable, being the only physician willing to ride the long and dangerous coastal mountain circuit to care for his patients. His perseverance and dedication were well regarded by all who knew him, and even crazy old man Clarke, who wasn't the least bit crazy, said Doc Roberts had the sharpest aptitude for the truth of any man he had ever met. That comment passed for something rare and unique, coming as it did from a man who went to great lengths to camouflage his own extensive scholastic credentials under the guise of partial but harmless derangement.

The doctor was a strongly built specimen with orderly, handsome features and a generous expression, a look that inspired instant confidence and respect in strangers. His dark hair and full mustache were set in fine proportions. His narrow, pale eyes habitually cast an expression of warm concentration and interest. His handsome and pleasant features, when crowned with a physician's social status, had enticed many a young woman to pass her hours in hopeful speculation.

Inventive feminine ploys had not gone unnoticed by the intended victim, so Doc forestalled all future attempts in that vein by sending for his young fiancée and marrying her at once. This one act did wonders for his respectability in Monterey. A family man of sober habits could be trusted not to desert his responsibilities to his patients. At least that was the model supposition of the day.

After six years of practice, from Monterey to the Big Sur, Doc Roberts had accumulated an inestimable treasure of gratitude, loyalty, and respect. In fact, Doc's rounds actually carried him from Santa Cruz in the north to the jagged mountains of the Big Sur in the south. But it was always in the heart of the Big Sur that he was happiest. If there was a trail—and if his horse, Daisy, didn't throw a shoe, refuse the hitch, or pretend to go lame—Doc Roberts would make his way to the sufferer without fail. His favorite mode of transport, if the roads were decent and the weather marginally dry, was his two-wheeled cart.

Doc's cart was a hybrid vehicle of his own design and fabrication. Because he was not particularly skilled in simple carpentry, Doc's rig presented a sadly slapdash appearance. He had purchased the frame, axle, and wheels from John Gilkey and had proceeded to build a crude pine box on top of the frame. No two boards matched; all were crudely nailed; and when the wood had fully dried, all the knots fell out, leaving holes everywhere. Doc said it made for better drainage in the rain.

Tom Doud once witnessed Daisy kick up a fit and take on a bit mulish while Doc struggled in vain to maneuver the wary animal into her hitch. Tom Doud was an earnest and forthright rancher who took the opportunity to express the opinion that no self-respecting four-legged beast, regardless of species, would want to be seen near Doc's cart, much less be caught pulling it anywhere.

He told Doc to his face that his cart was an eyesore, more fitted to the transport of plague victims than the conveyance of a successful doctor. As far as he was concerned, it was no wonder the poor animal wanted nothing to do with the bargain. The humiliated creature shivered and hung its head with shame at the prospect.

Tom laughed and said, "Your mare may be only a simple dumb beast, Doctor, but she's not downright stupid." This insight didn't particularly amuse Doc Roberts at the time, but Tom Doud almost soiled his pants laughing at his own quip. Tom told the story affectionately for years. Secretly, Doc was forced to admit to himself that Daisy much preferred the saddle to the hitch, but the cart carried more supplies and there was room to convey a serious patient to the little hospital in Monterey if necessary. So, as far as Doc Roberts was concerned, Daisy would eventually have to bow to public service when required, just as he did.

IN THOSE RUGGED DAYS THE MONTEREY COAST shouldered more than its fair allotment of scoundrels, but even among this callous fraternity there was one character who was rigorously shunned, even by the rest of the roguish brotherhood. He was a perfidious and miserly old rancher who ran a pathetic spread out of a dilapidated house atop a promontory then known as Grace Point. His lair was approximately fifteen miles south of the Big Sur River. Everyone agreed that the old man's livestock (cattle, horses, pigs, and chickens) were of the most deplorable sort and condition. These sad creatures looked as though they longed for immediate dispatch from the miseries of this world in favor of the relative peace and tranquility of the smokehouse, tannery, and bone mill.

The malevolent old man had a name, but nobody chose to use it. Everyone referred to him, when at all necessary, as "the old Stoat." This discerning appellation not only characterized his weasel-like attributes, but also alluded to his controversial acquisition of a young bride of eighteen. The girl was a shy, penurious child from the streets of King City with little understanding of the world.

Rumor had it that the Stoat treated her unmercifully and did everything in his power to break her simple spirit. The Stoat was also widely known for his liberal use of the foulest language possible. It was said that he savored and unleashed his sharpest thorns on his child bride, habitually reducing her to defenseless tears. These anecdotes were commonly acknowledged by his neighbors, so it would not seem strange that almost everyone found something detestable in the Stoat's character. In fact, it might have been fair to assume that most people would have celebrated his timely reunion with the primordial dust from which he sprang.

Doc Roberts was usually too preoccupied with his own business to affect much interest in gossip, so he was only marginally prepared with intelligence when one day he found himself summoned to the side of the crusty old rancher to treat a badly broken leg.

Young Ned Murray had brought word of the accident when he came into town for supplies, so Doc Roberts determined to take his cart in case the old man required surgical attention in Monterey. The doctor was not one for unnecessary amputations.

Having assembled the requisite medical supplies, Doc hitched up Daisy and made his way south. Since Daisy knew the way down the old coast road without meddlesome interference, Doc secured occasional opportunities to read his medical journals, eat sandwiches, or drink coffee without reference to his course. He had often napped in the back of his cart in full confidence of Daisy's discretion.

The doctor sometimes stopped to greet a friend or patient on the road, but more often than not, the route was barren of incidental traffic. The occasional tinker or peddler sometimes camped by the way, and these dusty gentlemen of the road always received a civil greeting and a few moments' conversation from the doctor. He had discovered that commercial travelers often held keys to all manner of useful intelligence.

About a half mile north of the western cutoff to the Stoat's homestead, Doc Roberts came across just such a fellow. Mr. Elysium Shellworth Grey, as he styled himself, was a traveling vendor of patent medicines and numerous varieties of everyday pharmacopoeia. A sign on his highly decorated box wagon announced the vending of trusses, braces, crutches, and prosthetic devices at reasonable cost.

The duster-clad Mr. Grey was in the process of greasing a troublesome axle when Doc Roberts pulled up with an amiable greeting. A few moments' pleasantries revealed that the peddler had just come from the doctor's destination.

Mr. Grey shook his head slowly and rolled his eyes to

heaven. "That crusty old bastard is a real piece of work and no mistake. I could have saved myself the trouble of visiting the bloody old pike. They said up at Notley's Landing that a rancher had broken his leg. I thought it would be a kindness to go out of my way to see if I could be of service. I'm not a doctor you understand, but I do dispense a very fine tincture of laudanum that would have alleviated his pain until medical services could be rendered."

Mr. Grey wormed the wheel back onto the greased axle while he talked. The effort made him grunt by way of punctuation. "You should have heard the man swear and scream at the audacity of my uninvited visit. After calling me every name he could remember, he shouted that a real doctor would be on his way, and that he would tolerate no traveling villains on his place. The old reprobate possesses the vocabulary of a ship-bound bosun. I do assure you I've never heard the likes of such language from anyone who wasn't waiting to be hanged. Then the old heathen turned his extraordinary venom on this young girl. I was dumbstruck to discover the wretched creature was the ogre's wife. The poor thing just shuddered and wept like a whipped spaniel. Pretty little waif too. Sad to see her so ill used. Well, not content to abuse the child, he rounded back on me with lewd accusations indicting my presence as having something to do with his child bride. I swear I never laid eyes on the youngster before in my life. That evil old crow is crazy, I'd bet my life on it, but he's falling off his perch and that's no mistake. Then suddenly the antique bushwhacker pulls a horse pistol from under his pillow and threatens to kill me if my wagon isn't rolling out of his yard in ten seconds. I decided not to test the old man's resolve in the matter. I bid him a brief farewell and beat a hasty and thankfully bloodless retreat. I don't imagine many people of his acquaintance are that lucky. His broken leg might have slowed him down a bit, but I'm grateful to the Almighty all the same. So, are you the doc the old scoundrel is waiting on?"

Doc Roberts smiled, pushed back his hat, and wiped the grit from his face with a new bandanna. "Yes, and it's been a long pull for the two of us," he said, indicating Daisy's hangdog disposition. "The patient may happily mend his own damn leg for the price of a casual insult, but sometimes acute suffering may cause a being to act in a most outrageous fashion. One must refrain from sudden judgments in my line of work."

Doc Roberts touched his hat in farewell and snapped the reins, but something came to mind and he halted to ask the peddler a question. "I believe you mentioned that you carry a reputable tincture of laudanum. Were you serious? I also stand in need of a pint bottle of dark rum, a small bottle of vanilla extract, and oil of cloves."

The thought of making a sale after his humiliating retreat animated Mr. Grey as nothing else could. He left the hub bolt, wiped his greasy hands on a rag, and jumped into the back of his wagon.

Doc Roberts listened as the man rummaged through his stock in search of the required items. Doc was amused to hear the peddler talk to himself while he did so. After two minutes Mr. Grey emerged clutching the exact items requested. He was genuinely pleased to have been of some profitable service, perhaps the last of the day.

Because the doctor was obviously a professional man with influence, Mr. Grey thought it prudent to discount market value for his wares in hopes the doctor might return the kindness one day. Doc Roberts paid, stowed the bottles in the cart, waved good-bye, and drove on south.

The turnout to the Stoat's ranch was framed by a warped gate that swung in the wind. It made forlorn sounds on its dying, rusty hinges. A few hundred feet down the overgrown road, Doc's cart came to a deep depression that had once been a wide streambed centuries before. From this vantage point Doc could see neither the high road nor the house and he, in turn, could not be seen. Here Doc Roberts halted Daisy and made his preparations. From a carpetbag, he extracted a large, empty medicine bottle that still sported a cryptic medical label. He always carried such items to hold fluid samples or dispense medication. Into the bottle Doc poured a measured amount of laudanum, a healthy dash of vanilla extract, and a few drops of clove oil to give the blend a medicinal bite. Lastly he added a quarter pint of the dark rum. He recorked the concoction, shook it twice, and placed it in his medical bag. Once satisfied, he continued the short quarter mile to the house.

Daisy appeared to confront the ramshackle buildings with the same sense of trepidation that Doc Roberts was presently feeling. Emotionally unstable patients often made simple doctoring a precarious endeavor. Doc Roberts steeled himself against the darker possibilities and slowed Daisy's pace.

There was little to differentiate the barn from the house except windows. In fact, all the outbuildings wore a shabby weatherworn pallor that gave the whole vista an air of ceaseless desiccation. One sensed the salted winds and sea mists would soon erode the bleached boards and shingles into rotting splinters. It had probably looked that way for years.

Doc guided his cart to the front of the house and called out his own name by way of introduction. He waited without dismounting and then called out again. After a few moments the door opened and a bedraggled girl stepped out on the porch with her arms crossed guardedly across her chest. She stared up at Doc Roberts with a curious expression of child-like expectation.

Doc asked the doe-eyed girl if an injured man lay within, a man with a broken leg. He found it difficult to believe that this simple child could be anyone's wife. The girl nodded without speaking and gestured toward the open door. Doc stepped down, unloaded his bags from the cart, and unhitched Daisy from her traces. The mare pranced away from the cart rails with a nervous skip, and Doc led her to the water trough before securing her halter to the porch rail.

The girl had placed the doctor's things within the door and waited for his return. As he approached, Doc Roberts took a chill that made him shiver, as though he were leaving a world of warmth for a realm of frosts. He hefted his Gladstone and allowed the girl to lead him to a fetid bedroom that occupied the far end of the dilapidated house.

The wild-looking old man lay fully clothed in a stained sweater and filthy, patched overalls. He must have lain that way for days. He sweated upon an ancient mattress that sagged in the straps of a rust-chipped iron bed frame. Whatever his animated outbursts might have been with Mr. Grey, the old rancher was now quiet and obviously suffering from a level of exhaustion only chronic agony can induce.

As Doc approached, the old man's eyes flinched and narrowed suspiciously in his direction. A hooded prospect of misgiving clouded his brow, but the pain in the man's leg was the greater distraction, and he surrendered to it with a wincing groan.

Dr. Roberts introduced himself formally and set his bag on a rickety table placed by the bed. The old rancher's expression tightened with consternation, but he nodded his rawboned head in acknowledgment and then inclined it toward a bloody patch of blanket that covered his right leg. Doc Roberts lifted away the soiled covering to reveal a blood-soaked and putrid pant leg. He opened his medical bag and removed a folding instrument case. From this he withdrew surgical shears to cut away the clotted fabric. As Doc had expected from the amount of blood, the broken bone had penetrated the skin badly, and it would prove no easy task to reset the leg. The shock alone could kill a man of his years and dissipated constitution. The old man propped himself up on his elbows, but Dr. Roberts ordered him to lie back and save what little strength he had. It was obvious to the doctor that his patient was incapable of untroubled cooperation. Doc hoped the rancher's young wife would not prove helpless as well.

Doc reached into his Gladstone and took out the concocted medicine bottle. He uncorked the stopper and handed the preparation to the old man with instructions to drink as much as he liked. It would help kill the pain and give some relief before the leg was treated. The old pike sniffed the bottle skeptically, but his eyes widened at the sweet alcoholic aroma and he took a swig.

One sip lightened the old man's anxious expression. He next took a long gurgling pull on the bottle and lay back on his greasy pillow with a sigh of long-sought relief.

Doc Roberts announced that he would see to his horse and return in a few minutes when the medicine had taken effect. Turning to the girl standing in the door, he gave instructions to have a generous kettle of clean water boiled immediately. With that he left to attend to Daisy's needs.

Doc retrieved a clean canvas bucket from his cart and filled it with sweet oats. This he lashed to the hitching post for the mare's convenience. He curried Daisy with a stiff brush while she ate and covered the grateful animal with a stable blanket against the damp sea air before returning to the house.

After Doc Roberts had washed up and returned to his patient he found the old man almost comatose. He had consumed half the bottle of adulterated rum and lay happily insensate on his rat's nest of a mattress. Doc summoned the rancher's wife to bring the water and assist in other small matters. When he had sheared off the pant leg, Doc washed the ugly wound thoroughly and painted the whole area with a malodorous disinfectant that stained the skin an unattractive ocher. Then Doc Roberts had the apprehensive child bride secure the patient's right hip with heavy pressure while Doc pulled and adjusted the limb in a painfully prolonged attempt to set the withered leg properly. The problem of resetting was made more complex by the irregular nature of the break.

Luckily the old rancher's only response to these excruciating manipulations was an occasional stupefied groan. The patient's opiated state allowed a slight margin of error in the matter of shock, but Doc admonished the girl to see that her husband received plenty of clean water to drink at all times.

After suturing part of the muscle with catgut, Doc Roberts closed the wound with more gut, disinfected it again, and applied a clean bandage. With the girl's hesitant assistance Doc managed to lace up the broken limb in a long, heavy-canvas and whalebone-reinforced splint. This device had been artfully manufactured by a company that made ladies' corsets, and it retained many similarities in the manner of support and lacing.

When he had finished his ministrations, Doc Roberts repositioned the incognizant old man on the soiled mattress in a manner that would give the greatest relief to the leg while keeping the patient as immobile as possible.

He took the opportunity to remove the old man's pistol from under the pillow. Opiates and firearms were a bad mix, to Doc's way of thinking. The gun was hardly the cannon the peddler had described, but Doc unloaded the revolver all the same. He sequestered the weapon and ammunition in the bottom drawer of the rickety old dresser, knowing full well the old man couldn't possibly get at it. When Doc looked up, the girl was gone, nor could he find her in the rest of the house. He shrugged, but thought little of it.

Removing his valises to the kitchen, Doc sat at the kitchen table and set up three small bottles from his bag. Checking them for cleanliness, he arranged them on the table. From his Gladstone he withdrew a small silver funnel, the laudanum, the vanilla extract, oil of clove, a jar of distilled water, and the bottle of rum. He poured the laudanum into the bottle of rum; then, using the funnel, he filled the first bottle two-thirds of the way, the second half, and the last a third. To each of these he then added two tablespoons of vanilla, clove oil, and then topped off each bottle with the distilled water.

He corked the bottles and numbered them 1 through 3 in order of their potency and the order of their administration. Then Doc sat back, loaded his Wellington pipe, and contentedly reveled in the sweet smoke. After a few refreshing puffs, Doc pulled his medical log from the Gladstone and carefully noted down the pertinent facts of the case. Doc imagined that unless some external factor took precedence, the old man would walk with a severe limp for the rest of his life. But many unforeseen complications might yet arise that would substantially alter Doc's generous prognosis. The old man was hardly out of the woods, and in these unsanitary conditions the odds looked none too charitable.

Doc drew a long pull on his pipe and blew a ring of apple-flavored smoke. The floating ring was absurdly imperfect. It always was.

Reflecting upon the girl once more, Doc Roberts speculated that the rancher's young wife had probably let her squeamish nature get the upper hand and had most likely taken herself off to recover over a bucket. Many otherwise brave people fainted dead away at the sight of a suture needle piercing flesh. Their prostrate bodies complicated matters from a medical standpoint, so Dr. Roberts usually discouraged their participation.

Suddenly the front door opened and the silent young girl entered carrying the plucked and gutted carcass of a chicken. Her hands were covered with blood and bits of clinging viscera. Doc's speculations on the subject of squeamishness withered like his smoke rings. He smiled at the child. She smiled back.

While the rancher's wife stoked the rusty iron stove to life, Doc explained the numbered bottles. Her husband was to have one bottle every four days in the order indicated. Did she understand? She smiled and nodded. The child bride blushed slightly and said she knew how to read too.

Doc told her that was just the ticket and went on to explain other necessary procedures to follow regarding the splint and the wound. The girl followed the explanations carefully and repeated every detail accurately when requested to. Doc was satisfied that she understood the responsibilities involved, and with a nod he carried his two bags to the cart.

Meanwhile the girl deftly cleaved the chicken into quarters, dusted the pieces with flour, and fried the batch up in fatback, adding onions, wild mushrooms, and peppers at the end. Doc could smell the obliging fragrance while he packed and rigged his cart.

He allowed Daisy her repose until the last possible moment, but just as he was about to remove the mare's blanket, the rancher's wife emerged from the house with a large wooden platter of hot savory chicken and fixings. It was more than Doc Roberts was prepared to resist.

The girl motioned to the only chair on the porch and handed Doc the trencher and a fork. Like most men, Doc carried his own knife. He sat down on the ancient rocker with the generous platter athwart his knees. Moments later the girl returned with a mug of steaming, sweet coffee that he took gratefully.

Doc was in heaven. He hadn't had a good hot meal in two days, and he knew this would lift his spirits. The girl reappeared with her own small portion and sat on the porch steps to eat.

Together they watched the ocean and the wheeling birds while they enjoyed their meal. The view of the water was striking, but deceptive as to distance because of the cliffs on which the property sat. The homestead simply ended abruptly a hundred feet west of the porch at a sheer sandstone cliff that fell away to the rock-strewn surf ninety-five feet below.

The goats had cropped the grass neatly to the edge of the precipice, so the illusion of great distance and height was splendid and unique. The long drop, however, guaranteed sure fatality to the unwary. The pair quietly watched as large pods of gray whales breached and played just a few hundred yards from shore.

The rancher's wife at last stood and came to take Doc's trencher and fork. He smiled, complimented her on the food, and thanked her for the delicious hospitality. She smiled sweetly in response and turned to go. As an afterthought, Doc Roberts politely asked her name, her maiden name, of course. The girl turned, but did not choose to look at Dr. Roberts directly.

"Mary . . . Mary Rose . . . Mary Rose Dolan. . . . But now my name is . . ." Mary Rose Dolan elected not to finish the sentence. Instead she carried her burden to the kitchen.

Doc Roberts had no difficulty coaxing Daisy into harness. Indeed, one would have held the impression that it was all her own idea. The mare's intuitive faculties were highly developed, and immediate departure was her preferred option. She twitched her ears about as though divining malevolence from every quarter.

Doc climbed up on the cart and took the reins to calm the sensitive creature. Mary Rose reappeared carrying a small cloth bundle that she handed up to Doc Roberts. "It's only some leftover chicken and biscuits," she said meekly. "But you might find the need of it before morning." Doc smiled and accepted with gratitude. "Thank you very kindly, ma'am. Now, you just remember everything I told you to do. I have patients to see farther south, but I will return in a few days to change the dressings and check the splint. Try to keep your husband quiet in the meantime. Just make sure he gets plenty of clean water to drink, especially if he takes a lot of the medicine I left. Thanks again for the food. It's much appreciated, I assure you. . . . Good-bye."

Daisy needed no snap of the reins to inspire departure. She cocked her ears east and set off at a strong trot the moment she heard the word "good-bye." Doc was about to lift his hat to the rancher's wife in farewell, but he found himself attending to a horse with a serious itinerary. The combination of event and gesture had a comic effect that, Doc noticed, induced a broad smile to blossom on the doleful girl's face. Mary Rose watched Daisy prance off, bouncing the cart along with little regard for the good doctor's dignity, balance, or comfort. Daisy seemed determined to put leagues between her and that forlorn splinter of land.

Doc Roberts had brought Daisy to a better understanding of her equine obligations by the time they joined the broad coastal trail. Her first instinct was to head north toward Monterey, so Doc Roberts had to exert some authority to direct her to the southerly route. When the willful animal had settled into a known and trusted course, Doc left the minor details of the road to Daisy's circumspection. He loosely tied the reins through a knothole in the kickboard and lay down in the bed of the cart with his bedroll for a pillow. Within moments he was fast asleep. Daisy preferred to travel without supervision and when left to her own devices provided a gentle excursion. She had learned to avoid most common obstacles and could be trusted to sojourn on her own account for hours without amendment unless hunger or thirst intervened.

Doc awoke as darkness fell. Daisy had become halting and more judicious in her progress, so Doc Roberts hung a kerosene lantern from the kickboard. The flame distributed a reassuring arc of soft light that encouraged the mare when traveling at night. Doc opened Mary Rose's gift and chose a chicken leg with which to pass the time. Then it began to rain.

It had been an inclement month, so Doc had come prepared with oilskin ponchos for both himself and his horse. As long as Daisy could remain essentially dry, she would work on, but once soaked she would just stop, hang her head with a despondent air, and wait for Doc's compassionate intervention. Once wiped down with dry straw and covered with the oilskin poncho Doc had especially fashioned for her, Daisy would set off again with renewed vitality.

For the next six rain-soaked days Doc Roberts attended to his far-flung patients, some of whom were recuperating from a stubborn strain of lingering influenza. When the trails became too muddy for the cart, Doc left the rig at Tom Doud's place.

At this time of year, Doc always carried his old saddle and tack in the cart for just such an eventuality. He pared his medical kit down to those items he could carry in his saddlebags, bedroll, and haversack. The mud-washed tracks would never tolerate the cart, and there was always the danger of landslides obliterating the route altogether. Daisy appeared satisfied with the decision and became almost cooperative in a disinterested sort of way.

Over distended saddlebags, which were in effect dispensary, surgery, and consulting library all in one, Doc tied Daisy's sweet oats. His modest bedroll was secured over the pummel along with canteen straps secured over the horn. Doc had to admit that his saddle was always a bit crowded with cargo, and he determined for the hundredth time to look into the acquisition of a solid pack mule to carry all the necessary gear. It would mercifully lighten Daisy's burden and go a long way toward reviving her formerly lighthearted disposition.

After a modest breakfast by lantern light with Tom Doud, Doc and Daisy bent their course south just as the first light halos of dawn picked out the hills to the east.

The rains had tempered and scrubbed the air. Every molecule sparkled as the sun rose butter yellow over the mountains. Every dusty barn was rinsed of its dung-colored mantle, every painted house looked almost new, and every pasture and hillside vibrated with vigorous green shoots that had emerged only within the last few hours. The birds too had taken on a display of enthusiasm. The dawn was thick with their greetings, warnings, and gossip.

Doc's thoughts at last turned to his patients. He'd had several hard cases he'd promised to make calls upon, and in the end he was grateful that they had fared better than he had hoped. They all appeared to be on the mend. Doc was always pleased not to have to make any final pronouncements that would affect the future of friends or clients.

Doc's two-day journey back north to Doud's ranch proved relatively uneventful, and for that he was truly appreciative. At Tom's ranch he hitched Daisy up to the cart, which put the animal in something less than a cheerful frame of mind, and headed out toward Monterey.

On the trip back, Doc could not help but think about the old rancher and his child bride. He knew their next meeting would be the most discomfiting stop of his trip home. Daisy appeared to be of the same opinion once she recognized the route to the cliffs at Grace Point.

The Stoat's compound reserved to itself a singular air of fateful abandonment. The ocean breezes fifed through the bleached boards of the barn and sheds, the corral gates hung ajar on sprung hinges, and the only livestock in sight (three pigs, eight goats, and a score of chickens) scattered at his approach. There was scant sign of human habitation, no smoke from the chimney, no laundry hanging out to dry, no chores in progress.

Doc called out to the house, but there was no answer. He dismounted from the cart, unhitched Daisy, and led her to the corral before letting her drink her fill. In spite of the signs, Doc Roberts was sure he was being watched, and when he turned, he saw the rancher's young wife standing silently amidst the split shadows within the ragged barn. She was holding a baby goat. The kid nestled happily in her arms.

Though slightly taken aback by the sudden appearance of the girl from the shadows, Doc managed a smile and a warm greeting. "Mary Rose, I didn't see you standing there. How are you doing, child? Is my patient still with us? Come now. Help me with these things." The girl set down the kid and moved to lend a hand. She spoke only to answer direct questions. Her rejoinders were as brief as she could make them, and she never forwarded a personal sentiment on any subject.

Doc learned that her husband still complained of great pain. He had taken to drinking home brew since the medicine ran out. He had finished that off in no time. The old man wouldn't allow himself to be bathed, and all he did was yell, complain, and curse. At least the liquor kept him quiet now and then.

She had tried, when possible, to feed him the foods recommended by the doctor, but the old man would have none of it. He also believed gangrene had set in, and blamed Doc Roberts for not taking better care to see he had plenty of that medicine for his pain.

But for all the fuss and shouting, Mary Rose believed that her husband must be on the mend. He had yielded up to his previous habits without slack. She refused to say more, and soon after they entered the house she disappeared again.

Doc entered the old man's bedroom and was immediately assaulted by the stench of filth and decay. It wasn't the fetor usually present in cases of gangrene, but it was no less repugnant for all the medical difference it made. Doc Roberts propped up all the windows, allowing a steady cross breeze to scour the thick effluvium from the room. The old man came to his senses with a healthy burst of curses and grievances.

He thrashed about like an upturned crab until Doc Roberts calmed him down through superior moral will and natural authority. The old brigand wasn't afraid of much on the surface, but Doc knew the man was a coward at heart; he gained ascendancy over the fellow without too much trouble.

Doc checked and cleansed the wound, disinfected and redressed the leg, and then relaced the whalebone splint to give greater comfort. As a reward for his relative passivity, Doc Roberts presented the malodorous convalescent with another bottle of his special medicine, this batch substantially weaker than the last, though persisting in all the tang and whip of the original thanks to the rum, clove oil, and vanilla.

Doc admonished the old man to do something straightaway about the abominable state of his hygiene. He went on to suitably frighten his credulous patient with chilling tales of rampant infections and, of course, premature graves attended by grieving but prosperous young widows. Doc Roberts had seen it all too often, sad to say. Hopefully his patient would not be counted among that small number of complete fools who failed to take reasonable precautions. The old man was cursing and shouting out for hot water before Doc Roberts had finished tinting this portrait of impending doom.

Exhausted by the emotional excitement of Doc's chilling anecdotes, the rancher swigged a long pull on the concocted medicine and fell back on his filthy pillow, muttering dark curses under his breath.

Doc retired to the kitchen to find Mary Rose already heating two large kettles of water. She stopped to hand Doc a mug of strong coffee and a large sweet biscuit. He thanked her and retired to the porch to refresh himself. Mary Rose soon joined him. They stood watching the ocean for a moment. Doc cleared his throat by way of punctuation and said that he had calls to make up in the Los Burros district, but that he would return in a few days to check on his patient. For the moment he would be content if Mary Rose could get her husband just to clean himself enough to avoid an infectious disaster. Mary nodded and after a moment returned to her chores.

Doc sat on the porch steps to drink his brew and ponder his patient. He was unfortunately being drawn to the same verdict as those he had accused of jumping to ignorant conclusions. The Stoat was an extremely poor excuse for a *Homo sapiens*, and of that there could be little doubt. Doc had heard that the evil-mouthed villain couldn't even keep a hired man about the place for more than a week. No one would work for the parsimonious old cur. He never wanted to pay his hands on time, so they quit. He had a wicked mind and wicked ways, and there were none to care if he just fell off the earth one day. This led Doc to worry about Mary Rose, but her situation was really none of his business. She would have to look after herself. She had managed this far, and Doc had other patients who needed his ministrations every bit as much as the flinty old rancher.

Doc Roberts was pleased to find his other calls less tiresome, though the trek into the mountains was made more difficult than usual by the several rain-hammered landslides. These difficult patches were traveled under threat of constant peril, so Doc got out to lead Daisy through these hazards. The mare perked up, perhaps in the hope that a precedent was being set.

Manchester was a relatively prosperous mining town nestled high in the Santa Lucia range. It formed the hub of the lucrative Los Burros mining district. Mining, by its very nature, was a precarious and risky affair. Accidents of every imaginable variety were commonplace, and Doc always left town in profit. Unlike some of his other patients, miners always paid cash on the barrelhead for everything, including death, and they expected the same courtesy in return. Their expectations were always backed up with sidearms. In fact the only people who still went about fully armed were miners and lawmen. Over the years it had become almost a tradition to rob immigrant miners in California. As a result they had become edgy and unpredictable. One just came to expect that every miner had a gun on his person and acted accordingly.

After making his first rounds, Doc Roberts usually put up for the night at Willie Cruikshank's little cabin in town. Willie was rarely in residence, preferring to sleep rough near his mines to discourage ore poaching. Doc took his supper at the Gem Saloon as usual and passed the evening trading stories with local friends and acquaintances.

Hard rock miners were a breed of true raconteurs. Storytelling was considered an art form in Manchester, and a man without a ripping good yarn to impart was rarely invited to share the hospitality of the host's bottle.

The next day Doc made his stitch-splint-and-patch rounds out at the mines and, after passing a cheerful hour with his erstwhile host, Willie Cruikshank, Doc turned Daisy's head west and followed the sun out of the mountains. Doc took Willie's timely advice and traveled a different course out, an old but well-cut track down Plover Canyon. This wagon trail had survived the storms with little apparent damage, and it made a pleasant, shaded descent for both man and beast.

They crossed two swollen creeks, so Daisy refreshed herself easily and foreswore her usual objection to regaining the trail. Their course met the main track running north just as the sun crossed into its last quarter. There was a passable drover's shed on the banks of Little Grass Creek about three miles ahead, and it was there that Doc planned to bunk down for the night.

The creek fed a shallow meadow rich in clover and sweet grass and Doc knew that Daisy would find the extravagance only a fair exchange for her devoted services on his behalf.

The track north led back into a narrow canyon and down into a miniature, canopied glade of scrub oak and storm-twisted cedar. Suddenly, just as they were about to enter the bower, Daisy stopped dead and threw her head from side to side. Doc peered into the twilight shadows but saw nothing overtly sinister. He coaxed Daisy forward, but she complied only under protest. They hadn't traveled but a few yards when Doc spotted a strange movement by the side of the trail thirty feet ahead.

Doc reined in and watched carefully. He fixed the movement once more. Its motion was low to the ground and lurching, but it was the pattern and color of the form that seemed oddly familiar. Doc dismounted and, leading Daisy, walked toward the movement with every confidence that the situation was benign. He didn't know how he had come to that conclusion, but he followed through with it nonetheless.

Suddenly Doc released Daisy's bridle and rushed forward. He had established the figure as being that of a man struggling on his hands and knees. He was wearing a filthy plaid shirt and carried a thin bedroll tied across his shoulder. His boots had more holes than leather, and his jeans were torn and bloody.

Doc Roberts immediately recognized the symptoms of advanced exhaustion and dehydration. He at once retrieved his canteen and medical kit from the cart. Doc insisted that the thirsty man sip the water very slowly while he tended to his other injuries.

It was obvious that this poor derelict could not possibly walk, and without food, water, warmth, and rest, his hours on earth were numbered.

It took some applied effort, but Doc managed to haul the broken figure up into the cart for the short ride to Little Grass Creek and the shelter of the drover's shed. Daisy managed all quite nobly, even though she was somewhat spooked by the incident. Doc would see that she got a special ration of sweet oats to go with the fresh clover and pure creek water.

It was during the short journey that Doc learned that he had delivered a transient cowboy who had walked north all the way from San Luis Obispo to find work in Salinas. His name was Jersey Dean, and he hailed from Santa Maria.

He said that he had started out adequately equipped for the journey. He had purchased a sturdy burro, and the creature had bravely shouldered all his gear for many miles. But five days ago they had been attacked on the trail by a very large bear. The beast had killed the burro with one mighty bite to the neck and had driven Dean off.

He had spent a rain-soaked night in a tree. Dean had tried to retrace his steps the following day in an attempt to regain his gear, but the bear had dragged the animal away, gear and all. He was lucky to have found his blanket, and he was not prepared to contest his remaining possessions unarmed—Dean's old Colt pistol had unfortunately been packed on the burro, which gave the bear the edge in firepower. Doc laughed at the quip and commended the cowboy for his discretion.

Doc found the drover's shed in good order. It was really little more than a large, three-sided log hut, but it had a solid roof and four plank bunks against the facing walls. The fourth side of the shed was open to a broad stone hearth sheltered from the elements by the extended eaves of the structure. The fire reflected its light and heat into the shed by virtue of a stone screen erected behind the hearth. A secondary lean-to at the side of the first sheltered a good supply of dry wood, and as soon as Doc had put Dean to rights on one of the bunks, he set about building a substantial fire to drive the foggy chill from the shelter's interior.

The lack of food was a problem with few remedies. Doc rarely carried anything substantial in the way of rations for the trail. The smell of cooking or tree-stashed provisions was a magnet for predators, and Doc generally preferred to shelter without their company.

He did possess two pounds of venison jerky, black tea, salt, sugar, various condiments, and a large cake of portable soup, but he carried little in the way of utensils to prepare the same. A collapsible tin cup and an old army mess kit served his purposes, but allowed for limited entertaining.

The shed came equipped with a bucket, an axe, and a large rendering kettle that would serve to heat water once it was clean.

Doc cut fresh cedar boughs and made a more comfortable berth for his new patient nearer the fire. He used his own blankets to cover the branches and made a passable pillow from

Daisy's oat sack. Then he helped the grateful Dean to bed down more comfortably.

Doc took the kettle down to the creek to clean it with wet sand and did the same with the bucket. He set the first on the fire to scald and disinfect. Then he topped the bucket from the creek and set water on to boil. When the first kettle had boiled to the point of sure sterilization, he poured it off into the bucket, let it cool somewhat, and then bathed and dressed Dean's cuts and abrasions.

The cowboy blessed all the saints to have found such a Samaritan on the threshold of certain extinction. Dean swore he would repay the doctor for his generous kindness if it took a lifetime. Doc Roberts allowed that his patient's offer was more than attractive, but totally unnecessary. Hard money would do. Doc's fee was two dollars cash or eight live chickens, but terms might be arranged for a responsible client with steady employment.

Young Dean smiled for the first time in days, though it hurt his cracked lips. Doc noticed the boy wince and promised to be less entertaining until he recovered somewhat.

For sustenance, Doc cut up venison jerky into small pieces and cooked it with a large cube of portable soup in boiling water. He garnished the brew with meadow chives he found while staking out Daisy to graze.

When the venison had made a proper broth and been tenderized for a weakened constitution, Doc slowly fed a portion to Dean. Though frail, Dean was ravenous, and it took some effort to assure that he paced his intake. Doc Roberts also insisted that he drink small amounts of warm sugared water often.

The next morning brought dense fog, cold, and intermittent rain. Doc thought it best not to risk traveling under those conditions, especially with his patient still in such a feeble state. So rather than idle away his time, Doc set about seeing to their common comforts now that there was daylight to work by. First he built up the fire and went to fetch Daisy from her breakfast in the meadow. It wouldn't do to have her stand out in foul weather all day. That kind of thing always put her in a contrary frame of mind.

Doc brought her near the fire and rubbed her down with fragrant grass and cedar boughs and, when she was nominally dry, covered her with her blanket and installed her at the back of the shelter where she could remain warm and dry. On such a day she appreciated the consideration.

Jersey Dean slept so soundly that no disturbance could possibly penetrate his dreamless refuge. Doc took his pulse several times and was content that the cowboy still remained among the quick. Exposure and exhaustion were not simple conditions to remedy in a drover's shed in the middle of the wilderness, but Doc always liked challenges and he was tenacious as a problem solver. He contemplated the slumbering figure and recalled that only innocent children and octogenarians were blessed with true rest. To that list he would add exhausted young cowhands.

Doc recalled having seen fresh rabbit pellets in the little green meadow where he had allowed Daisy to graze under the trees. Doc never hunted for sport and only rarely out of necessity. He carried an old navy Colt in his saddlebags, but that was for scaring off curious predators.

He wasn't sure he could hit anything with it if he tried, and he judged the caliber too large to leave behind much rabbit if he should prove lucky enough to hit one. Somehow Doc needed to come up with reasonable rations if his patient was to gain enough strength to make the journey north.

At last Doc fetched a small reel of fishing line from his kit; selected flexible sticks from the woodpile; and with the help of his razor-sharp pocketknife, proceeded to manufacture six of the neatest rabbit snares one could imagine. Banking the fire with dry wood, Doc went off to set his snares. He discovered a generous ring of edible mushrooms, iris bulbs, and a robust little patch of cress at the edge of the creek. He gathered as much as he needed to enhance the evening's meal.

When he returned, Doc found Dean awake and hungry. Doc boiled water in the kettle and allowed the boy a cup of sweet tea and a soft tack biscuit to start with. Again he prepared a strong broth of venison, cress, and wild scallions. Dean voraciously inhaled the steaming brew and happily asked for more.

Doc could see that the boy was on the mend as far as appetite was concerned, but he insisted that Dean drink more water to rehydrate his system.

After filling his belly Dean flattened back into a childlike oblivion of healing sleep. Doc sat by the fire and recorded the day's events and medical observations in his journal.

The rains stopped in the late afternoon, and Doc led Daisy out to graze by the creek. Dean never stirred from his berth, but slept as though drugged. Doc felt that Dean's health was by no means a foregone conclusion. He had a premonition, based on years of experience, that the boy's constitution was about to be tested again. His weakened condition could prove fertile ground for any number of serious infections.

Doc was awed, proud, and surprised to discover that his snares had bagged three plump rabbits and a ring-necked pigeon the size of a prize pullet. Doc had no idea how a pigeon found its way into a rabbit snare, but he was grateful to an all-seeing Providence just the same.

On his return to the shed Doc proceeded to transform his catch into a noble repast. Two of the rabbits became a fine stew cooked with wild mushrooms and chives. The meal was also flavorful because Doc always traveled with plenty of condiments. Salt, pepper, dry mustard, chiles, and herbs were often the difference between good food and tasteless trail rations, and Doc liked his food savory. However, he would see that Dean's portion remained relatively bland so as to put as little stress on his digestion as possible. Doc roasted his own portions of rabbit and pigeon on wooden skewers, seasoned with a fulsome bravado of condiments.

Dean slowly awoke to the rich fragrance of hot food. Propped on his elbows, he asked Doc where he could relieve himself. Doc pointed to the great wilderness, held out a small shovel he carried in the cart, and humorously bade him choose any king's throne he pleased.

When Dean returned he looked flushed and there were slight beads of sweat on his brow, though the temperature was crisp. Doc made no comment, but portioned out hot rabbit stew, which Dean enjoyed to the last morsel.

Doc told the young wrangler they would have to make their way north in the morning. He said that he feared complications if better accommodations were not found quickly. As he curled back into his warm bunk, Dean assured Doc Roberts that he could make it the rest of the way if he had made it this far.

Again he blessed Doc for his kind intervention and promptly fell back to sleep. Within moments he began to snore softly while Doc ate his supper by the fire.

Doc disposed of all the food scraps in an old gopher hole and collapsed the entrance in lieu of formal burial. He retrieved Daisy from the meadow and stabled her at the back of the shed for warmth. It looked to be a damp, foggy night, and Daisy deserved every possible consideration. She would have to pull double duty in the morning. Better to be warm and flexible than cold and stiff when called upon for major exertion. After building up the fire, Doc made himself comfortable on his bed of cedar boughs and went to sleep covered with his trail duster and poncho.

He dreamed of the journey north. He dreamed that all the arduous and perilous obstacles had been removed from their path and replaced with a wide smooth avenue to ease their way. It wound beautifully like a broad, black velvet ribbon along the hills above the shore. The moonlight gave it a shimmer like cut jet, and it was warm and firm to tread upon.

Doc awoke in the morning to find Jersey Dean already up and about. Creek water was heating in the camp kettle for tea. Dean had packed and tied off his bedroll and burned the cedar boughs that had formed his mattress. The smoke gave off a lovely aroma. Dean had also given Daisy a hatful of sweet oats before watering her at the creek.

Doc Roberts was impressed and grateful, but he knew that in spite of Dean's supposed vigor, he was suffering the first giddy effects of a growing fever. Doc administered a dose of willow salts, which Dean swallowed obediently, and after swilling down his own tin of hot tea, Doc hitched up Daisy and loaded his gear.

He insisted that Dean wear Doc's rain poncho for warmth, since they had little else that would serve to insulate him from the elements.

The trip north was anything but swift or pleasant. As Dean's fever worsened, Doc found it necessary to make many stops to rest and water both his patient and his horse. Daisy was not used to hauling two passengers, and though Doc was proud of her steady forbearance and tenacity, he could not allow her to suffer while struggling over the rougher terrain. Thus he found himself walking a great deal more than he would have wished.

Poor Dean kept nodding off in a semifeverous haze of half dreams and hallucinatory ramblings that were mostly gibberish. Doc had to keep a close eye on the cowboy for fear he might pitch out of the bed of the cart unexpectedly.

Doc wished for a wider track along the coast. A trip that should normally have taken twenty hours, on saddleback, would now consume the better part of three days, possibly more. Three days without suitable shelter or provisions could prove dangerous for his patient.

For a while it seemed there was no viable way to haul Dean to the hospital in Monterey without killing him in the process. Daisy also stood in sore need of decent fodder and rest if she was to continue as well.

Doc considered the problem and at last remembered the unused bunkhouse on the Stoat's place. Doc decided to tempt the devil. At the appropriate juncture he would cut west and make straight for Grace Point.

He could see to the old man's needs easily enough and get Dean bedded down with some decent food and shelter before it became too late for effectual ministrations beyond a shovel, the Good Book, and a headstone.

A tattered sunset had commenced to streak below the clouds when Doc Roberts led Daisy up to the barn at Grace

Point. A faint movement in the barn was revealed by the shafts of light coming through the wide cracks between the boards.

While easing Dean down from the cart, Doc called out to Mary Rose. She stepped from the barn clutching a small tattered basket of eggs. Doc Roberts had no difficulty communicating the urgency of his predicament.

Mary Rose set down her basket and rushed to help the doctor move the partially conscious cowboy to the bunkhouse. This was a slap-dab, lean-to affair nailed up against the side of the barn.

The accommodations, such as they were, had hardly been kept in a hospitable state. Everything in sight was mantled in dust and decay. There were two rickety rope-spring bunks with thin horsehair mattresses, a rusted potbellied stove, an ancient table and a chair with a broken back. All this luxury came with a kerosene lantern and a slop bucket as amenities. Doc and Mary Rose laid Dean out on one of the bunks to rest. Doc gave the girl specific instructions about preparing some hot broth and begged the loan of a few blankets.

Returning to the barn, Doc unhitched and attended to Daisy as best he could. Retrieving his bag and bedroll, Doc did his best to clean out the hovel by the light of the kerosene lamp. He finally decided to surrender the chore until the following day. After making the semidelirious Dean as comfortable as possible, Doc repaired to the ranch house to see the old man and attend to his leg. In his state of footsore and road-weary fatigue, it was not an errand that Doc Roberts looked forward to with any enthusiasm.

Sixty feet from the house, Doc heard the old man shouting. He was cursing up a tornado at his wife and complaining that he was not getting all the attention and respect he was entitled to. He swore that when he was up and about again, things would go very differently for certain people.

Doc interrupted the old man's diatribe with all the professional authority at his disposal. It wasn't good for much leeway, but it stopped up his wicked tongue long enough for Doc Roberts to complete his examinations, redress the wound, and adjust the splint. Doc noticed that in spite of his entreaties to the contrary, the old man's hygiene was not much improved. His breath also smelled of raw spirits, but how he should come by such goods without the connivance of his wife was a mystery.

While he still had the old man cowed, Doc mentioned the cowboy he had saved on the trail and had only now installed in the old man's bunkhouse to recuperate. Doc mentioned the rancher's growing medical bill and suggested that they might strike a deal if the cowboy were allowed to receive room and board until he recuperated.

The rancher wasn't at all enthusiastic about the arrangement, but since he hadn't the cash to settle the doctor's bill, he deemed it best to acquiesce. But only until the saddle-tramp was on his pins again. Then the cowboy would have to be on his way. Doc agreed and retired to the kitchen to see to Dean's broth and the other requested items.

Mary Rose had all in readiness. Besides a pitcher of rich broth for his patient, she had prepared a brace of mutton chops with onions for Doc Roberts. Gathering up the blankets and assorted little conveniences, she helped the doctor carry the lot down to the bunkhouse. Once they had made up the better of the two bunks, Doc stripped the limp figure of Dean and tucked him down under clean warm blankets.

Mary Rose carefully fed Doc's patient spoonfuls of the nourishing broth while Doc coaxed the potbellied stove to harbor a vigorous little fire to chase the ocean chill from the air. When all that could be set to rights was seen to and Mary Rose had returned to the house, Doc sat at the rickety old table to eat his chops. After supper he sat by the light of the smoky lamp and worked on his journal. Dean's fever required some attention, but he seemed to calm down when Doc bathed his brow and wrists with cold water. This procedure continued until Doc fell asleep about midnight.

In the morning Doc awoke to find his patient sleeping peacefully. The fever had broken in the early hours of the morning, but between the rigors of exposure, exhaustion, malnutrition, and now fever, it would be some time before Jersey Dean would be up on his "pins" again, as the old man had phrased it.

While Dean slept, Doc prepared medications for both his patients. For the old man, he concocted a batch of the usual, but with only ten drops of laudanum to a pint of vanilla-flavored, clove-laced rum. Again he filled the bottles with diminishing amounts of the brew, topped up with water. Doc figured that this demi-placebo would keep the old man quiet if nothing else. Some people refused to believe they were being properly doctored unless they had a bottle of medicine to prove it. People found it difficult to comprehend the body curing itself with a little patience and care. They needed the medical props and potions to nurture their wilting self-confidence.

It was all the same from a medical point of view. What the brain believed, the body would believe as well. To harness the two in a harmonious fashion was sometimes a matter of psychological wizardry, but nothing unethical. Certainly nothing as unethical as what he would have liked to have done to the old reprobate, but Doc had not practiced that kind of venality since he was a child of six. Now it was too late to remember.

Dean's medicines were another matter altogether. His instructions for their administration were precise, and some discipline would be required to see that Dean did not forego the prescribed course of treatment in a premature show of youthful bravado. He made sure Dean knew that he had placed Mary Rose in charge. Then Doc worked on his journals, looked after Daisy's needs, and nursed Dean for the rest of the day.

Early the next morning Doc took Dean's pulse. The patient still slept, though exhaustion mixed with bad dreams caused him to toss about on occasion. Then Doc Roberts packed his kit for the ride north. On the way to the house, he stopped at the barn to see to Daisy. She seemed content enough with her oats.

Doc delivered the old man's medicine to the house with an admonition to take it by the spoon, not by the gulp. It would have to last the two weeks until Doc returned with more, if indeed it was still needed.

Doc also cautioned the rancher to treat his ailing guest with kindness for the sake of his medical bill. He calculated that the old man owed him more than all the chickens, goats, and pigs on the place, so he had better keep his end of the bargain.

The old man grunted and fumed, but said he would hold up his end of the deal. The checked anger in the rancher's voice told Doc that he was scarcely delighted with the arrangement, but he knew the old cripple would comply out of fear, if nothing else.

Doc found Mary Rose in the laundry shed kneading soiled overalls on a homemade washboard. He asked her to join him for a short talk. Mary Rose wiped her hands on her apron and followed Doc to the bunkhouse. He handed her his written instructions and asked if she could understand them. Mary huffed and said she could read quite well, thank you. She even owned some books. Doc praised her literacy and went over the list with her point by point.

When they entered the bunkhouse, Dean was just coming awake with a terrible thirst. Doc gave him all the water he could hold and then explained that he was about to leave. He said that he had made certain arrangements for Dean to recover his strength on the ranch. He was to do as Mary Rose instructed without argument or complaint. Doc said the rancher's wife didn't need any further vexation than was already at hand up at the house with his other patient.

Though weak, Dean smiled and thanked Doc Roberts for all his many considerations. He owed Doc Roberts his life and would work hard to show his gratitude. Doc waved off the sentiment and said that he could best show his indebtedness by obeying Mary Rose. He had left specific instructions and expected them to be adhered to religiously. Dean looked at the rancher's wife, blushed slightly, and agreed to all the doctor's requirements.

Doc Roberts knew he couldn't make it all the way back to Monterey in one shot, but he would travel as far as he could before Daisy lost patience. It took some effort, but Doc got as far as the Pfeiffer spread before night fell. He decided to beg a bath and a bed from his old friends.

The stress of the last week on the trail had caught up with the doctor, and he needed a good night's rest on a decent bed before continuing. A generous hot meal, of anything but rabbit, would find a hearty welcome as well. He would see that Daisy got all the attention she could stand. Fresh fodder, sweet oats, and the company of her own kind would go a long way toward improving her disposition. Daisy was in favor of the decision to stop over. She shivered with delight the moment she felt her rig go slack. Doc rubbed her down and gave her a couple of apples before he retired to the bathhouse to pass a long-anticipated hour in hot soapy water, smoking his pipe, blowing imperfect rings, and thinking of wife, home, and hearth.

TWO WEEKS LATER DOC ROBERTS TRAVELED down the coast again. After making visits to the Grimes outfit and the Dani place, Doc was asked to stop down at Partington Cove to treat a sailor who had broken his arm loading tanbark on a schooner.

Old man Clarke had appeared out of nowhere, as he usually did, and told Doc about the injured sailor. Doc had been friends with Clarke for years. Though he lived in the wilderness as a hermit and few people saw him about, he had a way of knowing everything that went on in the Big Sur.

After treating the sailor's arm to a custom-made splint, Doc spent the night at Tom Doud's ranch. In the morning he borrowed one of Tom's faster saddle horses to make a quick visit to check on the well-being of Jersey Dean and the old rancher. Since Daisy obviously hated the place, Doc saw no reason why she should pull the cart that distance when she could frolic in Doud's lush pastures and roll in the dust with acquaintances.

The trip brought Doc to Grace Point in midafternoon.

The first person he spied was Jersey Dean. He was sitting in front of the bunkhouse repairing Mary Rose's butter churn. He looked happy and well when Doc first spotted him, but the moment Dean spied the doctor, he took on a glum and sorrowful expression.

Doc dismounted at the barn, and Dean joined him to help put up the horse. Doc easily sensed that something was wrong. When Doc asked how he was getting on, Dean replied that he was slow coming up to snuff, but with time he hoped to be fully recovered.

Doc made a perfunctory examination of Dean's vital signs and came to the private conclusion that the cowboy was malingering just a mite. He asked why Dean had not taken the first opportunity to move on to fresher prospects. There were plenty of spreads that claimed a need for good hands this time of the year, and even the Devil knew that Dean's present host was hardly the most congenial of men.

Dean toed the dust with his newly patched boots and struggled for a spontaneous-sounding answer, but none was forthcoming. Then Dean said sheepishly that he rather liked it where he was, but the old man showed no signs of wanting to take on help. The place sadly needed a qualified hand while the old man was laid up, and Dean said he had done his best to be helpful. He had taken over the heavier chores from Mary Rose, who seemed to have her hands full just taking care of her husband.

Dean had even fabricated a pair of padded crutches so the old coot could move about more easily, but the rancher expressed no gratitude for the gift. In fact, the old man had even showed the temerity to complain that Dean was nothing more than a saddle-tramp looking for a free handout. He had heard the old man say the same to his wife on several occasions when he was sure that Dean would overhear his comments.

Doc said he would look into the matter and then made his way to the ranch house with his medical bag.

As Doc mounted the front porch, he heard the old man swearing up a storm. This had become so usual that Doc paid little attention, though he found the old man's constant use of profanity just a little more than he could stomach. It was one thing for men to rage at one another in such a manner, but to use such wicked language to a woman was unforgivable regardless of provocation.

The moment Doc made his presence known the old man ceased his ranting. He might try his will on others, but he was afraid of Doc Roberts and almost became obsequious in his presence.

Mary Rose was happy to see the doctor and managed something like a smile when he entered. Not wishing to pass the time of day with the old man, Doc set to work directly on an examination of his injuries. While this was being accomplished, Doc suggested to the old rancher that, though his leg was steadily improving, it would still be quite a while before he could run the ranch again. If his patient had any sense, he would hire Jersey Dean to work the place until the rancher was able to saddle up for himself again.

While the old man would have treated this suggestion with scorn if it had come from somebody else, he was willing to consider the recommendation since it came from the eminent Dr. Roberts. Mary Rose seemed pleased by the suggestion as well and encouraged her husband to accept for the sake of the ranch, which at present was going to the dogs without a man to oversee the stock and repair the fences.

When Doc returned to the barn to fetch Tom Doud's horse, he found Dean setting out slop for the pigs. Doc told Dean that an arrangement had been agreed to. The old man would pay thirty-five dollars a month with room and board, and Dean would work the spread until the old man could take over again.

Dean appeared pleased, but tried not to show how much. He thanked the doctor for his assistance in the matter and went back to his chores with a tenacity that belied his earlier grievance of lingering ill health.

Doc bid Dean farewell as he mounted. He said he would be riding circuit again in about three weeks. He expected to find some improvements to the place when he returned. Dean happily waved good-bye and returned to the barn. Doc Roberts spurred Doud's stallion in hopes of making it back to Tom's spread before moonrise. Tom had promised him a thick sirloin steak for supper if he got back in time, and Doc could almost taste the promise. Doud's stallion needed little encouragement to make a fast passage back to his own paddock. The animal seemed just as anxious to depart the old man's property as Daisy had been.

THREE WEEKS LATER, true to his word, Doc Roberts was again found jigging a reluctant Daisy toward the Grace Point ranch. When he arrived, it was to discover the homestead looking somewhat better, but noticeably deserted. Doc stabled Daisy, gave her a light measure of oats, and made his way toward the house.

When he was only a few yards from the porch a commotion of unusual verbal violence broke out from within. Doc thought he had heard the worst the old Stoat could generate when it came to vulgarity, but he now acknowledged that the old man had only skimmed the surface in the past. His well of obscenity was almost unfathomable. Doc Roberts had known men shot down in saloons for far less.

Not knowing what to do at first, Doc loitered, listening, not wanting to insert himself into the situation. His lingering embarrassment and chagrin at the low degree to which his patient had descended made him feel as though he might have avoided the exercise of ministering to the old reprobate in the first place.

Certainly the old man was an obscene aberration, but Doc Roberts maintained rigid scruples and would do nothing out of professional character. In spite of his personal feelings, it was not in his nature to be vindictive or vengeful. A patient was a patient and ethical considerations aside, his predisposition was keyed to curing people, not judging them.

The rancher's enraged and wrathful voice mounted into a tirade of truly hideous proportions. It reached a crescendo with the sharp report of a slap and a brief stifled scream. Doc was about to change his mind and enter the fray before any more violence erupted, but he was too late. A melee exploded with a shattering crash of furniture, screams, shouts, and curses. Before Doc could reach the door, it splintered off its hinges with a bang, and out rocketed two figures. In the lead was the old man, screaming and flapping his arms like an earthbound albatross. At first Doc couldn't believe any old man with a broken leg could move that fast until he noticed that Dean had the rogue by the collar and crotch and was giving him the bum's rush. The Stoat weighed as nothing in Dean's strong grip, and though the old man railed and waved his arms about, he was powerless.

While Doc watched, fascinated, Dean raced the old man

across the yard, over the goat-trimmed grass, and toward the cliffs. Dean screamed that this would be the very last time the old blackguard would beat a woman this side of hell and with that parting sentiment, launched the old sinner out over the cliff like a bag of wool.

Doc Roberts stood agape. The old man seemed suspended in air for a moment, flapping his arms in the most optimistic manner. Then he disappeared like a rock, squeaking his last mortal profanity, something to do with excrement, as Doc recalled.

Dean didn't remain at the precipice to inspect the scene below, but turned as though he had just thrown out the trash and walked back to the house. Doc was surprised to witness an expression of mature determination and resolve on Dean's boyish face.

As he walked by, Dean looked up and noticed Doc Roberts for the first time. He nodded as though Doc had just witnessed a commonplace occurrence. He didn't even take notice of Doc's profound look of astonishment and dismay.

"Glad to see you, Doctor. How've you been keeping yourself?" Dean grasped the doctor warmly by the shoulder and walked him toward the door like a favorite uncle. Doc was still in something of a stuttering daze, but Dean continued to ignore it.

"Oh, but look at you, Doc! You're surely a soul who could probably use some coffee. Won't you come in and share a pot?"

Doc allowed himself to be seated at the kitchen table. The only remaining evidence of the lethal struggle was a broken chair and washbasin, and these were being gathered up by Mary Rose as they entered.

Mary Rose looked well enough, except for an angry-looking red welt the size of a saucer on her left cheek and eye.

Despite this, she smiled at Doc, nodded, and proceeded to pour three cups of coffee without a word of explanation or comment. Then she sat down with her own cup and looked thankfully toward her young benefactor.

Dean turned his chair around and straddled it like a horse. He rested his crossed arms on the back of the chair and smiled broadly. "Of course you'll be the best man at our wedding, won't you, Doc? We couldn't have a wedding without you. Mary Rose wants you there special. So do I."

Doc looked up from his coffee and gathered his thoughts. Then he closed his eyes and grinned. "Yes. Yes, I'd like that. Thank you both for asking. When's the happy day to be?"

An hour later Doc and Daisy disappeared east down the road while the new couple waved farewell. Doc noticed at once that Daisy's gait had lost its agitated prance. She tossed her head with modest gaiety, as though amused by some cryptic witticism only a horse would appreciate.

Doc Roberts spent a considerable time pondering that day's events. He wondered what kind of future the couple could expect with a homicide weighing in the balance. Either way, he wouldn't be the first to mention it. But if, indeed, anyone should ever inquire what he knew of the matter, Doc Roberts would shrug and reply that as far as he knew, the old man simply fell from grace under the weight of a lifetime of ponderous iniquity.

In point of fact, Doc was never questioned about anything. No one seemed to care, one way or the other.

As a gesture to honor his new bride, Dean changed the name of the homestead to Rose Point, and Mary Rose changed her last name to Dean.

THE DARK WATCHER

PROFESSOR SOLOMON GILL SAT AT HIS DESK surveying his impatient pupils over the wire rims of his reading glasses. He had paused in his presentation of an article by Dr. Herbert Nash on aboriginal commonalities as they pertained to the indigenous coastal peoples of California.

His restless students took the hint and stopped their fidgeting when he paused in his reading and iced them with an expression of profound disapproval. His pupils bent every effort to stop squirming, but it was beyond expectation. This was their last class, on the last day of school before the commencement of their 1933 summer recess.

San Jose was a beautiful campus set in a landscape of abundance. Her scholars felt privileged to study under her ivied auspices, but summer vacation was summer vacation, and little mattered beyond thoughts of escape, freedom, and leisure.

It was a magnificent afternoon. Small, picturesque clouds skipped across the Santa Cruz Mountains to the west. Through the open windows of the classroom the calls of robins, jays, and sparrows penetrated the academic veneer with promises of long summer days of deliverance. For most students and faculty it was a joyful liberation from the routine demands of university life. The entire world waited in delighted anticipation, all save poor Professor Solomon Gill.

The hour chimed from the bell tower just as Professor Gill concluded his reading. He dismissed his class and formally wished his students a pleasant and stimulating sabbatical. The professor resolved his semester's best efforts with a caution to keep up on their reading. This last statement went mostly unheard in the clamor and commotion of the swift mass exodus.

His pupils joyfully shouted their parting sentiments and vanished like spooked deer.

In seconds Professor Gill found himself sitting all alone, while through the windows he watched the quadrangle fill with a flood of exuberant youth making good their escape before fastidious professors suddenly remembered some parting summer assignment. In minutes his vista showed scant signs of academic life of any kind.

The professor was tall, angular, and slightly stooped at the shoulders. He sported a full head of brown hair that spurned all attempts at reasonable grooming, in short, a semianimated example of a forty-three-year-old bachelor. His slightly dusty, threadbare appearance and worn boot heels endorsed his unmarried state.

Except when officiating from the lectern of academia, where he exhibited reasonable skill and wielded absolute power, Professor Gill had a tendency to display pronounced symptoms of social reticence. His great aunt, Miss Honoria, often likened him to a youthful Abe Lincoln: "Very distinguished, to be sure, but I'd feel encouraged if he'd say something useful now and then."

Her insensitive remarks always made Solomon blush with suppressed indignation. Many of his students, on the other hand, thought the professor closely resembled a wrathful Ichabod Crane and used to call him "Black Ichy" behind his back.

As Solomon Gill rose to harvest his notes and stuff them into his worn briefcase, one of his female students entered again and begged a moment of his time. The young woman needed sober advice on an academic matter, and she thought Professor Gill best qualified to render assistance.

Professor Gill squinted over his glasses and said, "Yes, of course, come in, Miss Castro. What is it you wish to know?" Solomon Gill continued to stuff papers and books into the case, but it appeared unwilling to digest the total volume.

Miss Castro approached, almost as shy as the professor himself. "My parents said they would sponsor me to accompany one of two expeditions this summer, and I still haven't made up my mind which would be most rewarding. Dr. Rice, at Stanford, is leading a small group north to the Salmon Island excavations, and our Dr. Holt has been invited to muster a party of students to work the diggings at Casa Grande. Which trip would you recommend as the most rewarding, Professor? As an anthropologist, I mean, would you have a preference of one above the other?"

Professor Gill flushed slightly, more at his inability to close his briefcase than from the complexities of the question. "That's hard to say, Miss Castro. It quite depends on which direction you wish your course of studies to take. As an anthropologist, as you say, I think I might be attracted to both expeditions equally, like yourself. But if one were to judge the caliber of events by the quality of the instructor, I would have to choose Dr. Holt. He is one of the most illuminating interpreters of post-Clovis native cultures in America, and a very sympathetic gentleman as well. Dr. Rice, though credible in every degree, has a reputation for being something of a martinet in the field, and it's a long, wet, walk home from Salmon Island."

Professor Gill cleared his throat nervously. "By the way, Miss Castro, what were the expenses quoted for Dr. Holt's junket, if I may ask?"

"Not at all, Professor. Each student is expected to pay one hundred dollars for the three-week course. That includes all travel and boarding expenses, of course. Were you thinking of joining us, Professor?"

"I'm afraid my summer recess is spoken for," said Professor Gill. "But I look forward to hearing about your many adventures next semester, Miss Castro."

The girl smiled. "Yes, thank you, Professor, and thanks for the recommendation. I'll talk to my father tonight. Good-bye. Have a pleasant summer, Professor." Miss Castro disappeared like the others, and Solomon Gill's world was again tranquil, accompanied only by distant birdsong and the pace of his own labors.

Professor Solomon Gill had lied. He had nothing in the least interesting to do during his vacation, primarily due to the problem of funds. College professors, especially the younger variety with only modest tenure, were not highly recompensed for their services. Inherited wealth was almost a requirement to survive on a teacher's salary, and Solomon Gill was his aging mother's sole support. There was little left for anything like adventurous forays into the desert to study the digs at Chaco Canyon. Solomon couldn't even afford a weekend of museums in San Francisco, much less a trek to Salmon Island. And, if the truth be known, the professor was jealous, almost crestfallen at the thought of the injustice of it all.

The professor wallowed in these unhappy speculations all the way home on the trolley car. He remained earnestly steeped in his melancholy all through Mrs. Hammel's pot roast. His landlady had always prided herself on her Friday evening pot roast, and her boardinghouse was popular in that regard.

Mrs. Hammel had become used to Professor Gill's prolonged silences over the years, but he seemed particularly withdrawn at present. She tried to tempt him out of his shell with her famous rum-raisin bread pudding, which he accepted and took to his room.

Mrs. Hammel shrugged, shook her head sadly, and continued her conversation with her other three boarders. The twilight's afterglow found Solomon sitting and looking out of his bedroom window at the backyard; the rum-raisin bread pudding remained untouched upon his lap.

Solomon twitched at the sound of the distant doorbell, and the spoon slipped from his saucer of pudding. A moment later he came to life and bent to retrieve it. He twitched again when the knock came at his door and Mrs. Hammel announced that a package had been delivered by hand.

Professor Gill thanked her and asked that she deposit it on the table next to the door. When he rose to brush his teeth and make ready for an early evening, he remembered the package, a book as it turned out, a slim volume wrapped in brown paper and string and containing a note from his friend Professor Wick. He sincerely hoped that Professor Gill might find the obscure text of some interest.

The text, though dry, focused on Native American hunting societies in central California, so Professor Gill propped himself up in bed and began to read. It was almost one o'clock in the morning when he put the book aside and turned off his light.

He had been particularly absorbed by descriptions of Rumsen and Esselen coastal hunting and gathering techniques. He had discovered an interesting cross-reference that mentioned the existence of cunningly fashioned hunting camps that were used year after year.

A gentleman by the name of Bert Stevens claimed to have discovered two such sites in the company of the Partington brothers while surveying for a logging operation. He stated that the arrangement of the camps was unique and well thought-out. They seemed sturdy and strong, though no one knew when they were last occupied by their innovators. Mr. Stevens was quoted as saying that the garbage middens were large and remarkably diverse in discarded material.

Professor Gill became curious when he could find no credentialed testimony corroborating the existence of these sites in the book. Evidently no other qualified observer had ever seen or cataloged them.

Solomon Gill digested the text all through his sleep and in the morning awoke with a firm desire to know the truth about some of the things he had read the night before. After a light breakfast of coffee and toast, the professor caught the trolley and eventually made his way to the university library. He spent four hours in serious research and left with an expression of self-congratulatory success.

Gill returned to his boardinghouse just long enough to pack a small bag, retrieve a stashed purse containing his emergency funds, and bid a temporary farewell to Mrs. Hammel.

She seemed somewhat flustered at first, but Professor Gill said he was only going down to Carmel and the Big Sur for a week to do some research. That explanation appeased her, and she set about putting up a little food for the professor's long stage ride to Monterey. Perpetually short of resources, the professor was grateful for any and all material assistance.

The first portion of his trip was accomplished by scheduled bus, an uncomfortable, home-built, rattling affair that broke down twice. After Monterey, Solomon Gill knew it would be pretty much a matter of improvisation since his destination was rather remote. There was a motor stage that made its way up and down the coast on the new road, but its scheduling was informal and unsure. The professor thus had hopes of finding a generous soul to give him a lift to Carmel. Luckily he spotted old Sam Trotter gassing up his truck across from the little Monterey bus depot. The professor had met the renowned Mr. Trotter the previous year when the professor had traveled down to see his old friend Dr. Hedgepoole.

In fact, it was Dr. Hedgepoole whom Professor Gill was traveling to visit first.

Dr. Hedgepoole had been retired for some years as a result of poor health. He rented a graceful little cottage on San Carlos Avenue in Carmel from Mrs. Hammel's aged sister-in-law. There he led a tranquil existence amongst his books, port, and pill bottles.

The myopically studious Dr. Hedgepoole had been something of a mentor to Solomon Gill at Stanford. His lectures on clinical disciplines applicable to anthropology had drawn respectable audiences above and beyond the student body, and the doctor's knowledge of local native lore was thought considerable, though unpublished in the main.

Sam Trotter happily transferred his load of provisions to the truck bed, wedging them among some cement bags so that Professor Gill might enjoy the comfort of the cab. Solomon and Sam talked about incidentals for a couple of miles, and then Gill led the conversation around to Indian encampments in the Big Sur. Sam Trotter was about the best woodsman the coast of California had ever produced. If he didn't know where something was, then it probably didn't exist.

Sam had heard the stories, of course, and he had found several small locations, but nothing that quite fit the published descriptions Professor Gill quoted. The Partington brothers were responsible men, not known for salting the mines of accuracy. The Partingtons had ranged over a wide stretch of land in that part of the county, from Partington Cove, with its hand–chiseled tunnel, all the way up to Partington Ridge in the mountains.

Sam Trotter smiled, nodded, and agreed that there might be quite a bit of stuff up in those hills nobody had ever seen. People had talked of Indian gold caves for generations, but folks in the high Sur kept to their own a good deal and never talked to strangers about such things if they could avoid it.

After an introspective moment he returned to his subject. "Rumsens and Esselens were known to be very secretive hunters. For obvious reasons their encampments and blinds would be well concealed, mostly within natural occlusions. They were disguised well enough to deceive more than just passing game. Stealing food from rival clans was always a popular form of mischief."

Sam scratched his head. "But it's not an easy ticket, Professor. Over the years, there have been any number of people who've searched those mountains for one thing or another, boundary stones, lost cattle, game, Indian gold, you name it.

But I never heard anyone mention that they found much evidence of permanent settlements up in those hills. It wouldn't surprise me to find that coastal Indians moved about a good deal, followed game and fish migrations and all."

Sam let Professor Gill out at the top of Ocean Avenue. He apologized for not taking him down the hill, but he was afraid his old truck wouldn't make it back up again with the load of cement bags in the back. The grateful professor grabbed his bag, waved farewell, and walked down toward San Carlos Avenue and Dr. Hedgepoole's cottage.

Solomon Gill had long craved a plausible discovery he could call his own. Perhaps he had come upon a workable anomaly in the form of the long-overlooked and forgotten narrative. He yearned for any result, no matter how nominal, that might assist in his discovery of one of the hidden Indian camps. He foresaw a modest scholarly publication to follow, but one sure to note the exploit and bring credit to his years behind the lectern.

Unfortunately, the professor's total budget for this peculiarly spontaneous expedition was now reduced to fifteen dollars and seventeen cents. Hardly a princely sum, but all he could scrape together at the last moment. He had started with his emergency twenty-dollar bill, pursed and secreted in the toe of an old boot. His round-trip coach fare had substantially eaten into that fortune. His future efforts would require practiced frugality, but Solomon Gill was quite familiar with the skills necessary to fashion silk purses from sows' ears.

DOCTOR THADIUS HEDGEPOOLE WAS SITTING in his small garden reading his mail when Solomon Gill shuffled across the dirt street and planted his bag on the abalone shell wall that guarded the old doctor's roses. Hedgepoole looked up over his reading glasses, but since he was expecting no company, it took a moment to recognize his road-weary friend.

"By all that's holy, Solomon Gill, what are you doing here? I didn't expect to see you until . . . But come along there and have a seat by me. Mrs. Ogden is due with some port and hot tea any moment. It's my favorite time of the day. So what brings you to these parts, young Prometheus?"

Solomon found it difficult to come to the point at first. He insisted on talking about minor irrelevances, but saw he was boring his host, so he moved on to the crux of his visit. The short of it being that, yes, Dr. Hedgepoole had known about the text reference to Indian hunting encampments and, no, he had personally never seen or heard of one being discovered.

"If they still exist as reported," Hedgepoole continued, "they would now presumably be heavily overgrown and probably invisible to the naked eye. I once talked to Frank Post, years ago it was, about Indian fishing camps on the Carmel and Big Sur Rivers. He said that as far as he knew, the locations changed all the time, because the rivers and the good fishing changed all the time. But come to think of it, Frank did mention a place his mother had taken him to when he was a child. It was up near Pico Blanco as I recall. Rumsen hunting parties traditionally gathered there in the spring and autumn. But Frank distinctly said he couldn't remember exactly where it was. It seems his mother, Anselma Onesimo, stopped taking him when he was six or seven. He was always getting himself in some mischief or other, so she finally left him at home when she went off to be with her own people."

The tea and port arrived, and it was decided that Solomon

would have the small guest bedroom for the night. Captain Balycott, an old friend, kindly stopped by with a basket of fresh sand dabs as a gift. Dr. Hedgepoole was overjoyed and begged Mrs. Ogden to grill the delightful creatures for supper. It was later agreed, over fine Cuban coffee, that Mrs. Ogden had certainly outdone herself in their preparation.

Once warm in front of the fire, Solomon continued a rambling query roughly centered on the subject of semipermanent Indian enclaves in the mountains. Hedgepoole came to understand that his friend was eager to have a look for himself and, though somewhat skeptical about the possible results, said nothing to discourage him from his little sojourn. In fact, he took the time to compose a note that would introduce Professor Gill to the people down at Pfeiffer's Lodge. Dr. Hedgepoole thought they might be helpful in seeing to it that Solomon found his way about safely.

"Very good people down there," he said. "Talk to any Dani or Grimes you come across. Their families have worked that territory since the year one. If there is something to find up in the Sur, they will know where it is. Perhaps you'll strike the mother lode where others have failed. I have known it to happen on rare occasions."

The next morning Solomon caught the motor stage south at the top of the hill and found himself deposited at Pfeiffer's Lodge by three o'clock, two dollars lighter, but content. The weather had been excellent. The sunlight lanced through the trees in honed, piercing shafts, and the ocean vistas glittered with dancing whitecaps and wheeling seabirds.

A fragile perception of the impending adventure was slowly beginning to bore into Solomon's academic shell. He was commencing to enjoy himself. He even traded amusing small talk with Corbett Grimes, the hearty and garrulous stage driver. This was very unlike the professor's usual shy reserve with strangers.

Dr. Hedgepoole's note opened all doors at Pfeiffer's Lodge. For a very modest fee they supplied Professor Gill with rustic accommodations, food, a saddle mule named Doughboy, a good map, a bindle of trail rations, and a parting admonition to stay with the mule at all costs.

Doughboy, a creature of mature sensibilities, knew his way about the mountains far better than Professor Gill. To give the animal its head was to find the way home automatically. To let the beast roam about unattended was equivalent to a long walk home. Doughboy had an abiding passion for the comforts of his own snug stall and would find his way back to it through a blizzard, if such an oddity should ever come to pass.

In either event, Professor Gill was warned against the perils of spending the night on the trail. The Pfeiffer's stockman said, "Best you return before Doughboy starts cutting up stubborn. The dear creature is a real handful when deprived of his oats, blanket, and warm stall." Professor Gill was in complete sympathy with the mule's sentiment, but said nothing that might reflect humorously on their mutual affection for the simple comforts.

The next morning Professor Gill again faithfully promised to remain diligent about marking trails and to keep to a rational schedule. With help, he mounted the mule, waved a cheerful farewell, and took the trail that led north by east in the general direction of Pico Blanco.

Pinky Ransome, who was then visiting, remarked that the professor looked somewhat akin to Abe Lincoln with his long legs dangling down the sides of old Doughboy. Solomon overheard the comment from a distance and silently fumed. It seemed the observation was destined to become a popular assertion. He cringed at the thought and spurred the mule on. Doughboy didn't bother to respond.

The rugged slopes of Pico Blanco, mentioned in the obscure text, were far too distant to consider a journey there and back in a day. Indeed three or four days might be required, but Solomon only wished to familiarize himself with the lay of the land as much as possible. He hoped to take in the broadest probable vistas for later reference, and even made crude sketches on a small pad for later study.

The lodge had kindly loaned the professor a copy of a homemade map of all the roads, game trails, and paths in the area, a courtesy usually reserved for their seasonal hunting clientele. Professor Gill suspected that any evidence of semipermanent encampments would necessarily be within a walking radius of running water. Where water and established trails crossed, viable locations might exist on all compass points. The rest was a matter of looking for the right signs.

The professor followed the Big Sur River east-northeast for a while. Where game trails crossed fordable creeks, he would ride a wide circuit around the area looking for natural blinds or high points that might command a long view of the approaches. He looked for areas where a small band of hunters could conceivably find shelter and concealment while they dressed and jerked their kills for transport.

The mule moved with a certain and steady gait, never too fast and never too slow. The animal seemed to understand what was required and suffered the professor a wide latitude of blind trails and dead ends to be retraced. Every now and then, Doughboy would come to a dead stop, pull up his head, and focus his long slender ears in all directions. After the mule had repeated this maneuver several times, Solomon automatically started to listen as well.

On two occasions he thought he heard the whinny of a distant horse, and on two other occasions he swore he detected a mounted figure, a mysterious rider spying on him from the dark recesses among the hills above. Then about five o'clock, soon after he had turned Doughboy homeward, Solomon observed the solitary horseman again. This time the rider was way ahead of Solomon on the next rise.

Professor Gill was at a loss to explain how the rider crossed the intervening ground so quickly without being seen or heard. Perhaps there was more than one horseman.

Doughboy was as good as his reputation and, with no prompting from Professor Gill, came within sight of the lodge just as the supper gong sounded. The mule's timing was impeccable.

That evening the professor ate well and was entertained by several thirsty locals who dropped by to swap wine and tall tales. Some showed serious interest in the professor's theories and shared what they knew of the puzzle, but in the main, it was Solomon's opinion that the Pfeiffer outfit had little but speculation to offer. They had seen sites that might fit the professor's description, but the native groups that had used them were a shrewd and crafty lot. The company agreed that any significant example of such handiwork would have disintegrated and disappeared by now.

"All except for the dark watchers of course," said "Dozer" Dutch, grinning. "And the fog ghosts that guard Indian graves." The professor sensed impending yarns and moved to sidestep that eventuality by thanking his hosts and bidding everyone good night. He expressed the wish to ride out again first thing the following morning and pleaded the need for rest, since he was not accustomed to the saddle in the normal course of everyday business.

He was cheerfully hailed off to bed as a good fellow and wished a peaceful night. He did not mention or inquire about the lone horseman who had shadowed him through the hills. He wished to avoid too much attention being focused on his endeavors or his concerns.

Like most academics on the sniff for publishable research, Professor Gill played his cards very close to the vest. Theft of scholarly assets was rife in his profession. He often reflected upon the outright venality and treachery of which fellows of his calling were capable. University dons all grazed in the same small meadows, and academic quarrels occasionally led to intellectual bloodshed. It was rare, if not impossible, to find a lifelong pedagogue who could not exhibit the scar of at least one stab wound in the vicinity of the spine.

Unfortunately, Solomon Gill had anything but a peaceful night. His sleep was marbled with stalking phantoms; images of a shadowed horseman pursued him through endless hills, and he awoke in a troubled sweat. For a few moments he seriously considered returning to San Jose, but the bouquet of fresh-roasted coffee and ranch bacon marshaled warmth and fortitude back into his stiff joints.

As he dressed, Solomon contemplated the logic that had prevented him from discussing the curious horseman. While shaving he decided that it had indeed been wise not to garner a reputation as one who sees visions in the shadows. Mysterious sightings would undoubtedly ring the death knell for his career. He would say nothing until he knew with reasonable certainty what he had seen. The horseman possessed motive and purpose and was concerned with the presence of Solomon Gill. He was almost sure of it. That thought continued to goad him as he went down to the bustling ranch breakfast.

Before his departure on the back of old Doughboy, Professor Gill begged the loan of a pair of field glasses. He had neglected to foresee the usefulness of a good pair of binoculars when planning his adventure. Sadly, the only available solution to his problem lay in a pair of tarnished brass opera glasses that had belonged to a forgetful guest when Adelaide Pfeiffer ruled the roost. One lens was slightly cracked, but they were marginally serviceable. The professor accepted the loan with thanks and a promise of their safe return at the end of the day.

With food and water bindled to an aged McClellan saddle, Professor Gill and Doughboy set off. They headed farther east than north to follow the heights above the dry tributaries that fed the ancient river courses.

The Pfeiffers' map indicated a likely area for Solomon's hunt near a plateau overlooking a confluence of four game trails and two brooks. The geology of the place looked promising. Many archaic watercourses were still to be found where their flow had worn away the limestone. Every hour of trekking through this primeval landscape only further convinced Professor Gill that he might be getting closer to something tangible.

Then Doughboy stopped and rotated his tall ears in all directions. Solomon Gill went rigid as he caught sight of the horseman on a rise some ways to the north. Half an hour later, Solomon again found the rider on a crest south of the river. Solomon drew out the opera glasses and focused, but the distance and angle of light prevented a clear view. The mysterious rider appeared again in the north, and Professor Gill became genuinely uncomfortable with the constant reappearance of the apparition.

There appeared to be no overt hostile intentions on the part of the specter, but Gill began to question whether the local legends of the dark watchers might not, indeed, be true. Perhaps this secretive figure was a true source manifestation of the myth. . . . But then he thought he was just letting his imagination get the best of him. Either way, the professor almost shivered when the mounted figure materialized again on another rise to the north of the trail.

Rather than be confronted at every turn by the shadow presence of the horseman, Solomon Gill decided upon a sly maneuver of his own design. He was angry that the rider had proved such an emotional distraction for two days. The horseman never approached close enough to be identified or confronted, and this struck Professor Gill as bluntly contentious. He had abandoned several promising destinations because he had felt intimidated by the distant horseman's watchful presence. Now he felt like turning the tables on his shadow. Yes, he would do it, if only to move the game piece one square in his own favor.

On the assumption that he was always being watched, even when the rider was not in sight, Solomon turned northeast through a dense grove of scrub oak and weathered pine. His obvious destination to anyone spying upon him was a narrow plateau a quarter mile away. Solomon assumed, judging from recent behavior, that the rider would contrive to appear on a rise above him on the adjacent ridge to the east.

When the professor and Doughboy were well hidden in the grove, he reined the mule to a halt and waited quietly until the blue jays had ceased their raucous warnings. When he thought the timing appropriate, he reversed the direction from which he had come. Knowing that the rider would soon discover his mistake and retrace his course to hold the advantage, the professor dismounted and posted himself in a natural blind at the southeast corner of the grove. His purpose was to confuse the shadowing rider and force him into revealing himself.

Solomon took a moment to clean the opera glasses and adjusted the sloppy focus to the point where he suspected the horseman might reappear. It amused Professor Gill to recognize that he was using ancient native hunting techniques to grouse out his elusive phantom.

The professor didn't have to wait for long, but what he ultimately witnessed was something of a shock. The truth, unfortunately, did not conform to any speculations he had loitered over these past two days. What the professor saw was no apparition, but a half-naked Indian galloping astride a black stallion across a shallow depression a quarter mile to the east.

The Indian looked truly savage. He wore nothing but a breechcloth, loose Indian leggings resembling chaps, and a dark cloth headband. His hair was long, black, and streamed out behind as he raced along. The Indian managed his mount with obvious expertise and rode using only a saddle blanket and a rope halter. He easily cleared every hazard and obstacle, as if his equestrian stunts were mere child's play.

There were a few moments when Solomon caught sight of the features on the Indian's face. The warrior's severe aspect was strong, gaunt, and almost classical.

The professor judged the rider as possibly dangerous if provoked and thus decided that his safest alternative was to remain invisible until the horseman moved on. The professor focused closely and determined that the Indian appeared unarmed. He carried the normal sheath knife of course, but Solomon spotted no firearms—and that was a reasonable blessing, to his way of thinking.

In a few moments, the Indian's stallion had outrun Solomon's simple binoculars. The rider galloped to the crest of another rise and stopped. Solomon refocused and watched from cover as the Indian slowly surveyed the vista in all directions. After a minute or two, the horseman decided on the southwest and disappeared over the ridge.

It was a while before Professor Gill thought it safe enough to pull Doughboy from cover and, with some difficulty, remount. They then traveled roughly in the same direction that the Indian had taken, except that Gill remained to the north and well behind. He decided that the best policy would be to allow the mule to choose the route. Solomon reflected that every course he had chosen during his search had come to nothing. Perhaps the mule could find what he could not. The professor happily let the reins go slack, sipped water from his canteen, and daydreamed while Doughboy moved purposely along a trail of his own choosing.

Eventually the mule carried Solomon down and out of a small stand of scrub oak. The trail led across a shallow plateau to an ancient, dry creek bed that had once flowed into the Big Sur River beyond. The mule halted again, and Solomon thought for a moment that Doughboy had sensed the near presence of the Indian's stallion; but the mule's ears flopped forward, and his head hung down with an air of world-weary forbearance.

Professor Gill looked about and, noticing nothing out of

the ordinary, dismounted to serve the needs of nature. This relieving opportunity allowed him a few moments for closer examination of the ground on which he stood. After a few seconds he noticed a complex arrangement of stones hidden under the browning vegetation. He gazed about and noticed still other symmetrical orchestrations of rock masonry, piles of stones that were once part of a greater shelter, now all well camouflaged by generations of plant life and natural erosion.

Professor Gill, now the enthusiastic hero of his own dreams, worked his way through the underbrush and found a score of foundation holes cut into bare rock and anchor stones that had once held the sprung boughs and bent ridgepoles of small temporary dwellings. He was elated beyond all imagining.

After a short search, Gill discovered a location that very likely served to support jerking racks and dressing trees for game. He walked across a shallow clearing to the edge of the hill and found the location of a probable midden. He knew garbage deposits spoke volumes about ancient cultures. To the south the view down to the dry riverbed was perfect for spotting game. In fact, he thought he heard an animal at that instant. Something large moving off down the trail.

Solomon suddenly went rigid. He looked into his hand and spun around to discover his worst fears realized. He had permitted himself an unforgivable distraction in the immediate passion of his discoveries and had dropped his mule's reins.

During this unattended interval, Doughboy, finding himself at liberty, had decided to go home for supper. He had obviously found no compelling reason to give notice of his intentions. Professor Gill groaned painfully, rolled his eyes to heaven, and palmed himself in the forehead. After this spontaneous celebration of his own stupidity, Gill quickly decided there was nothing for it but to follow the mule as quickly as possible.

Poor Professor Gill left his discovery behind and made his way down the broken trail with all the dispatch allowed a man of sedentary habits. He was distressed to discover how easily the splintered ground fatigued his frame and thwarted his progress. He was forced to rest by the trail often, nursing his swelling feet and cursing his fate. He also came to regret that he had not carried his canteen instead of lashing it to the mule's saddle.

As he worked his way down the trail Solomon attempted to make mental notes of his location, but he soon realized that any rediscovery of this remote site would be a matter of pure luck. His map didn't show the location; he was sure of that. And for someone with his poor sense of direction, retracing the way would prove difficult at best. Doughboy knew the way, of course, but he was a creature who kept his own counsel.

Happily, Doughboy wore distinctive iron shoes, and following his tracks was not difficult as the earth softened farther down the trail. Though Solomon realized that after sunset, even that exercise would become useless without a torch.

Lamentable prospects inundated Solomon Gill. The weather held promise of chilly evening winds, very possibly fog, and Solomon hated the thought of a night in the wilderness without food or shelter.

His darkest fantasies were further invigorated by visions of a wild, mounted Indian stalking him after sunset. Then Solomon remembered that he didn't even carry a small box of matches. He didn't use tobacco and had never considered the need of a fire in case of an emergency.

Professor Gill grew more nervous and despondent by the

moment, but he rippled even further when he heard the Indian's stallion whinny in the distance. Solomon couldn't be sure, but he imagined that the sound came from the direction in which he was traveling. The thought gave him few prospects he wished to contemplate in depth. He reflected on the possibility that perhaps he had read too many pulp adventures as a youth. His imagination, though now tempered with education and experience, was still faintly littered with childhood images of bloody scalps, burning cabins, and waves of screaming, painted braves.

Another half hour of footsore travel and the trail flattened and became more bearable. Suddenly the professor thought he caught the scent of smoke, but then it was gone on the breeze.

He was hiking through a landscape of strange shadows and stranger perspectives. Every detail seemed contrived to impede any immediate view of his surroundings. Distances became impossible to judge. Then the fragrance of pine smoke drifted across his path once more, and he stopped for a moment to judge its source. That proved impossible.

Professor Gill limped down the trail until he came to a clearing in the trees. What caught his eye astonished him. There stood old Doughboy, reins secured to a tree limb and hind leg cocked in repose. Doughboy was slumbering the sleep of God's innocents. A little fire burned in a small stone circle neatly cleared of all surrounding combustibles. The professor's food bindle had been laid out neatly on the ground like a table-cloth. Closer examination revealed that his packed lunch, which he had neglected, had been partially liberated. Two pieces of fried chicken and two johnnycakes were missing. The professor's canteen had been set upright on the bindle cloth and he noticed that the collapsible cup was still moist with use.

Though he waited cautiously, no one appeared from the shadows to claim responsibility, and there were no further appearances from the mysterious Indian horseman, for which Professor Gill was prayerfully grateful. Relieved at finding his transportation secure and quiescent, Solomon sat on the ground next to the spread bindle and ravenously consumed the last of the chicken and the remaining johnnycakes. Whoever had caught and tethered Doughboy had been generous enough to leave half the rations intact. Solomon was grateful for both.

When he had finished refreshing himself, Solomon packed his bindle, mounted the reanimated mule, and moved off down the shadow-laced trail with a prayer of sincere appreciation upon his lips. Doughboy and the professor finally made their way back to the lodge about nine o'clock. Both rider and mule were warm and fast asleep within thirty minutes of their arrival.

Solomon Gill rose upright in a cold sweat at five-thirty the next morning. He had heard a sound in his dreams that had frightened him. Suddenly he heard it anew, and it sent chills up his spine. It was the sound of a horse whinny in the distance.

Solomon pulled on his pants and went to the window. A wrangler leading a string of five shaggy cow ponies was coming up the road. The professor sat on the bed to pull on his boots. He was disturbed by his startled reaction to the sound of the horses, and he was forced to concede that the experiences of the last two days had not been all that he might have wished. The fact that he had been spooked by the phantom Indian gave Solomon pause to consider his own suitability as a field researcher. He missed his books and the simple comforts Mrs. Hammel's establishment was pleased to provide. He had long since become accustomed to the secure precincts of academia. It hadn't been an acquired taste, either. He had fallen into it quite easily. The vistas might not be as broad and spectacular, but the dangers were correspondingly lessened by the mundane constraints of campus life.

The professor took his little five-and-dime notebook from his jacket pocket and looked at the scant few notes he had made in the last couple of days. There seemed pitifully little to show for his adventures except a possible Neolithic campsite he could never find again and a strange tale of a half-naked Indian horseman that he was sure no one in his right mind would credit.

Within seconds, Solomon Gill had talked himself out of any more expeditions into the hills. He would take the next available transport back to Monterey. If he didn't arrive too late, he could catch the night coach to San Jose and be home in time for breakfast. The idea became more attractive every moment, so he cheerfully began preparations for a timely departure.

The professor's fortunes were on the rise. As chance would have it, the motor stage north was due to stop by around nine o'clock. There would be plenty of time to enjoy a ranch breakfast of venison and eggs at his leisure.

The bill for Professor Gill's stay at the lodge came to a grand total of six dollars and forty cents. He left the change to buy Doughboy a treat. Sixty cents worth of apples or carrots he thought a fitting gratuity for a mule. He left another dollar as a housekeeping tip. Then he took his bag and went outside to the veranda to await the stage in the morning sunshine. Little Anne from the kitchen brought him a second cup of sweet coffee to enjoy while he waited.

At 9:05 the motor stage rattled to a stop in front of the lodge with a grinning Corbett Grimes at the wheel. Next to him sat a young girl he introduced as his daughter, Mary, called "Toots." He said he was taking Toots to a friend's birthday party up on the Palo Colorado. Grimes was in a garrulous frame of mind and full of good-natured quips. Toots laughed at everything.

Being the mail-stage driver made Mr. Grimes the first herald of all local tidings. His catalog of idle gossip seemed endless. Grimes loaded the professor's bag in the boot of the stage with the mail, smoked wild boar hams for Frida Sharpe up at the Bixby Inn, and a roll of uncured deer hides for the little tannery in Monterey.

Solomon thought he would be the only passenger until the cowboy who had delivered the string of ponies earlier came out of the lodge, greeted Grimes with a chuckle, and climbed into the front passenger seat next to Toots.

The cowboy was dressed in the Spanish mode. He wore a black bandanna on his head in seaman's fashion and a flat-brimmed black hat. He sported black leather leggings that buttoned up the sides and took the place of chaps, a style Mexican vaqueros had long since made popular. The cowboy carried a beaded quirt with which he saluted when introduced to Professor Gill by Mr. Grimes.

The vaquero said, "A pleasure to meet you, Professor. My name is Castro, Roche Castro. Have you enjoyed your stay in our wild country?" He spoke well, but maintained a lissome accent that sparked with Latin embellishments.

During the ride north Mr. Grimes and Roche Castro exchanged tall stories like trading cards. Occasionally Roche would turn to share exceptionally colorful details of some story with the professor, but for the most part Solomon Gill kept to himself.

He wasn't impolite, just reserved, and Roche went out of

his way to make the shy professor feel included. He asked Gill where he taught, but not what. When he heard that Solomon was a professor at San Jose State, Roche said that he had a second cousin going to school there, but never asked if the professor was acquainted with her. He was just being polite.

Roche preferred trading hot shots with Corbett Grimes. He was not one to chat up strangers except when boosting them at poker. Toots just sat there in the middle soaking it all in and laughing at the old jokes as her father spun them out.

God only knew how many times she had heard these tales in her young life, but she enjoyed them all the same. Grimes liked regaling strangers with his stories about Robinson Jeffers, the famous poet. One of the first locals to meet him, Grimes had driven Jeffers up and down the coast when he first came to visit the Big Sur.

Professor Gill didn't care much for poetry, but he listened politely while Grimes spun out yarns about the old days. Grimes had known George Sterling and crazy Jimmy Hopper too, but these names meant nothing to Solomon, so he let his mind wander out over the vast green ocean flecked with white. The sunlight was clear and sharp and defined the stark coastline in superb detail. The professor drifted in his reverie until Roche Castro said something about "the dark watchers." Instantly the professor surfaced with a belated, "What? What about the dark watchers? What were you saying?"

Roche turned around and said that Corbett had been talking about this story he heard about a tool-drummer from Santa Cruz who got lost up the Little Sur River. When they found him he was jabbering on about being haunted all night by dark figures that watched his every move, but would not come out of hiding. They had been seen for centuries, Castro said. All the local Indian legends related similar stories about the dark watchers.

Grimes cut in, shouting over his shoulder to make himself heard over the loud rattle of a particularly bumpy turn. "That's the truth, Professor. Seen 'em myself once or twice of a moonlit night. Ain't that right, Toots? You can ask Olive Steinbeck over in Salinas. She used to teach school in the Sur. A well thought-of woman, and you won't find anybody as hard-nosed and stone-bound practical-Irish as Olive Steinbeck. There's no malarkey tolerated with that woman, but she's seen them, plenty of times. Told me so herself a few years back. She said she had spotted them when she was riding the high trails in the evening. Told me she made a habit of leaving small baskets of apples at special locations. The apples were always gone when she returned, but the baskets were never touched or taken. The dark watchers have never harmed a soul as far as anyone can recall, but Olive said that several greedy old prospectors had disappeared mysteriously while looking for Indian gold in the high canyons; fat chance of anyone finding Indian gold up there. Have you ever seen them, Professor? The dark watchers, I mean."

The professor didn't answer at first. He couldn't. He was about to say "No" when the stage made a wide turn around the base of a hill. On the bluff above the road overlooking the Pacific, mounted on his black horse, stood Professor Gill's private Indian nightmare.

Solomon felt cold perspiration bead on his temples. He wanted to say something, but his throat constricted and the words wouldn't come. Solomon desperately needed to know whether the other passengers could see what he saw, but he found it impossible to make himself understood. When Roche

Castro turned to better hear the professor's answer to the previous question, he was confronted by a disquieting sight. Professor Gill was almost blue, sputtering and pointing a shaking hand to indicate the mounted figure high on the bluff ahead.

Professor Gill was not remotely prepared for what transpired next. Suddenly Corbett Grimes, Roche Castro, and Toots all caught sight of the figure on the hill. They began to wave and hoot wildly. Grimes blew the rusty Klaxon horn and waved his hat out the window while Toots crawled across Roche's lap, propped herself out the passenger window, and waved both arms with delighted enthusiasm. Gill was then double stunned to see the half-naked Indian dismount, smile broadly, and wave back. In a few moments the motor stage had banged and popped its way down through the next turn and the apparition was gone. Solomon heard Roche Castro's voice as through a fog. "Are you all right, Professor? Professor? Are you feeling well?"

Professor Gill at last found his voice. "Yes. Yes, thank you. It was all something of a jolt, well, a surprise at any rate. I've seen that man before and, obviously, you are all well acquainted with him. Who is that Indian, sir? I'm confident we have crossed paths before."

Roche Castro turned with an amused knit to his brows. "I shouldn't be surprised, Professor. But he's no Indian, though he knows the local Indians better than any man in California. That was Dr. Jaime De Angulo. He bought a ranch from me a few years back. He's a famous anthropologist, studies Indian languages for one thing. I've heard said Dr. De Angulo knows twenty-five dialects, maybe more. He's an expert on the Pit River tribes. I'm surprised you never heard of him, being a professor and all."

Professor Gill sat back with the expression of a poleaxed calf. His jaw dropped, his eyes rolled to heaven, and his head nodded like a Chinese doll. After a few moments Solomon Gill reached into his pocket to retrieve his handkerchief and wipe his perspiring brow. When he withdrew it, his little notebook emerged in the folds. He looked at the cheap marbleized-paper cover for a second and then tossed the fluttering pages out the window into a ditch.

In late August Dr. Hedgepoole sent a letter to Professor Gill. The message communicated the doctor's disappointment at not hearing from his friend since his trip into the Big Sur. The letter also related the news that a local anthropologist and noted Indian linguist by the name of Dr. J. De Angulo had discovered a remarkable network of Native American hunting encampments in the Big Sur.

Dr. Hedgepoole had been told the discovery took place in approximately the same area Professor Gill had supposedly investigated. Dr. Hedgepoole went on to state that he had never met the man personally, but was apprised that Dr. De Angulo was understood to be quite the character and that the Big Sur locals all seemed to know the man well. Dr. Hedgepoole asked if Solomon had met Dr. De Angulo while staying at Pfeiffer's Lodge. He closed his letter by asking for news of his friend as soon as it was convenient.

It was almost four months before Dr. Hedgepoole heard from Professor Gill again. One day he was surprised to receive a letter postmarked from Chicago. The professor apologized for the long delay in replying to the doctor's previous message. He went on to explain that he had decided to accept a more lucrative teaching post at a prestigious women's college in Illinois. Unfortunately, his move had required considerable dispatch and thus afforded little time to catch up on his parting correspondence.

Professor Gill's letter went on to relate various trivial details about his decision to move east, but one aside did manage to catch Dr. Hedgepoole's attention. In the vast fertile plains of anthropological study, Professor Gill had finally decided to focus on an unusually obscure and unpopulated field of study. Dr. Hedgepoole didn't quite understand it all, but the gist had something to do with early grain cultivation, arthritis, and dental ware in prehistoric European populations: obviously a field of study offering little competition. Professor Gill's letter noticeably avoided any mention whatsoever of his journey into the Big Sur, or his singularly bizarre encounter with fellow anthropologist Dr. Jaime De Angulo. *Sic transit gloria mundi.*

BLIGHTED CARGO

~~~

EVEN BY THE SLIMMEST OF ACCOUNTS, young Simon Gutierez O'Brian was said to be fractious, deceitful, ill bred, and dangerous. Born a cold, selfish, and resentful scion of an indifferent bloodline harboring similar tastes, he was thought well suited to bear the malformed, sapless branches of his malignant family tree.

The O'Brian clan of San Jose, such as it was, had long dedicated its meager endeavors toward diverse forms of petty and not-so-petty villainy. At any given time, half the O'Brian tribe was abroad taking the cure at some state-run correctional facility.

At fifteen, young O'Brian had already grown gaunt and leaden with sin, but his greatest criminal talent always manifested itself in cultivating some witless blockhead to shoulder the blame for his own calculated misdeeds. On those lucky occasions when he could get away with bearing false witness, O'Brian took his deliverance as a sure sign that his skillful duplicity was beyond the mastery of the local authority, and for the most part, he was right.

At sixteen, O'Brian ran away to sea to avoid prosecution for serious crimes he could not blame on others. This gave the San Jose constabulary much-needed breathing room, but it did little to modify the boy's basic inclinations. Even aboard ship, O'Brian found ample opportunity to employ his dark gifts and in no time at all was up to his eyeballs in petty crime.

Unfortunately a particular instance came about when his cunning miscarried badly. As a rigger's mate aboard the coastal schooner *Queensland*, bound for Seattle, O'Brian had been caught stealing medicinal brandy from the spirits locker, which in turn he was selling to his mates at rudely inflated prices. He might have escaped with a fine and demotion if he had not been so impetuous as to attempt to lay off the true guilt on the bosun.

The inculpable bosun, wide-eyed casualty of O'Brian's black accusations, turned out to be a first cousin to the captain, who knew only too well that his kin had taken "the pledge" the previous year at the behest of his dying wife. After summary justice before a captain's mast, O'Brian was ignominiously put off the ship without pay or rations and left to fend for himself on a lonely stretch of beach south of Coos Bay, Oregon. O'Brian swore never to be caught short of a credible patsy again.

By pretending to be an officer of a passing ship bound for the sealing grounds and cruelly washed overboard in the dead of night, O'Brian cozened the sympathies of two aging

Catholic priests, soliciting their aid to finance his journey north to Portland.

The castaway spuriously represented himself as part owner of the lost vessel the *Saints* and warranted the captain, his brother-in-law, would make for Portland when they discovered he was missing. As a ship's officer, O'Brian avowed he would be pleased to sign a promissory note for all funds advanced, with modest interest of course, the funds forthcoming as soon as he returned to his ship.

The two priests were gulled into believing that the castaway was a good Catholic and a gentleman of his word. O'Brian played upon their sympathies until they happily offered to subsidize his journey north with two hundred dollars in Mexican gold.

O'Brian repaid their credulous generosity by pocketing the cash, stealing valuable church silver, and skulking out of town hidden in the back of a northbound goods wagon. In all, he thought himself far better off than if he had stayed aboard ship.

In a Portland dockside gin mill, O'Brian elaborated upon his sly story to a sinister audience in the person of a scar-faced Portuguese schooner captain late out of Macau and the China trade. Though obviously an accomplished officer, the captain (in O'Brian's estimation) had all the charm of hard-boiled leather. He correctly accounted the "Portugee" a dangerous man from all quarters, but also lucky enough to have survived and prospered in his chosen field of roguery.

Like most old hands, the Portuguese captain was highly suspicious of every sailor's self-appraisal. Nonetheless, the captain hinted that he might be in need of a rated hand, but specifically a mate having special knowledge of the more remote landfalls south of Santa Cruz, California. O'Brian at once claimed such knowledge and more besides.

There was little doubt in the captain's mind that O'Brian might possibly hand, reef, and steer if pressed to it, but the balance of the braggart's professed credentials he dismissed out of hand as so much oakum and smoke. However, it was not the Portuguese's actual intention to take on deck crew, but rather to snare a blackleg, a soul-skinner and Judas goat with a morbid dependence upon lawless enterprises. The applicant should also constitute a fitting dog's body to take the axe when the cards turned sour, as they sometimes did. But the Portuguese sea wolf hardly thought it prudent to apprise O'Brian of that particular eventuality.

As a ship's master who had survived ten years on the China station, the captain had, by necessity, developed a keen sense of character, or lack thereof. Aptly discerning that O'Brian had little or no real integrity to contend with, the captain offered up a post with the stipulation that O'Brian learn to master his mouth. The excruciating alternative to the captain's code of silence was beyond contemplation. He hinted that his lascars knew more about pain and death than any scoundrels in the world. He also indicated his willingness to demonstrate those subtle arts the first moment O'Brian stepped over the line or opened his mouth to so much as a bedbug.

With a raised glass and a warped smile, the Portuguese declared that on *his* ship, even the vermin had ears and they all reported to the captain's mast.

O'Brian gulped down his brandy like one about to cheerfully face the noose, then signed articles with a handshake. To solemnize the contract, O'Brian poured his new captain three fingers of Mexican brandy, a treacherous distillation that corroded the blood in mere seconds. The Portuguese shrewdly noted that O'Brian had a prodigious thirst for strong spirits.. To the captain's way of thinking most sailors were sworn to perpetual inebriation, but happily it made them remarkably pliable when moral fiber required acute flexibility.

It was thus that Simon Gutierez O'Brian began a new career as a blackleg smuggler. Not just a common contrabandist of uncustomed rotgut, but a bootlegger of souls. He had come under the sway of a captain who made his trade smuggling Chinese "illegals" into the numerous mining enclaves of California and the Baja coast.

It would be O'Brian's task to search out prospective customers for the Portuguese and, once landed at some clandestine location, lead the hapless Chinese off to the mine contractors. Five or six times a year O'Brian would meet the captain off a prearranged point and guide the Portuguese's ship to a secluded landing where the contraband might be transferred ashore out of sight of the authorities.

WHEN NOT ENGAGED WITH THE CAPTAIN'S BUSINESS, O'Brian would occupy his time with nefarious schemes of his own devising. He judiciously never showed his face in Monterey or King City, where awkward questions might be asked if he were picked up on charges.

O'Brian's favorite haunt was a notorious perch on the Monterey coast called Notley's Landing. This curious enclave was comprised of a humorless cluster of bleached wood structures haphazardly braced against the ocean winds on a rugged span of coast south of Carmel Highlands, at the mouth of the

Palo Colorado canyon. It was there, in the arms of frontier depravity, that O'Brian squandered his spare time, his money, and his health.

When not engrossed in planning or executing minor felonies, he could be found with the ladies at the bar of Notley's infamous dance hall, the most uproarious establishment of its kind on the Monterey coast. Other occasions might find him laid up for a few days at the Chinaman's, where he indulged in numerous pipes of opium to medicate the ills acquired asserting a dissolute lifestyle.

One day, as expected, a message came down that the Portuguese would await O'Brian off a lonely beak of coast on a certain moonless night in August. The captain wished to land a cargo ready for delivery to the Los Burros mines in Manchester.

The town of Manchester, if it could be called that, was a loose but lucrative community set high in the Santa Lucia Mountains. Like most mining enclaves, Manchester exhibited a robust appetite for bargain labor. The mine shafts, often haphazardly constructed and poorly maintained, took their customary toll in blood. The turnover in labor was high. Coastal Indians, Mexicans, Filipinos, and Chinese made up the bulk of the sacrificial feast, but there were also professional miners from Wales, Italy, Poland, Hungary, and Germany. Tin miners from Cornwall were especially regarded as thoroughgoing bastards and the best shaft bosses to be had, but even they quickly succumbed to the rigors of frontier mining at an amazing speed. The Italian and Portuguese miners happily murdered each other at a prodigious rate, so turnover was relatively high for them as well.

Manchester was a dangerous place to make friends and a worse place to make enemies, but O'Brian fit right in. The town saw him only when he had contraband Chinese in tow, and this made him rather popular with the mine bosses.

By way of business, O'Brian made it a habit to go fishing by himself on evenings when the weather permitted. To disguise his real purpose with an innocent avocation, he would hire small fishing boats from the locals, who were always in need of a few coins. He made a point of becoming a familiar face to other fishermen as he worked a dory in and out of the shallows and inlets. O'Brian's well-known pastime was intended to camouflage those particular occasions when his catch would be far more lucrative than fish.

On appointed evenings, O'Brian would row out with a hooded signal lantern to await the captain's old schooner in the offing. Contact made, the wily Portuguese would personally barge the Chinese ashore and await O'Brian's return with the money. To expedite matters, the mine owners were often encouraged to send their own men to a prearranged site near the landing. There they took possession of their cargo for the long march back into the mountains. On other occasions O'Brian made deliveries personally.

On the evening in question, O'Brian sat quietly, rocking and smoking in his hired dory. He nursed the kerosene flame in his lantern and warmed his hands periodically over the blackened stack. The coming night was well suited for phantom fishing, so he sent down several bottom rigs on hand lines in case he was being watched or was hailed by strangers. His general indifference to any possible catch proved irresistible to the fish and his slop box soon boasted sixty pounds of flounder and five robust sea bass. This too he would peddle to the miners to feed to their Chinese conscripts.

Like many sailors, O'Brian couldn't swim an oar's length.

Nonetheless, he always felt at ease afloat. The sea gave some small repose to his madness, but it did little to lessen his bodily discomforts. To that end he swallowed a small bead of opium against the chilled pain in his joints and followed that with a long, satisfied pull on his brandy flask. After a short belch he beamed like an anointed cat. He carefully checked the shore's rocky points of reference every few minutes and deftly countered tide and drift with long strokes on the sweeps. He had acquired the simpler rudiments of coastal navigation from long exercise waiting for the Portuguese.

The ocean chop became docile as the onshore breezes died. The sound of shallow waves scuffing against the bows became quite soothing, and O'Brian allowed his head to sink almost to the point of sleep. But only a few seconds would elapse before he looked up again to check his bearings, his hand lines, or his pocket watch. At the appropriate time he began to flash his signal from the lantern. Standing in the dory, O'Brian flashed his number in a sixty-degree arc out to sea. He did this three times in a row, covered his light, and sat down to check his lines. He waited ten minutes before repeating the maneuver. On the fourth attempt he became worried, on the sixth sullen, and on the eighth angry.

It was just as he had decided to sweep back for shore that O'Brian noticed a dense, swift-moving fog bank overtaking his flanks from the northwest all the way to the lee shore. It came upon him at first like a wall against the horizon and stars. Then it consumed the constellation of Leo and boiled on to embrace every visual reference. O'Brian felt iced fingers of panic climb his spine and make his scalp twitch. Beads of perspiration erupted from every pore and chilled instantly to magnify the effect.

Forgetting his tackle, O'Brian rowed for the shelter of his hidden cove, but before he had pulled a score of desperate strokes his world was enveloped in an impenetrable vapor. It was a fog so dense and a sea so temperate that every sound traveled under protest.

O'Brian's first instinct was to listen for the breakers on shore and then test for the set of the tide. Using a hand line and a cork float he set out a log and was relieved to find a slack tide on the verge of turning. O'Brian took advantage of the tidal shift to row farther out to sea. He wanted to keep a safe leeway under his stern in case he was unhappily obliged to make a night of it. Such things had happened before. If the fog cleared by late morning he would coast in on the next turning of the tide.

After an hour of slow rowing with occasional listening stops, O'Brian relaxed. The vapor cocoon was densely still and the slap of water almost akin to his pulse. He tested his signal lantern, but the light barely traveled the breadth of the oars. There were long moments when he lost sight of the stern of his own boat and all sound diminished to muted echoes or remote reverberations of distant surf.

O'Brian sat quietly in his fog-bound dory, content for the moment to let his brandy flask hold up its own end of the conversation. A thinning of the veil channeled echoes from indeterminable directions. Suddenly surprised, O'Brian coughed on his foul pipe as two heavy splashes erupted, seemingly nearby.

Then came the ghostly tones of men speaking almost inaudibly. O'Brian jumped to his lantern and made his signal in every possible direction, but the light refused to travel. It returned as a billowing specter of itself.

Out of frustration, O'Brian called out. "Is that your anchors, Portugee? Ahoy, ahoy there! Is that you, Portugee? Damn your eyes, masthead! Sing out there! It's me, O'Brian!" But there was no response. His voice seemed to travel no farther than his light. He didn't call again for fear that it wasn't his captain's ship. Revenue cutters used the fog to catch smugglers in the act sometimes. He had no wish to attract their attention.

Resigned to long hours of waiting, O'Brian decided to let the ill wind blow his way for a change. He rebaited his hand lines with small squid and stationed the rigs over either thwart. The sinkers dropped almost sixty feet before being spooled off the bottom a short span to entice the big flounder. Marking the line with a drop knot, O'Brian would use this measurement to gauge his progress inshore when the tide turned.

UNBEKNOWNST TO O'BRIAN, the Portuguese captain had ghosted under reduced sail for almost six hours. The unseasonably heavy fog banks had overtaken his schooner off Point Ano Nuevo in the early afternoon, and though there were infrequent sunlit breaks, it had proved a menacing run across the top of Monterey Bay with all vessels as fog-blind as himself.

Once south of Point Lobos the fog lifted briefly and it appeared that summer stars would govern the night's run down the coast, but five miles west-southwest off Yankee Point the ship was engulfed and fog-blind once more.

The dense ocean mists blotted out all visual references and stifled all but the loudest sounds. Within seconds the stars were gone and only the glow from the ship's binnacle remained to illuminate the tendrils of fog drifting through the rigging and curling about the decks.

The Portuguese listened for all warning horns, but refused to betray his position by sounding any of his own. He shrouded or extinguished his brightest lights, determined to sail on under wraps until his logs brought him off his estimated point of rendezvous with O'Brian.

While the schooner stood off and on in the vicinity of her destination, waiting for the impenetrable soup to clear, an incident of sinister distinction drew a pall of apprehension over the entire ship. Halfway through the starboard watch a lascar came to the Portuguese to report that two of the Chinese in the hold had died of some kind of pox and that the rest were in a state of great agitation.

The Portuguese fumed, but gave his orders instinctively. He called for the bodies to be brought on deck at once, but only the Chinese were allowed to touch the corpses. Once his lascar had herded the anxious Chinese porters back to their hold, the captain approached and inspected the dead coolies. Though he refused to touch the cadavers with anything but a rope's end, he detected the telltale skin blotches that forecast a profitless journey or worse. The Portuguese ordered a lascar to eviscerate the bodies to prevent bloating and rising and then had the corpses rolled unceremoniously over the side with a boat hook. A sad moaning arose from the Chinese in the hold when the sound of the splashes echoed through the ship.

As the Portuguese cursed the fog before, now he blessed the veil concealing his presence. With luck, he might depart without ever being seen in the area. The Portuguese quietly ordered the schooner to a new course, west-northwest, so as to raise a position convenient for hailing China Cove the following evening. He was passably sorry about missing O'Brian, but the fragile condition of the cargo demanded a quick sale, and the only paying customer within a day's sail was the Carmelo Land and Coal Company.

The Carmel Highlands boasted a number of working mines, and they exhibited a normal craving for cheap labor. Fatalities were to be expected anywhere men dug into the earth, but there always remained the dilemma posed by surviving widows and orphans. Very sad and very expensive if a whole shift perished at once. The Chinese were far less burdensome when it came to accidental extinction. Under the shadowy circumstances of their labor, families, if they existed, rarely came forward to request compensation.

The Portuguese cast his thoughts back to his stray goat, O'Brian, and wondered what had happened to the duplicitous brigand. It wasn't like O'Brian to bungle a rendezvous worth hard cash, but then no one had foreseen the fog or the dying Chinese. Being a naturally superstitious creature, the captain preferred to believe it was all a portent of impending misfortune. Discretion, therefore, dictated a need for an immediate departure from these phantom-burdened shores. In particular, he wanted to put a fair stretch of water between his ship and those dead Chinese.

Standing at the taffrail looking back into the fog, the captain contemplated granting O'Brian a small share of the Highlands commission for this night's aborted efforts, but he ultimately decided against it. He had already lost two Chinese, and that was enough expense. The Portuguese always decided against generosity in the end. It hadn't come up often as an alternative. The Portuguese crossed himself out of habit and called for more sail in the hope of a freshening breeze.

Five minutes later the fog bank parted and fell away behind the ship. The sky again became a stunning congregation of re-assuring stars. A cold hand lifted from the hearts of captain and crew. They felt the broken spirits of the dead drift away with the fog in the wake of the ship. The captain called for liquor rations all round to celebrate their deliverance. He insisted the bosun pour a measure of rum into the waves in the Saint's name, and then crossed himself again.

The Portuguese reigned over a polyglot crew of lascars, Mexicans, Madras Indians, and sundry local wharf rats no less superstitious than himself, so it did nothing to settle their collective nerves when from out of the tunnel of fog created by the ship's passage, some distant tormented soul screamed a strangulated cry so laced with fear and despair that every man on deck drained off his rum ration with one swallow. Again the Portuguese crossed himself and silently prayed for protection from the murky, vengeful shades of the sea.

He also prayed that O'Brian hadn't been taken by the sheriff's men. The captain knew O'Brian for what he was and justifiably feared being sold out for leniency if things went badly for his pet goat. It was exactly what the Portuguese would do in O'Brian's place. Still, the captain found O'Brian a profitable man to know and hoped providence would not squander such an asset. Mystery would have to attend his speculations indefinitely, for he never saw or heard from O'Brian again. Indeed, no one ever saw O'Brian again.

There was the standard conjecture from the locals when O'Brian and the dory had not returned, but most thoughts rested upon the whereabouts of the boat rather than on the possible fate of its occupant. O'Brian had never sought out or cultivated friendships of any kind. In fact, he disdained even passing familiarity, so naturally little time was spent pondering his destiny. Most people just assumed he tumbled over the side and would eventually wash up if the sharks didn't find him first.

One heaven-sent appeal was acknowledged, however. Four days after its disappearance, the dory was discovered floating free and intact. There was scant sign of O'Brian anywhere in the vicinity. His slop box of fish was relatively intact, barring the predations of gulls, and his hand lines were still cast off on either side of the boat. All looked as normal as any ocean-borne mystery may, but there was one disquieting apparition that cast a passing shadow over the dory owner's delight at repossession.

When the port hand line was hauled up, it brought with it the head and half-eaten carcass of a prodigious great flounder that might have weighed in at eighty-five pounds before the dogfish discovered it. But the other line, which was not paid out more than twenty feet, brought up the disemboweled and grimacing corpse of a Chinese man. The hook was snagged neatly under the left arm so that the corpse rose gaping from the waters pointing directly at the person hauling in the line. The dogfish had inevitably discovered the Chinese gentleman as well. Both lines were instantly cut free and the dory was towed back to shore.

THE PORTUGUESE PROVED TO BE A MAN blessed with considerable good fortune. He managed to unload his tainted cargo on a rapacious mine owner in the Carmel Highlands before anyone should be the wiser. He then sailed off with the intention of working a different shore until events cooled down. Except for one documented sighting off San Francisco, the first week in September, neither the Portuguese nor his greasy schooner were ever seen again this side of the Pacific.

SING FAT AND THE IMPERIAL DUCHESS OF WOO

A FEW DENIZENS OF THE BIG SUR were now and then molded by events into locally celebrated figures, while still others, by design, focused all their native genius on remaining unobtrusive, if not invisible. There was one such enigmatic character who chose the latter course with such studied diligence that no one ever guessed his true purpose or identity. How and why this mysterious figure came to accept the Big Sur as his asylum, the following narrative will attempt to explain.

THE PILGRIM'S NAME WAS SING FAT. He was born in central China to a powerful family that could trace its ancestry back to the sublime creation of the Middle Kingdom. His forefathers, so it was said, had mustered great legions against the barbarian hosts that surrounded the celestial perfection of the Empire.

The whole clan aspired to continue in this honorable endeavor until the end of the Tenth World.

Like most male children from his station in life, Sing Fat began his education early and with intensity. In this regard he showed exceptional promise, especially with languages and mathematics. He demonstrated a studied ear for perplexing dialects. Even as a child, Sing Fat easily conversed with household servants from remote provinces in their own tongues.

A renowned Taoist abbot who had traveled extensively throughout the kingdom assured Sing Fat's proud father that the boy would certainly grow to be a pillar of wisdom and prudence on which the Empire would come to depend and venerate.

But when he was thirteen, Sing Fat's entitled world tumbled from its ordered axis. Bloody civil war crested like a terrifying wave over much of the Middle Kingdom, and when it was over, Sing Fat was the only member of his immediate family left alive.

Within days of the final destruction, the promising seed of a great patrician tree had become little more than a wretched plowboy, a peasant slave fettered to his own inheritance.

When he was sixteen, Sing Fat decided to adopt a perilous subterfuge by changing places with a recently deceased field coolie who had been sold by the new landlord to an Imperial labor contractor. This broker, in turn, fed his impoverished countrymen to the ravenous mines and railroads of the Americas. The dead man had chosen suicide rather than depart China. He had no wish to die under the "gold mountain," far from his ancestors and lost in the savage lands to the East. With this sad event the degraded orphan found an opportunity to escape a humiliating bondage in service to his family's enemies. As a unit of contract labor he would be packed into a cargo ship like a chest of illicit opium and transported to a place his people called "the mouth of the mountain"—in fact, San Francisco. From that fearful destination, he had often heard, few souls ever returned to mother China.

Having judged the bleak alternatives, the boy reasoned that the prospect of laboring for the barbarous roundeyes, with the ever-present possibility of escape, could be no less abominable than the certainty of a slow, excruciating death at the hands of his own people. It was thus ordained by the fates that Sing Fat should come to San Francisco (Tai Fau), California.

From the dark, fetid holds of nameless ships, the numberless Chinese laborers were transferred to straw-bedded cattle cars and deposited like weary livestock at the foothill placer mines northeast of Sacramento (Yi Fau). For five years Sing Fat labored like a canal mule in the mud of the gold fields. Like most Chinese, his pitiful salary never seemed quite enough to cover his debts at the company-controlled concessions.

Sing Fat soon forgot what it was like to be dry and clean, or to wear garments that had not been patched by previous owners. Most of the donors had died at their picks from exhaustion, been blown to bits by faulty blasting charges, or had fallen afoul of some terrible Western disease. Sing Fat draped his hungry frame in the last bequests of the dead, and he honored their generosity every time he patched a seam or tear.

There were singular occasions when Sing Fat might have made good his escape from the mud and privation, but he had no idea where to escape to. He couldn't truthfully say he really knew where he was to begin with, much less where to find refuge if he chose to make a bid for freedom. He prudently decided it would be best to wait until he had acquired enough useful information to effect his emancipation without consequence. The last thing he needed was to have the mine police hunting him down through the wilderness like a stolen horse.

In the meantime, Sing Fat made the acquaintance of a fellow coolie, a cagey old man from his own province of Baoding. This astute, elderly fellow, who remembered Sing Fat's family by reputation, instructed the young man in a covert skill that happily made employment in the placer fields more profitable than the mine owners might have wished.

The old man showed Sing Fat how to glean small amounts of gold from the mine tailings. If one were patient and unobtrusive it was possible to harvest a modest income from the discarded waste of the placer mining process. If he came across a healthy nugget now and then so much the better.

The magic involved the furtive reprocessing of supposedly dead tailings to reveal the minutest traces of residual gold. The technique was similar to panning for gold except that the method involved the use of clear whale oil and a Mason jar. The fine, dried tailings were spooned carefully into the jar of whale oil, which allowed the lighter soil to remain suspended while the heavier gold particles sank to the bottom of the jar.

It was a painstaking skill to pick out the flecks of gold with a thin reed tipped in pine tar. When the process was finished, the oil was filtered through cloth for reuse. Since there was little else to do in one's spare time, gleaning gold became something of a recreational enterprise. At the close of his eighth year working the mines, Sing Fat had accumulated approximately $3,300 worth of gold dust.

Sing Fat's nest egg was always secured within a wallet belt that he had fashioned from waxed canvas. This belt he carried about his waist, securely bound under his smock with stout leather thongs. It would have required considerable effort for a thief to remove it even with the aid of a sharp knife. The same venerable gentleman had also advised Sing Fat to learn as much of the roundeyes' strange language as possible. He admitted that much of their barbarian tongue was unpronounceable, and therefore useless, but what the roundeyes were pleased to call pidgin English would suffice for most transactions. Indeed, it was all a poor Chinese coolie was really expected to speak under the circumstances.

The old man confided that true mastery of the barbarians' language would draw only suspicion and scorn from both sides of the gate. It was best to remain obsequious and invisible in a land of strange morals and unpredictable dangers.

He reminded Sing Fat that in his present situation—lost, bound, and alone in a land of spiritually unbalanced roundeyes— it was no particular crime for those barbarians to rob or even murder a Chinese. It happened all the time without intervention from the authorities.

Sing Fat and his gold would not long prosper if he drew attention to himself. Wisdom dictated caution. The shrewd man adopted a faceless and nameless demeanor if longevity was to be one of his goals.

After what seemed an eternity of backbreaking exertion, Sing Fat had acquired enough basic information to conclude that it was time to take his modest earnings and disappear. The inherent dangers implied in an escape were of little consequence to a man in search of the freedom to choose the pattern and place of his labors. Life without choices equaled bondage, and Sing Fat had sufficiently explored the depths of servitude.

Over the years since his arrival in the gold fields, Sing Fat had made subtle queries among his fellow workers. He discovered that there were substantial Chinese enclaves not only in

San Francisco, but also in Santa Cruz, Watsonville, Salinas, and Monterey. It might be possible to find refuge and employment in such places. If one possessed a little capital, the prospect of securing an honorable place within those communities would prove all the easier. Sing Fat decided to vanish at the first practical opportunity.

His chance came sooner than he expected. One hot August morning a hundred laborers, including Sing Fat, were piled onto ore wagons and hauled down toward Sacramento and the American River cargo landings to work as stevedores, off-loading heavy mining equipment from three riverboats.

During the dangerous transfer of loads from boat to dock, a cargo sling snapped free of its shackle and swept Sing Fat and twenty Chinese coolies off the riverboat and into the river. Sing Fat could hear their shrieks of distress even underwater as he struggled to regain the surface against the weight of his wet clothes and his belted treasure.

Many of the laborers could not swim and were drowned almost immediately. Sing Fat, who had been taught to swim by an uncle when he was a child, managed to rise to the surface just under the loading docks. When he came up gasping for air, he found he was holding on to one of the pilings and was therefore hidden from general view. He clung fast there against the current, waiting to regain his breath.

It suddenly occurred to Sing Fat that if he didn't show himself prematurely and made no noise, his masters would naturally assume that he had been lost with the other nameless victims and swept downstream. Confident that liberation was close at hand, Sing Fat clung tenaciously to the hidden pilings for the rest of the afternoon and into the evening until it was safe to extricate himself. Luckily the water was not deathly cold, thanks to the August heat, and though uncomfortable after many hours of immersion, he did not fear for his safety. When it was dark enough to escape notice, Sing Fat allowed himself to drift downstream with the current until he found a secluded place to haul himself free of the river. There he rested in hiding among the reeds for the remainder of the night.

The next morning, after discarding those elements of his attire that specifically identified him as a mine coolie, Sing Fat made his way west on foot as best he could. Sacramento hosted its fair share of Chinese laborers, as well as other minorities, and the fringes of the city supported a tattered network of shacks and shanties that passed for dwellings. Like the rings of a tree, every consecutive layer represented a different minority. The Chinese enclave was relegated to the farthest location, and all except household domestics were exiled to this outside ring. Thus they had the farthest to travel to and from their labors.

Sing Fat eventually came upon that outermost ring, and there he at last found invisibility and safety among hundreds of his own countrymen. He sought out and followed a relatively prosperous-looking laundryman named Lee Me Fong. This particular gentleman proved very amenable and truly sympathetic.

He happily exchanged clean clothes, sturdy sandals, two blankets, and twenty dollars in Yankee currency for a modest amount of gold dust. To show his good faith, the laundryman even drew a map of the roads leading toward San Francisco and Salinas. Lee Me Fong was proud to acknowledge close relatives in both locations and presented Sing Fat with a card bearing only one character: "mulberry." The laundryman begged Sing Fat to tender his deepest respects should he happen upon any of his illustrious relatives.

After a generous meal, and the purchase of rations for the road, all farewell formalities were acknowledged. Sing Fat then departed on his journey into a wilderness inhabited, he was certain, by ogres and demons prepared to beguile and destroy the unwary foreign traveler.

Upon studying his handmade map, Sing Fat decided that San Francisco was too big and too close to the arena of his last employment. He thought it prudent to travel farther south to Santa Cruz, Salinas, or Monterey, where the chances of being detained by labor authorities would be minimal.

This could not have been an easy choice. The distance in miles was beyond the scope of his understanding for the present, but he began to appreciate the general concept after three weeks on the road found him only halfway to his destination. By then he had repaired his sandals at least a dozen times. When conditions allowed he walked barefoot to save wear on the over-worn leather.

For a man whose cultural predilections leaned heavily in favor of demons and devils, the journey south proved frightening. Sleeping rough in the wild, where any creature alone drew the attention of strange beasts, was akin to a journey into hell. Sing Fat would occasionally be offered some small assistance by a passing Filipino field-worker in a wagon or a poor Mexican sharecropper.

From such as these, Sing Fat might purchase a few rations or a night in the shelter of a barn, but he was careful never to reveal any sign of his wealth. He would always proffer a few coins in exchange for his needs, but these he would pour from a worn leather pouch to show that these few coins were all he possessed.

He shunned all contact with roundeyes for fear that some white man would guess his secret and have him taken up to be returned to the mines. The probability of such an occurrence was extremely slight, if not totally improbable, but Sing Fat did not know this and so kept his distance from all barbarians on principle.

At night, while he took shelter in a grove of scrub oaks or a culvert, the sounds of the creatures of the night haunted his fertile imagination to such a degree that sleep often proved impossible. On several occasions he found it prudent to take his ease in the branches of a tree to avoid the marauding packs of coyotes that haunted the dark. Often their distant, nocturnal howls set his hair on end as he fantasized them to be anything but what they were. It might be taken as an indication of the terrors of the journey, or perhaps a natural reticence to speak about himself, but for the rest of his life, Sing Fat chose never to speak about those arduous and frightening weeks.

Always fearful of bandits or beasts, starvation or thirst, Sing Fat had worn away layer upon layer of courage and resolve until he thought his soul would cave in upon itself.

When he did at last arrive on the outskirts of Salinas one dry, star-choked night, he was no more than a wraith, with little to show for his long ordeal except an empty stomach, a hollow-eyed expression of total fatigue, and bleeding feet.

Like every town he had skirted on the way south, Salinas had delegated her laboring minorities to isolated enclaves, and it was there that Sing Fat at last sought refuge. He knew himself to be suffering from exhaustion as well as maladies that had come upon him as a result of his withering life on the road. So at the first opportunity, Sing Fat appealed to an old charcoal vendor for directions to an apothecary where he might purchase medicine.

He thought he was becoming delusional when the old

man pointed out the way to Chow Yong Fat's venerable establishment, not six doors away near the corner of East Lake Street. The old vendor added an endorsement to the effect that the elder Chow Yong Fat was the finest doctor in the valley. His store of medicines and cures was superior to anything white men could provide. Chow Yong Fat was also a sage of the mystic needles, that most esteemed of the healing arts. Sing Fat bowed weakly, thanked the old man, and half stumbled in the direction he'd indicated.

The vendor watched the stranger depart, noticed that he had cut off his braided queue, and shook his head. It was sad to see any creature in such a depleted and careworn state, especially a son of the Middle Kingdom who had resolved never to return to his homeland. But from what he had observed, the stranger would not live long enough to regret the folly of his choice.

Sing Fat found the establishment a few minutes later. The calligraphic sign above the modest shop was handsomely painted, but to Sing Fat's disappointment there was no indication of life within. Through the door's dusty glass panes, Sing Fat could see a small kerosene lamp, well turned down, set on the rear counter. It softly illuminated the interior and cast a warm veneer of amber light upon the countless pigeonholed drawers and porcelain jars containing herbs, ointments, and medicines. In desperation, Sing Fat knocked upon the door, but not a flicker of movement came in response. Sing Fat was about to knock again, but his spent constitution would tolerate no further exertion. With hand raised, he fainted from exhaustion where he stood.

★   ★   ★

As HE LATER REMEMBERED IT, Sing Fat was not brought around to consciousness easily, but rather floated ever so slowly toward sounds and light that seemed forever beyond his reach. Just as he sensed he might break free to the surface of apparent reality, he would slip once more into a pallid, murky insensibility. There he drifted helplessly like a mote of plankton until the light and sounds called him forth once more. But the faculty that finally netted him toward consciousness was smell, the pungency of ancient aromas, familiar but forgotten scents of home, of China, of childhood.

Each distinct odor was an amalgam of a multitude of different sources, some sweet, some piquant with a disturbing but familiar stench, all ancient, mysterious, and definitively Chinese.

Opening his eyes proved difficult and revealed an inability to focus on anything farther than a few inches from his face. He perceived detached precincts of light and dark, but little else. He could attest to neither movement nor sound, and he became aware of a creaking anxiety that tingled his bones. Sing Fat felt about in the gloom to find that he was laid out comfortably on a thick woven mat and covered amply with a sturdy, warm quilt. His head was cradled on a small wicker bolster. He tried to stir himself into a sitting position, but a firm yet gentle hand restrained him. A distant man's voice instructed Sing Fat to have no fear. He had been very ill, but if he followed a prescribed course of care he might yet live to bless one or two generations. Sing Fat, too devitalized to protest, did as he was told.

Moments later the same hand lifted his head, and a cup of warm but bitter medicine was placed to his lips. The remote voice encouraged the stranger to drink as much of the concoction as he could. It would aid in rest and make recovery more comfortable. Sing Fat accepted the brew without objection. Within minutes he noticed the mat began to feel like goose down and the coarse linen quilt became a fur-lined mantle. He slept for two days and awoke to visions unlike anything he expected.

At first, the light and shadow pattern of his surroundings appeared familiar, as was the detached voice of the man inquiring as to his symptoms and state of relief. What Sing Fat was not prepared for, however, was the extraordinary beauty, tranquil grace, and imperturbable serenity of the young woman who sat close by watching his every movement with clinical impartiality. To her right and across the room sat an older gentleman of somber aspect. This fellow labored at a worktable carefully preparing bewildering compounds over the coals of a small brazier.

Though he rarely looked up from his work, the wizard addressed the stranger with an informality that disarmed Sing Fat. But for all that, Sing Fat could not take his gaze from the girl for more than a moment. It was as though the sight of anything but her literally hurt his eyes, and he felt compelled to return his gaze to her as if gasping for breath.

Sing Fat had never experienced any sensation remotely like the spiritual commotion he was undergoing at that moment. He sincerely believed that he had been possessed by a supernatural being. Every detail of his existence was instantly in attendance upon every aspect and inclination of this creature.

It was all too much to sustain in his present state, so Sing Fat chose to shut his eyes before his heart fell out of his sleeve. The maneuver didn't work. The girl's image was burned into his retina like a flash of lightning on a black night. However he turned his eyes beneath his darkened lids, her likeness, etched in blue and violet sparks, floated to the center of his vision and remained there.

The next words that Sing Fat heard came from the apothecary and were spoken at his bedside. He instructed Sing Fat to drink an offered preparation at one go and to disregard the flavor. His reward would be a mug of sweet tea to take away the aftertaste.

Sing Fat opened his eyes and saw the man holding a small bowl of thick, brown liquid. His host now occupied the place where the girl had been. She now knelt by the hearth across the room. She was stroking a large white cat that reclined with its front paws splayed upon her lap. The girl's attention was drawn to a simmering clay pot set in the coals, but the cat eyed Sing Fat with the same dispassionate and thoughtful expression the girl exhibited. Sing Fat contemplated the similarity. It was as though the girl and the cat were two halves of the same being.

The apothecary centered his guest's attention with a pointed reminder about the elixir at hand and the necessity of immediate consumption to achieve maximum effect. Sing Fat blinked as though hearing the man's voice for the first time. He reached out for the medicine and became aware that he was dressed in a clean smock that was not his own. Instantly his hands rushed to his waist, but before a search commenced, Sing Fat heard the man say that there was no reason to be alarmed. His possessions had been safely set aside in a secure place. He might redeem them intact as soon as he was well.

The man smiled, and Sing Fat took the bowl and swallowed the odious blend at one go. The apothecary seemed pleased and rubbed his hands together with sincere satisfaction.

Good patients never labored their benefactors with objections or obtuse questions. Next he offered Sing Fat a small cup of sweet tea as promised.

The apothecary then called over his shoulder to the girl and asked that she prepare their guest a bowl of fish soup. Within moments the bowl was passed from girl to apothecary to patient. Sing Fat thought it was the most wonderful soup he had ever tasted, and he ravenously devoured it almost at once. The girl brought another, and this too he consumed.

The apothecary advised against gorging and insisted that the stranger take advantage of the opportunity to rest and sleep. Only then would his health and vigor return to him. Sing Fat nodded and thanked his host.

The vision he took to his dreams was that of the girl watching him. Her white cat reclined against her quilted jacket as though the girl's lap was its natural setting. The cat too watched Sing Fat and flicked the tip of its tail every so often as a display of applied feline disinterest. The last thing Sing Fat recalled, before a medicated sleep towed him under, was an innocent observation that hinted at a note of disquieting coincidence. The girl and the cat wore identical expressions and shared the same languorous bearing. One could almost believe that they were related by blood. With one last quizzical glance in their direction, Sing Fat surrendered to the apothecary's potions and drifted off in a warm, safe fog.

Sing Fat awoke the next morning with an exquisite sense of well-being, but when he discovered that he was all alone he became somewhat apprehensive. The fact that the girl and her cat were no longer watching over him brought on twinges of sadness faceted with relief.

For a few moments Sing Fat was forced to confront the

possibility that everything he had experienced in the throes of his illness might have been nothing more than a fevered dream, and yet the details of his present surroundings were as he remembered them. Now that the morning's light, cast from a small window high in the rear of the room, illuminated more of his environment, Sing Fat realized that he must have been attended to in the workshop and storeroom of the apothecary's establishment.

The worktable, with its myriad instruments, little boxes, and porcelain jars, was well within sight, but the back of the room, which had remained hidden in the dark, now revealed stacks of hinged wooden boxes and large jars perched on long shelves. Each was labeled with elaborate characters, but since he had never seen such ciphers, Sing Fat could not understand what they really contained.

As he rose from his low pallet and swung his legs to the floor, Sing Fat heard a door open to the accompaniment of a tinkling bell. He listened as two muffled voices conversed for a moment. Then the door behind him opened and a pleasant-looking old woman came in carrying a covered tray, which she placed on a low table next to Sing Fat's bed. The old lady nodded, said that she hoped the young master was feeling better, and encouraged him to eat while the food was hot. She then bowed politely and withdrew the way she had come.

The savory odor of the meal reached out and seduced Sing Fat at once. Setting aside all other considerations for the moment, he surrendered to his appetite. He could not remember the last time he had eaten so well. All the delightful flavors and aromas, so long excluded from camp rations, came back to greet his palate with childhood memories of bounteous kitchens and long tables of laughing people.

It was just as he set his chopsticks across the empty bowls that the door opened again and the apothecary entered carrying a paper-wrapped parcel and a bundle of clean clothing that proved to be Sing Fat's own.

The apothecary introduced himself as Chow Yong Fat and was truly taken aback when his guest responded with his own surname, Sing Fat. The elder Fat smiled broadly and said that the gods must have guided the young man's footsteps. Though there was no direct relation between the two men, the elder Fat insisted on calling the younger man "cousin" as an acknowledgment of their distant clan affiliation.

When Sing Fat hefted the parcel he knew at once that it must be his gold. When he unwrapped the canvas belt he found all the pockets still stitched and sealed just as he had left them.

He thanked the elder Fat for his diligence and kindness and further expressed his gratitude for the efforts expended to save his withered remains from certain death and an unmarked, roadside grave. He said that he would be honored to generously recompense the sage apothecary for all his masterful efforts.

The elder Fat bowed his head politely and said that while under his roof payment was not necessary, but if the young man truly felt an obligation, perhaps he could honor the debt with simple answers to a few questions. Sing Fat nodded his head in turn and declared a willingness to respond to any queries his host might have.

The elder Fat was most curious about Sing Fat's adventures. He was impressed with the young man's parentage and education and sympathized deeply with the story of his family's destruction. The apothecary knew only too well of the predations inflicted by the burgeoning class of petty warlords in China. He appreciated Sing Fat's resolution to escape the escalating bloodshed.

The apothecary himself had suffered from the military rivalries sparked by the end of the Boxer Rebellion and had chosen to come to America to help minister to fellow countrymen laboring like ants to build the local railroads.

But the elder Fat was most amused with the methods by which Sing Fat had amassed his little fortune. Gleaning discarded specks of gold from the waste of the placer mines required cunning, patience, and attention to detail. These qualities indicated a sense of diligence and perseverance not readily found in most young laborers.

The older man then tactfully inquired what Sing Fat's future course might be and, for the first time, found a degree of confusion on the part of his guest. Sing Fat shyly admitted that he was not sure what he should do. His first priority had been to escape the lethal labor of the mines. He had thought to go into business of some kind, but knowing so little of the country and the prospects available to a foreign stranger, he had set aside any contemplation on the matter until he became better informed.

Sing Fat freely admitted that he had chosen to take on the challenges one at a time and had hoped that after he had found refuge amongst his own people, some worthy elder might be able to counsel him on the best policy to follow. He was forthright when it came to self-criticism and expressed total ignorance in the ways of Western commerce. He had been groomed, he said, to take on the responsibilities of his ancestors' estates, and he knew little else. Now that such things were no longer possible, he would have to apprentice himself to a new profession and start all over again. He would be content with any occupation except mining, he said with a laugh. Outright slavery seemed preferable to mining in his estimation. The elder Fat chuckled knowingly in agreement.

During the length of the informal interview, Sing Fat had been bursting to ask the apothecary about the mysterious young woman who had attended him, but he knew that etiquette and custom frowned on a stranger's curiosity in these matters. Sing Fat had hoped that perhaps his host would incidentally mention her presence or her name, but that expectation went unfulfilled, and the prospect that he might never see the girl again tormented him to an extent he had never thought possible.

Sing Fat had little or no experience with women, at least with those not directly related to his family. He had never been counseled about what to expect from his own emotions in these matters. In fact, as a youth, he had been scrupulously tutored to keep his sentiments about women under tight rein at all times. A man susceptible to the vicissitudes of temperament and desire was considered vulnerable and at risk to all manner of reversals in life. Sing Fat now found it almost impossible to leap this hurdle of parental guidance, particularly as it had delivered him from personal calamities in the past.

The elder Fat mused upon what he had heard, looked up, and asked what profession seemed most appealing to the young man. Again Sing Fat shook his head and pleaded bewilderment. But any path, he said, that would lead a soul to a competent livelihood, providing ample ability to support a family, was worthy of consideration.

He was not proud or overly ambitious, he said, and entertained no desire to return to his long-dead social status. But he was anxious to nurture any blossom, no matter how small or solitary, of his truncated ancestral tree. If he could not do so in the heart of the Middle Kingdom among his own people, then he would attempt a minor resurrection of his clan abroad.

Here in the land under the Gold Mountain he would make peace with his ancestors and his fate.

The apothecary, having taken up his place at his worktable, looked up from his concoctions and studied the young man for some moments. Then he said that perhaps the gods had indeed led the young man to his present circumstances with a purpose. The elder Fat asserted that he was, at present, searching for just such a person to bring into his learned occupation.

The work required a studious and disciplined nature to be sure, but the future might shine brightly for a young man who understood the importance of such a meaningful undertaking. The people had great need for masters of the healing arts. He had hoped to draw upon the talents of his sons one day, but that day would never come. This last statement obviously pained the elder Fat, and it took a moment for him to regain his composure.

Chow Yong Fat said his beloved children had passed into the shadow world to join their venerable ancestors eight years past. They had died of an exotic malady contracted from the whites. Sadly the illness had proven unassailable and immune to all his medical skills. His poor wife had died of protracted anguish, grief, and shame a year later.

All his love, talent, and medicine had shown itself even less effectual in that instance. When her two beautiful sons died, the apothecary's despondent wife had abandoned the will to live. She expired under the darkest of all human veils, he said: self-recrimination, remorse, and illusions of culpability.

Since then he had carried on alone. Sing Fat could see these confidences distressed the elder Fat, but he chose not to interrupt with formal condolences until his host had concluded his story.

Chow Yong Fat had a few distant relations, he continued, but they lived to the north in Santa Cruz. After laboring on the Monterey and Salinas Valley railroad, they had taken to the fishing trade with only marginal success. Abandoning that vocation as too dangerous and unprofitable, some had taken on an even more perilous occupation laboring for the California Powder Works on the shores of the San Lorenzo River, while others worked as lime packers for the Henry Cowell Lime and Cement Company.

Unfortunately their endeavors had a marked tendency to narrow their focus to the health of their purses. They knew, or wanted to know, little else. Their children, he confessed, enjoyed scant education and seemed content, as did their elders, to make their living in the same traditional ways.

The apothecary said that he had welcomed several hopeful youths into the mysteries of his profession over the years, but in general they had shown themselves helplessly thin-witted and exhibited only a shallow inclination to improve their lot. They had all eventually returned to their nets or their beet fields.

It had saddened the old man, of course, but he ascribed their reasoning to an exile's mentality. It was as though life among the unsympathetic barbarians had weathered all the intellectual vigor and spiritual resolution from their souls. He did not fault them, however. He well knew what anguish and suffering his race had endured in the West. He understood that rudimentary survival was challenge enough for such creatures.

Perhaps in a future age they would find themselves and return to the path, but for the present, the apothecary was still in need of a suitable young man to bring into the profession. There was more work than time, and eligible candidates were as rare as flying teapots. The elder Fat began to shred dried go-takola leaves into a brass bowl as though he had said nothing of any real consequence.

Sing Fat was taken aback by the apothecary's informal proposition. While working the mines, he had hardly hoped to dream beyond the proprietorship of a laundry or a small-town market. Honest endeavors to be sure, but hardly the kind of occupation to animate the intellect or establish a venerable social standing to pass on to his children. To be of real service to his own people also suggested intrinsic rewards not found in lesser occupations.

If the apothecary's suggestion were to be credited, and Sing Fat saw no reason why it should not, there might also be a likelihood that he would see the comely and enigmatic young woman once again. That prospect alone ameliorated any lingering reservations he might have entertained. Though he would openly express concerns about his faculty to undertake such a singular enterprise, the prospect enticed him to savor the possibilities.

Returning from fanciful sparks of supposition, Sing Fat assumed a solemn expression and inquired if his host was seriously suggesting that a refugee and fugitive miner would make a suitable apprentice for such a lofty calling as medicine. Aside from his earlier education and an innate affection for mathematics, he had little to recommend him for such a scrupulous calling. Of course, Sing Fat was always willing to study and apply himself diligently to every task set before him. Such conduct was second nature to one raised a patrician, but that time was long ago and counted for little.

Sing Fat was polite but candid in asserting that if their positions were reversed, he would be far more circumspect about such an important decision. He said that his father and numerous uncles had been meticulous about social, political, and professional credentials.

Perhaps he must fault his own strict upbringing, but Sing Fat conceded that he was baffled by his host's brisk appraisal of a newcomer's aptitude for such a position. Especially an outsider whose only noteworthy qualification seemed to be that he had collapsed unconscious at his benefactor's doorstep. Sing Fat smiled and said he had never heard of a doctor asking a patient to assume the mantle of the arts by which he was cured.

This seemed to amuse the elder Fat. He said the question was worth scrutiny, but that necessity was the author of spontaneous decisions and he preferred to trust his own intuition in such matters.

Their congenial and tactful banter continued in this manner for some time, with tea offered as a pleasant intermission, but at the conclusion, Sing Fat found himself engaged as full-time apprentice and chartered student of the most estimable of professions. Sing Fat became slightly giddy with the realization and momentarily thought perhaps he was still hallucinating from weariness. The singular sequence of events, beginning with his escape from the mines, appeared to have been determined by the gods with some considered purpose. He would be worse than a fool to set himself against the rationale of *heaven*. As far as he was concerned, the seal was set. He was gratified and honored by the arrangement.

MONTHS OF COMPLEX AND ARDUOUS WORK followed Sing Fat's decision to take up medicine as a trade. The apothecary insisted that the young man keep detailed journals on every item and subject discussed. He said the annotations would serve his protégé admirably in the years to come. It always helped the visual memory to write things down in their minutest particulars.

The elder Fat found a modest accommodation for his new apprentice with a boardinghouse owner named Yee Get who operated an establishment near the corner of East Lake and Soledad Streets. It was a neighborhood known as new Chinatown, the older enclave having burned down in 1893. He also saw to it that Sing Fat banked his gold wisely with a venerated elder of the Quang Sang Company. That company's association with the prestigious Ning Yeung Association of San Francisco guaranteed the security of his funds and also allowed him the convenience of drawing against his deposit in American greenbacks.

The elder Fat also arranged for the barber Fong Kee to look after his apprentice's appearance, and the merchant Sam Wah supplied Sing Fat with new clothes at reasonable prices. Within a few months, Sing Fat had become a noted fixture in the neighborhood and was known for his cheerful, thoughtful, and modest demeanor.

When he judged his apprentice competent enough to understand such things, the apothecary began to take Sing Fat on his collecting rounds. Many medicinal ingredients could be acquired locally or from Monterey, but others could be had only from Chinese brokers like the ancient Ham Git or Ham Tung of the Wing Sing Company in Santa Cruz.

Myriad exotic herbs, pickled sea snakes and salt-cured turtle eggs, six varieties of dried sea horses, Asian blood toad skins, powdered Persian deer horn, tiger bones, tinctures of medicinal opium, and hundreds of other necessary ingredients could be obtained exclusively from licensed importers who shipped them in from Asia.

Since the elder Fat treated mostly the working poor, he could not, by any stretch, be confused with a wealthy man. He regularly found it necessary to barter with the venerable Ham Git in order to replenish his modest inventory of medicines. This was not as difficult as it might seem as Sing Fat's teacher had local access to any number of medicinal compounds that were difficult to come by, even in China, and trades were often arranged.

The apothecary knew where to unearth all manner of valuable substances locally, but the concentrated effort required to select and grade these items with assurance was by no means a task for the uninitiated. Sometimes it took days to gather, sort, grade, and value just a few bushels of tiny rock mushrooms, dried blue barnacles, or black mustard seed. The quality and potency of such goods were very much a condition of trade, and men like Ham Yin or Ham Git knew their business every bit as well as the elder Fat.

With his apprentice to help with these labors, the apothecary now toured the Salinas and Monterey countryside in his cart to gather, purchase, or barter for trade items. He had also contracted several Chinese farmers to cultivate specialty items like purple-foot sorrel, licorice root, black tiger weed, lemongrass, and leopard snails. In Point Alones or Pescadero Village he would sometimes barter his skills for deepwater shark livers and dried fins. The apothecary was always in the market for various marine specimens necessary to his practice. Other singular ingredients could be gathered only among the hills and along the rocky shores of the Big Sur. These goods therefore carried greater market value because of their rarity.

Sing Fat totally enjoyed these working adventures. He was learning wonderful things at an amazing rate. Every day brought forth new mysteries and amazing secrets. Because the apothecary was known and respected for his arts, Sing Fat also found many opportunities to meet influential people in the Chinese enclaves of Watsonville, Santa Cruz, Castroville, and Monterey.

The elder Fat always encouraged his pupil to write down the names of these men and their professions. Many times he would ask Sing Fat, strictly as an exercise, to record observations he might have about their general health.

He was required, of course, to base his amateur diagnosis on the Twelve Heavenly Principles of Balanced Health. These ancient canons were repeatedly rehearsed and discussed. The fact that Sing Fat was wrong two-thirds of the time did not particularly upset his teacher. He knew that practiced examination and study would eventually sharpen the young man's assessments.

With a twinkle in his eye, the elder Fat asserted that with study and hard work, his apprentice might bring up his average to something like three in five in twenty years. This joke always amused the elder Fat no matter how many times he trotted it out.

Sing Fat never dared argue a medical point with his kindly master, though ignorance and superstition sometimes lured him to consider it. Any reservations he might have entertained were consigned to private deliberations or his journal. For the most part, however, Sing Fat was profoundly content with his work and strived to grasp as much of the formal study as possible.

He was becoming aware that what he had often assumed

was simple common sense resounded like a slack drum when it lacked the authority of long experience. He took mental note and endeavored to restrain his native credulity. No easy task for a young, provincially pious landlord's son.

IT WAS AFTER one of their more successful foraging expeditions into the Big Sur that Sing Fat found himself in the apothecary's back room sorting dried willow bark and bee venom sacks for a special preparation. He heard the front door of the shop open with a chime of little bells and, a few moments later, the voice of the elder Fat called out to his apprentice.

Sing Fat set down his work, wiped his hands on a damp cloth, and moved through the curtains to the front of the shop. The bright afternoon sunlight streaming through the dusty windows made him look down and squint for a moment. When he looked up, he froze and melted in rapid succession, for there *she* stood.

The tender vision he had nurtured for months was again in the same room. Her white cat peeked out of a basket that she carried over one arm. She appeared even more fair than he had remembered or imagined, if that were possible.

For a brief moment, Sing Fat thought he might swoon with amazement. As soon as their eyes met the young woman smiled, bowed, and modestly cast her gaze to the floor.

The elder Fat cleared his throat to gain his pupil's attention. Sing Fat went crimson with embarrassment and stuttered a haphazard greeting, but he could not for the life of him take his eyes off the sublime object of his dreams.

The elder Fat proceeded to formally introduce the young

woman as Sue May Yee, the widowed daughter of a distant cousin who had lived and died in San Francisco. Sue May Yee now cared for her aging father-in-law at Point Alones Village on the shores of the bay in Pacific Grove. Her dead husband's family had been in the squid fishing and drying trade. Sadly, her husband, his three brothers, and one hired man had been lost during a gale that had scourged the waters white and sank many boats two years past.

As the apothecary explained, Sing Fat bowed to the young woman and offered his formal condolences while secretly rejoicing at her unmarried status. This conflict in his own sentiments did nothing to lessen his embarrassment. His crimson hue only deepened and prevented him from saying more.

The elder Fat, noting his pupil's predicament, smiled and continued the introduction. He said that Sue May Yee sometimes visited Salinas to obtain special medicines for her father-in-law and neighbors. She was also quite expert at gathering rare sea anemones whose stinging tendrils were sometimes used to help alleviate the symptoms of acute arthritis. Chow Yong Fat declared the young woman well versed in the uses of other natural medicines and said she often gathered specimens for him when she could take the time from other obligations. Now it was the young woman's turn to blush. Such high praise from one so esteemed and respected was not usual in her life.

The apothecary went on to say that Sue May Yee had been visiting when Sing Fat had made his unusual appearance. She had kindly stayed on to assist in his recovery. He maintained that in many ways she possessed as much intuition and native skill as any medical man he had ever known. Unfortunately, the profession was customarily closed to women, which the elder Fat decried as a great loss for all concerned. Sue May Yee bowed to acknowledge the commendation, but said nothing.

The elder Fat interrupted the rampant blushing all around with a request that his apprentice take himself off to Ah Kit's restaurant and see what his kitchens might provide in the way of a humble supper to celebrate Sue May Yee's safe arrival. He handed his pupil a few coins and sent him on his way with a pantomime kick. Sing Fat smiled and then was gone upon the errand.

In later years, Sing Fat would remember that in those early days he moved about as though walking upon magic sandals, his feet scarcely touching the earth. Rest from his labors appeared unnecessary, and his nights were visited with the most harmonious and auspicious of dreams.

The only occasions on which the elder Fat took meals with his apprentice were while working in the back room of the shop or when they were on the road together. On most other occasions he preferred to dine alone or with old friends. Thus Sing Fat naturally assumed that his master would take his meal in his rooms above the shop. Sue May Yee would share the meal in the traditional manner, but Sing Fat was on his own.

So while Ah Kit's cooks prepared his master's favorite dishes, the apprentice enjoyed a wonderful fish stew fortified with whipped egg and rich crab dumplings.

It proved a timely decision, for when he returned to the shop, Sing Fat discovered his teacher in a very animated frame of mind and full of instructions to be carried out at once.

While Sue May Yee served out spiced fish and steamed boa, the apothecary instructed his protégé in his immediate duties. He was to run to Ah Sing's livery stable and prepare the cart and mule for a long excursion. Sing Fat was to see that the canvas awning and side curtains were fixed to the bentwood frame that covered the cart bed. The elder Fat chuckled an aside to Sue May Yee lamenting the eccentric weather of past months. He wished to evade its extremities while on the road.

Chow Yong Fat returned to the subject at hand and advised his young friend to purchase ten days' ration of oats for the mule and to see to the condition of the harness, tack, and axles. He was to be particularly industrious where the axles were concerned. They needed a liberal facing of grease, and the grease bucket should be topped up for the journey.

Sing Fat was to do his best by the mule as well. The poor, moody creature might endorse the venture after a hearty bribe of carrots, or apples and sweet oats. Sing Fat was also to see that the contentious animal received a thorough currying and brushing. The apothecary insisted that the beast enjoyed a certain amount of normal vanity and preferred to be seen at its best in public. Last, the cart should be drawn up behind the shop in two hours' time, ready for loading. They would begin their journey that very afternoon.

The elder Fat made no allowance for the score of questions Sing Fat wished to ask. He simply began his meal and waved his apprentice off about his chores.

Knowing it would have been discourteous to intrude further, Sing Fat looked to Sue May Yee for some expression of understanding, but she was preoccupied with serving the meal and did not meet his gaze. With a slight bow and shrug of resignation, Sing Fat turned to leave. His teacher called him back and, with a fatherly smile, offered his pupil a steaming, sweet pork bun. The elder Fat insisted the young man's stomach would rejoice with gratitude. Sing Fat thanked his teacher, looked at the girl once more, laughed, and floated down the stairs.

Two hours later Sing Fat returned with everything in hand. Even the mule seemed relatively pleased to be sporting a brushed, shiny coat and freshly oiled harness. All was prepared just as his teacher had requested, with a few items attended to that his master had forgotten.

Sing Fat had cleaned and scorched the small water barrels before filling them afresh. He had seen to purchasing two extra iron shoes for the mule and had also inspected the road box to make certain that the appropriate tools were in good order. He had also stopped by his own quarters to prepare a bedroll, fresh clothes, and a few provisions for the journey.

The elder Fat pronounced himself well pleased with his pupil's enterprise and, still without a hint of explanation, gave instructions for the loading of the cart.

First a comfortable pallet of sleeping mats, quilts, and pillows was to be assembled well under cover, behind the seat. It was the apothecary's wish that Sue May Yee should ride in absolute comfort. Then little wooden chests brimming with medicinal herbs and tinctures were loaded carefully in front of the axle to soften their ride.

Next Sing Fat stowed food and other stores securely padded by the mule's grain bags. Lastly came the apothecary's clever, combination workbench and medicine chest, with its three-score drawers, intricate scales, and utensil trays. This was arranged in the back of the cart in such a way that, when the tailgate was lowered, the whole became a broad working surface on which to measure and prepare complex prescriptions.

With the addition of the master's traveling bag, all was set for departure. By three-thirty the mule cart was well on course west down the old road to Monterey with the other farm traffic. The sun would hang high for quite some time, but the elder Fat remarked that if they were pressed to it, they might stop for the night with Sam Wah's youngest brother, Kee Wah. Kee Wah owned a prosperous little berry farm just east of Monterey. He was in the apothecary's debt for services rendered the previous spring.

All seemed right with the world in Sing Fat's humble opinion, and though he would have appreciated knowing more about their present journey, he was content just to feel Sue May Yee's warmhearted presence riding behind him. Every once in a while he would attempt to steal a glance at her sitting in the back of the cart with the white cat curled up on her lap.

While Sing Fat drove, or rather encouraged the mule, his teacher perused his notebooks, apparently intent upon finding a particular article.

Notwithstanding his bubbling curiosity, Sing Fat asked no questions until his teacher had put away his notes; then he burst forth like a fountain of inquiry. The elder Fat looked at his pupil with a perplexed expression and said he thought that he had already explained everything earlier. Sing Fat nodded but claimed that he had been told everything except their destination and the motive for going. The apothecary scratched his head like a muddled old wizard and apologized. He muttered something about advancing age and forgetfulness, and then went on to explain his purpose as though recalling it from a distant page.

He disclosed that Sue May Yee had brought a secret letter from an old friend and patient. The gentleman worked and lived in a mining enclave southeast of Carmel Highlands. His name was Han Foo Yeung, and he owned and operated several

"Chinese cookhouse" concessions and was contracted to a number of prosperous mines.

The elder Fat assumed that his pupil was most likely aware, better than most under the circumstances, that newly immigrated or smuggled Chinese miners often sickened and died on a frontier diet of kippered meat, beans, canned vegetables, and hardtack. This insight, discovered only after a notable loss of coolies and money, encouraged the mine owners to subcontract their laborers' victual supply to other local Chinese.

These small businessmen, in turn, set up kitchens with Chinese cooks to prepare suitable rations at so much a head per day. With strong company affiliations, founded with the Hop Wo Association for instance, one could depend upon a solid and steady profit.

Chow Yong Fat winked and added that these same noble merchants gained considerable face and profit by servicing the needs of their less-fortunate countrymen. It helped if you were blind to their suffering as well. Han Foo Yeung was the best of that breed. An honorable man in the elder's estimation.

He went on to say that Han Foo Yeung had written to say that a number of recently smuggled Chinese had come down with a malady so alien to the white miners that they feared even approaching the victims, much less treating the symptoms. The miners had confined the stricken Chinese to a ramshackle toolhouse and, aside from water and some food, seemed content to let nature take its course without the expense of dubious medical intervention and public disclosure.

With a promise of fair compensation, the ailing Chinese miners had seized on Han Foo Yeung's suggestion and had humbly petitioned Master Chow Yong Fat to come to their aid as soon as possible. The apothecary was not sure what he could do besides make the men more comfortable, but he was more than willing to gamble his talents against the vacant response offered up by the mine owners.

Han Foo Yeung had also hinted at additional inducements. Several natural treasures had come into his possession, and he was willing to relinquish these cherished articles in exchange for services rendered. Any one of the Six Companies would barter handsomely to obtain possession of such natural rarities.

Discretion prevented describing these items in writing, but the sender had appealed for indulgence on a promise of good faith. The elder Fat frowned and remarked that he might have been suspicious of any other man's claims in such circumstances, but Han Foo Yeung possessed an astute and practiced eye in these matters. The situation must be very serious for a man of his predilections to exchange treasure for services.

Changing the subject and nodding in Sue May Yee's direction, the elder Fat expressed his wish for a tranquil and untroubled journey to Point Alones. Sue May Yee, he said, had always worked too hard. A day or so of leisurely travel with trustworthy gentlemen companions to care for her might pass for something like a pleasant distraction.

Sing Fat's teacher raised a finger and one sparse eyebrow to get his pupil's attention. He ordered due consideration be paid to her every request. The apothecary tactfully reminded the young man that he was under considerable obligation to Sue May Yee for his care and recovery. The elder Fat might have saved his breath.

Sing Fat felt a warm flush climb his cheeks with the memory, but he assured his master that everything would be done as he wished. He well understood his obligations. They carried the mandate of heaven, and his own secret desire was to prove worthy of her care. He said he would endeavor to make their honored guest's excursion as comfortable and safe as possible. The elder Fat smiled, nodded approval, closed his eyes, and soon fell asleep where he sat.

Ten minutes later, a deep cross-rut in the road violently jolted the cart and almost launched the dozing apothecary into a rock-strewn gully. Only Sing Fat's nimble response kept his master from serious harm. The elder Fat was most grateful, but somewhat flustered by a dream he was having at the moment of the accident. He thought he'd been thrown from the back of a great jade turtle flying through the clouds.

Sue May Yee, a woman used to taking charge where older men's well-being was concerned, immediately stood up in the back of the cart and gently insisted that dreaming, like sleep itself, was best savored in the prone position. She insisted that the elder Fat change places with her so that he might take advantage of his own thoughtful accommodations.

Sing Fat remembered his teacher's previous admonition on the subject of tender compliance and was pleased to find the policy so quickly applied by the master himself. After a moment's rearrangement, the elder Fat was comfortably tucked up among his quilts in the cart bed, and Sue May Yee, basket, cat, and all were now perched on the driver's bench next to Sing Fat.

For all his daydreams and aspirations, Sing Fat suddenly found himself speechless with bashful, boyish trepidation. One moment he felt so electrified by the girl's proximity that he thought he might jump out of his skin, and the next he floated, tranquil as a mist and happy just to smell her faint perfume of rain, roses, and smoke.

The couple sat in silence until the mule's distraction by tender roadside grasses forced Sing Fat to address the beast in rather personal terms. There was an innocent, humorous tone to Sing Fat's makeshift threats and entreaties.

Sue May Yee found the performance funny enough to laugh out loud, something she never did. Sing Fat also perceived the humor in the situation and laughed as well. This happy event opened the floodgates, and the two young people began to talk, at first cautiously and then continuously.

Occasionally the elder Fat would wake and listen from behind closed eyelids. To eavesdrop on the innocent gossip of the young gave him a guilty pleasure he could not resist. He listened to their gentle voices, and the sound conjured a memory of summer rain drumming softly on wood.

Sue May Yee told Sing Fat about her life growing up under the shadow of the Gold Mountain. She had been born in California and had never known her homeland at all.

Though willing to answer all questions candidly, she seemed genuinely far more interested in asking than answering. Though always polite, she proved insatiable, full of questions about Sing Fat's life in China as a boy. She also begged to hear about his escape from the mines and his dangerous journey south.

Sing Fat, like most men, was flattered by the attention. He told Sue May Yee all she wanted to know. But the elder Fat, listening with only half an ear, was far more intrigued by his pupil's omissions. Though he was straightforward in every other particular, Sing Fat never mentioned his treasure of gold dust, or how it was acquired.

Chow Yong Fat had seen many young courting couples in his day, and it was his considered observation that young men, like mating peacocks, flash all their plumage at once.

In the older man's experience, wealth had always been a primary feather in that raiment, and yet his apprentice had avoided all mention of the subject. The elder Fat profited from the insight at once. He was gratified to discover dimensions lurking beneath his young friend's wistful veneer. With this novel observation affixed for future reference, Chow Yong Fat laced his fingers across his chest and drifted off to the gentle swaying of the cart.

Sing Fat would always cherish the memory of that afternoon ride sitting next to Sue May Yee. He had never been so happy in all his life. The very recollection of those first hours brought forth sensations of complete joy.

The couple whiled away the sunset hours talking about every subject that came to mind while the mule plodded west. Their mutual interests and sensibilities, reflected in almost every utterance, soon made a score of little recognitions unnecessary where a smile and a nod would serve.

The sun had set by the time the mule found his way to Kee Wah's berry farm. By then the couple's friendship had been sealed. They shared an unspoken intuition that gave them the undoubted impression that they had known each other forever. Their mutual trust was spontaneous and innocent, and even the elder Fat could see that their reciprocal esteem was based on a foundation of admiration for each other's strengths and compassion for each other's obstacles and misfortunes.

Kee Wah made the venerable apothecary and his entourage as comfortable as circumstances would allow, and all hospitable formalities were generously observed. Despite Kee Wah's invitation to remain as long as they liked, the morning sun rose to find the cart entering the outskirts of Monterey.

Sue May Yee had accepted the invitation to sleep. She rested like a cargo of rare porcelain between fat quilts on a soft, straw pallet in the bed of the cart. The vigilant white cat stood guard over her mistress and her dreams.

Sing Fat had hoped to spend more time talking with Sue May Yee before their arrival, but the opportunity had not suitably presented itself.

Later, as he reined the mule cart down the narrow track that bisected Pacific Grove to Point Alones, Sing Fat's reflections fell under the pall of impending separation.

Sing Fat had seen and experienced a great deal for his years, and the ever-present danger of vulnerability had taught him to hold his emotions in check. He had discovered early that survival often required a detached response to uncertain dilemmas, especially painful ones, but the emergence of this haunting young woman into his life had profoundly influenced his thinking. His sense of emotional equilibrium rebelled against the heart-throbbing chaos. But it was no use. Sing Fat was smitten and therefore helpless. Eventually he would resign himself to eventualities, as if the choice were really his own to make.

The elder Fat, having observed the couple together, could find no objection to their friendship, but he worried about the cold realities facing their future. He knew only too well what thorny obstacles lay along the path should their companionship take root and bloom in true affection. But as befitting a man of his years and insight, the elder Fat shrewdly kept his own counsel and feigned complete ignorance. He indulged the forlorn hope that the fit would pass from his charmed apprentice before sober intervention became necessary.

Chow Yong Fat was well aware that many ancient customs and practices had been altered or abridged under the constraints of life bound by the Gold Mountain. He remembered being young once, to be sure, and he recalled that in his youth all things romantic appeared possible on the surface. He could happily admit that for once he had been fortunate in his choice of apprentices, but he had no wish to loose a serendipitous blessing to a spirited agitation of the blood. Privately, he trotted out every useful argument against such inclinations, even though he knew how powerless logic could be when outflanked by youthful ardor and purpose.

SUE MAY LEE AT LAST AWOKE and rose to stand behind the driver's seat just as Point Alones came into view. Now that home was in sight she proudly announced that she would not let her benefactors depart before she prepared them a worthy repast of the freshest fish the village might provide.

The arrival of Chow Yong Fat at Point Alones would be remarked upon by many. Sue May Yee insisted that it would be worse than inhospitable to allow such a venerable benefactor to depart without sampling her culinary gratitude. The elder Fat cheerfully relented to the invitation only because he knew Sue May Yee to be an extraordinary cook—a fact he had hoped his pupil might not have a chance to assess just yet.

The elder Fat saw no reason to advertise the young woman's virtues against his own better interests, though he knew that fate and circumstance ruled in these matters. As it stood, he was losing ground with every new revelation. In the end he knew that it probably would not have mattered to Sing Fat if Sue May Yee had never boiled water successfully. The elder Fat half remembered an Arabic proverb that stated, "Love viewed a one-eyed man as having a pleasant wink." He hoped it wasn't so, but knew better.

★   ★   ★

THE DAY OF THEIR ARRIVAL WITNESSED contrary waves and perverse winds on Monterey Bay. It discouraged all small boat work, so most of the fishermen of the village labored repairing torn nets or rehooked leagues of trawl lines while others patched and caulked their skiffs and sampans. Packers salted squid in barrels, while boys and girls turned the air-dried catch that lay spread over every rack and rock in the village.

Sing Fat found the odor of desiccating squid more intense than he had expected. Eyes tearing, he gagged back a cough every so often, but was determined to let no one gauge his discomfort. He looked to his teacher for guidance, but garnered little more than a reassuring smile and a pat on the knee.

Sue May Yee and her old father-in-law lived at the south end of the spindly fishing village. Though visited by sharp gusts and the odd wave, the location enjoyed the advantage of ocean breezes and thus smelled less like squid than anywhere else in the vicinity.

Old Jong Yee, Sue May Yee's father-in-law, still fished occasionally, but he earned his living primarily by sorting and bailing dried squid. He also fashioned net floats and crab traps when time allowed.

Jong Yee was sitting on his narrow porch rigging just such a trap when the mule cart drew abreast. The elder Fat bowed his head and offered a polite salutation. This was acknowledged with a smile and a slight bow in return. Sing Fat dismounted to hold the mule's head while the apothecary helped Sue May Yee dismount with her basket-dwelling cat.

She bowed and greeted her father-in-law with affectionate respect and then disappeared inside their weathered clapboard shanty.

Sing Fat could not help but notice that the rear half of the shack's rickety frame, like that of so many of its neighbors, was precariously balanced out over the tide-washed rocks. Each dwelling was haphazardly supported by an irregular latticework of asymmetrical poles and found wood. A stone's throw beyond the cantilevered rear porch, the raucous surf broke against an irregular shore.

The locale gave one the impression of constant hazard. It looked to Sing Fat as if every structure in the village was in perpetual jeopardy of being washed out to sea. But, oddly enough, they were still standing after several generations of such peril.

Sing Fat was given the usual instructions concerning the mule and cart. The elder Fat seemed comfortable repeating himself on subjects of trivial consequence while forgetting the least mention of topics of decisive relevance. Sing Fat had cared for the mule and cart for months. Every detail of that task was now second nature and needed no instruction.

Sing Fat had hoped to earn a few precious moments of conversation with Sue May Yee before the master decided it was time to continue their journey south, but the prospects dwindled with her devotion to the little feast she had promised.

He had wished to join her as she interrogated the neighborhood fish vendors about their freshest wares, but he had been directed to grease the cart axles again and to form a vigilant buffer against the predations of the vicinity's youngsters.

These sparrow hawks were a gregarious but light-fingered crew of little miscreants who were not able to resist the challenge of putting something over on the apothecary's apprentice. Urchin honor demanded such attempts, so Sing Fat was kept at odds playing the terrier while his teacher and the elder Yee shared tea and watched Sing Fat's torments with amused detachment.

The modest feast Sue May Yee had promised was served to the elders first. She would eat last as tradition demanded. But the odor of her cooking and the elders' loud praises heard from within the house only made Sing Fat salivate more. As instructed, Sue May Yee conveyed Sing Fat's portion to the porch so that he might maintain vigilance over his teacher's property. He had wanted to speak with her then, but she had time only to set down his food and then return to serve the elders.

His bowls of delicately prepared sea bass, crab and ginger, steamed rice, and pickled eel only confirmed the beguiling kitchen aromas. It proved to be the most splendid meal he had consumed in years. The daughter-in-law of Jong Yee, if nothing else, was a treasure who rivaled the abilities of any kitchen god.

Sing Fat wondered why this bright gem of a girl should have attracted no acceptable suitors, widow or not. She had even contrived to make honey-sweetened rice cakes, his favorite, and all from a meager brick hearth that served the shanty as both kitchen stove and central heating system. Central, only insofar as everyone slept in close proximity to its banked fires at night.

Sing Fat was toying with his second rice bun and devising a scheme to speak with Sue May Yee privately when his teacher suddenly appeared like smoke and announced that all preparations for departure should be made at once. Time was of the essence for safety's sake. He offered no further explanation, as usual.

Having fed and watered the mule upon arrival, there remained only the animal's harness anchor to be stowed before Sing Fat declared the expedition ready for the road.

Chow Yong Fat and old Jong Yee shared a few parting

words and a formal bow of mutual appreciation. Sue May Yee and her white cat appeared at the door. She carried a neatly wrapped cloth bundle that she handed up to Sing Fat on the driver's bench. She bowed and said that it was food for their journey in case the weather should keep them from a generous hearth for the night. Sing Fat stowed the bundle under the seat and thanked her.

With time pressing, he decided to shunt caution aside and share a personal sentiment with Sue May Yee. He wanted to tell her how much their long discussion had pleased him. He wanted her to know that he looked forward to future conversations, if she was amenable and custom allowed. But the words simply flew away as his teacher hastily mounted the cart, took over the reins with a grunt, flicked the mule's haunches with authority, and jogged off down the lane with clods of earth flying from the wheels.

The moon-eyed couple could share little more than a clasped gaze and self-conscious smiles before the elder Fat had rattled the cart onto the track moving east toward the coast road. The apothecary occasionally encouraged the mule, but aside from that the elder Fat drove on in silence.

As the cart pulled around the crest of a low bluff, Sing Fat looked out at the bay and clearly saw a broad storm head coming up from the southwest. The wind-driven whitecaps were now supported upon the shoulders of rolling swells of great length.

Near the horizon he could make out the smoke of steamers and the sails of coasting schooners as they raced for the shelter of Monterey before the storm overtook their wakes. Sing Fat recalled that the squid fishermen had said they had never seen a year so pregnant with storms. Their comments came to mind just as the wind began to shiver the heads of the taller pines. Sing Fat licked his lips. The moist air, even at this distance from the bay, tasted of sea salt.

The elder Fat drove his cart along according to a schedule all his own. As usual he had not bothered to share his purpose or destination. Sing Fat always assumed that his teacher had simply forgotten to mete out these morsels of information. Since the moment he climbed aboard the cart, the elder Fat had appeared grim and preoccupied. Responding to the threat of bad weather with distracted grunts or shrugs, he made constant visual reference to the changing sky and the increased vigor of the winds. Still he said nothing to enlighten his apprentice further.

Though confused, as was customary, Sing Fat took no offense. He much preferred to sit back and daydream about the incomparable Sue May Yee.

Later, when the cart ran over a downed tree limb by the side of the road and almost pitched both occupants to the ground, Sing Fat respectfully suggested that perhaps such dashing about was a bit perilous.

The elder Fat erupted with a gush of justifications. He hated repeating himself, he said, and wondered why his pupil didn't listen to significant information the first time. With a sigh of resignation the elder Fat went on to repeat what had never been said.

It was the impending tempest, of course. Was the youth blind as well as deaf? The venerable Jong Yee had been most instructive on the subject. Accounts of the approaching gale had been bayside rumor for days, but now its arrival seemed so imminent that even the seagulls were moving inland.

The elder Fat shivered, shook his head, and muttered on.

A rainy night or two of sheltering under the cart's canvas roof was one thing, but to suffer a mature storm on the open road was reckless in the extreme. Everything aboard would be soaked within minutes. The medical stores would be ruined, and he didn't foresee the mule taking up the muddy challenge with any perceptible enthusiasm. Even now the poor beast was twitching his great ears, a sure sign of agitation and the onset of a contrary disposition. The apothecary continued with his catalog of possible calamities. The coast roads and mountain tracks, difficult enough to pilot in the dry seasons, would become hazardous or even impassable with any appreciable rainfall. If the ground became thoroughly soaked, then landslides could be expected at the most inconvenient locations.

Ample shelter, obtained in a timely manner, was of foremost importance, and there was only one point along their route where suitable refuge might be found. An old friend, the elder Fat chortled, now fallen on prosperous times, had purchased a small coastal farm just north of the gully bridge in Pescadero Village.

His name was Jung San Choy, and the elder Fat considered him a capital fellow with a generous turn of mind. His house might prove a bit meager with four children prancing about, but Jung San Choy had recently raised a sturdy barn large enough to take the whole cart, mule and all. If the gods saw fit, they might still find sanctuary in Jung San Choy's barn until the storm moved on.

Traveling away from the shore and south toward the direction of Carmel Valley, the cart moved through a striking grove of gnarled cypress trees, which only added to the menacing character of the weather. As they traveled south, Sing Fat became fascinated by the dichotomy of the western sky. Everything north of a given line was bright sunshine and green sea peaked with bright white crowns. To the south of that same line the sky was dark gray and frothed with darker clouds boiling in from the southwest like lava. Here and there dense, broad shafts of black rain hung beneath their parent clouds as they paced across the sea in an angry cavalcade. The sea in turn reflected all the dark menace of the clouds and gave off colors akin to old hammered iron.

The cart at last came to a crossroads. The elder Fat turned right and came upon a leaning rustic structure called Lodge Gate. He jigged the mule and traveled south down a road he called "the Seventeen-Mile Excursion." When Sing Fat asked about the name, the apothecary snapped the reins, shook his head, and said it made no sense to him either, since it had little relevance to the distance traveled.

They were nearing their destination at Stillwater Cove when the mule, master, and apprentice all became aware of a distinct electric odor on the wind. It was a primeval scent that augured only the largest of storms.

Within moments the mule's ears twitched to the rumble and clap of distant thunder. This added some urgency to his gait in the hope his master had shelter in mind to reward his exertions.

Like Point Alones, Pescadero Village, which clung precariously to the rocky shores of Stillwater Cove, could be located by bouquet alone. Even with the rising wind, the odors of fleshed and dried sea life stuck to the village like a paste. Sing Fat was sure that not even the coming rains would scour the stench from the air.

The apothecary found Jung San Choy's little farm just as the first bloated raindrops struck the dusty soil. They were so fat that when they impacted the dry earth, they sent up little clouds like miniature artillery bursts.

Jung San Choy owned four large lots that ran from the road to the cove just north of the gully bridge. His house was tucked up in the southeast corner across from his garden, but his new barn and corral sat almost at the heart of the property, with the cove just two hundred feet beyond.

Jung San Choy was overjoyed to see the elder Fat. Three of his children had come down with slight fevers, and the venerable apothecary's presence at this time was truly a gift from heaven. He was happy to offer every available hospitality to his guests.

They were lucky in the way of shelter for cart and mule alike. Jung San Choy and his second cousin Foo Chong, who lived just south of the bridge, had shipped off their varied harvests the week before, so plenty of room was to be had in the barn.

There was an abundance of fresh-cut hay in the loft for bedding and, of course, Jung San Choy's wife would be honored to prepare all their meals if they so desired. The elder Fat thanked Jung San Choy for his timely generosity and said that they would continue their journey as soon as the storm passed.

Sing Fat noticed, when the cart was led into the barn, that acquiring straight or matching lumber had not been a keen priority in the building's construction. In fact, enough gray light entered through the chinks and gaps in the walls to read by, and the wind, which was growing in intensity, entered the same way.

The basic structure of the barn was sound enough, he supposed, and the broad roof and hayloft looked to be in good repair, so Sing Fat set to work with a whisper of celestial appreciation upon his lips. Notwithstanding present conditions, he intended to make this forced delay as comfortable as possible for his teacher.

While the apothecary assembled a few rudimentary medications for the children's relief, Sing Fat saw to the comforts of the mule.

The beast appeared pleased with the relative shelter and safety of a dry stall, and Sing Fat's application of the curry brushes nearly brought tears of joy to the creature's eyes. With a bucket of sweet oats thrown into the bargain, Sing Fat was confident the impressionable animal would endure the coming distress with reasonable fortitude. For warmth against the penetrating winds, he covered the mule with its own sturdy blanket and stacked hay sheaves against the side of the stall to hinder the chill drafts.

Master Chow Yong Fat announced that he would retire to their host's lodgings to attend to the children. Sing Fat was to make their environment as habitable as possible in his absence.

Before leaving, Jung San Choy pulled two kerosene lanterns from a wall box and handed them to Sing Fat with the undeviating Chinese caution against the fire devils that tormented the negligent and unwary.

The devils enjoyed a wicked appetite for hay-filled barns. Jung San Choy laughed cynically, winked at the elder Fat, and claimed the fire devils often chose Chinese barns when the barbarians were in a dither about one thing or another. Sing Fat bowed and agreed to be particularly vigilant.

While his master was gone, Sing Fat set about creating a

comfortable bivouac. The storm's winds had grown in strength, and the rain had begun a rolling tattoo across the roof. In an attempt to create greater protection from the strong drafts, Sing Fat retrieved the spare canvas from the cart and, with the use of straw sheaves, built a sheltered enclosure that included the rear portion of the leveled cart. Moving the medicine chest to one side and fashioning straw and canvas into a clever simulation of a mattress, Sing Fat managed to convert the bed of the cart into a comfortable snuggery protected from the blustering gusts of intrusive winds.

In the center of his straw stockade, Sing Fat cleared a space free of all combustibles, rolled out bamboo mats about a central hearth, and set up their small cast-iron charcoal brazier.

Within twenty minutes Sing Fat had boiled water for tea and was feeling quite pleased with himself.

Then the gale struck in force. There was no doubting the sincerity of its intention, which as far as Sing Fat could tell, was to blow everything upright off the coast of Monterey.

Every joint and board in the barn began to twist and groan, and the wind, which up until that point had been a chilly inconvenience, now shrieked, whistled, and moaned through the myriad gaps in the walls. The strength of the gusts actually piped generous portions of rain through the chinks in the boards to soak everything within three feet of the walls. The mantle of storm clouds had vanquished the last of the daylight, so Sing Fat lit and hung the kerosene lanterns and waited for his teacher in the meager cheer of their glow.

The sounds of the storm had lulled Sing Fat into a drifting slumber when the barn door crashed open with the wind and a cloaked specter entered. The vision, having appeared on the heels of a dream, frightened Sing Fat. The figure released a black oilskin cloak and revealed the elder Fat carrying a wrapped stack of bamboo steamers.

They all contained something hot and delicious, if the aromas stood up to scrutiny. Despite the escalating howl of wind, roar of rain, and rattle of shingle and board, master and student managed to share a most enjoyable meal sheltered comfortably about the glowing brazier.

When the drafts blew and it became even colder than anyone might have expected, the elder Fat felt obliged to use his arts to contest the elements. Searching through his satchel, he came up with a squat bottle of his own special elixir. It was a concoction that he claimed would, after a few small cups, render one immune to the frosts of winter even if one were stark naked. And so it did.

As the temperature dropped, two thimble-sized cups became four, then six, and so forth until both men at last could honestly attest to the fact that they felt little of anything at all, including the cold.

Indeed, even the strident hammering of the storm against the sieve-sided barn seemed to take on less importance. An aura of safety, warmth, and confident security appeared universal despite the constant crash of thunder and the occasional cannon report of a snapped tree. All might be chaos and tumult without, but within their shelter of straw sheaves and canvas all was warm, safe, and remarkably comfortable.

Another collateral immunity imparted by the elixir soon took effect, and after a while Sing Fat felt emboldened enough to speak to his teacher about the most delicate subject possible, Sue May Yee.

The elder Fat was caught off guard, though he should have

known his concoction might have just such an effect since it contained a goodly portion of Chinese brandy.

Though he did not wish to appear unsympathetic, Chow Yong Fat did not wish to be drawn into a matter that would obviously move against his own interests in time. The thought of his promising young friend wedded to Sue May Yee and immersed in the life of a Point Alones squid fisherman was far from attractive, or necessary. In any event, it was not a subject he wished to discuss at the moment.

It was his belief that deliberations of the romantic variety should always be postponed until the last possible moment. One never knew what changes of fortune might transpire in the interim. So rather than offend his optimistic pupil and possibly wound his spirit, the elder Fat chose the lesser of two evils and pretended to fall asleep during Sing Fat's disjointed overture characterizing Sue May Yee's unique attributes.

It didn't take long for Sing Fat to realize that he had lost his audience. He would have to broach the subject at some other time if he still possessed the courage. He decided to let it pass for the moment and proceeded to help the elder Fat to his bed in the cart. After carefully extinguishing the kerosene lanterns, Sing Fat made his own pallet on a mattress of straw that was screened from the elements. There he lay in the last light of the brazier's glowing coals, listening to the clamor of the storm.

That night the surf crashed on the rocky shore with such force that Sing Fat could feel the ground shiver through his straw mattress. The howling whistle of the wind through the gaps in the boards changed pitch and timbre as the agitated gusts altered direction.

The rain had not settled into a steady cadence, but rather

grew or lessened in intensity as conditions varied. Sing Fat's last thoughts, before sleep overtook him, were of Sue May Yee. Perhaps it was his own depth of feeling, singularly reinforced by his master's extraordinary tonic, but Sing Fat had conceived a certainty about his future, and the keystone of his vision was the incomparable Sue May Yee.

No matter what happened, or who objected, Sing Fat knew that one day they would be married. Drawing these happy thoughts about himself like a quilt, Sing Fat went to sleep while the storm pressed on through the night.

The morning, which came early for master and pupil, witnessed the gale's bruising fidelity of purpose. It was a wonder that everything was still standing upright. Through a space created by a wrenched board, Sing Fat watched and marveled while the ocean shattered itself about the little bay like a maelstrom in a bucket.

Stillwater Cove, normally temperate in stiff conditions, had become an affliction of wind and waves. Vigorous, frothing breakers collided with the shore and churned back on the next incoming waves. It was chaos incarnate.

The gully just south of the Choys' garden and toolshed, which was dry most of the year, had matured into a respectable river with currents running in both directions simultaneously. The resultant collision of runoff, tides, and waves inundated part of Foo Chong's property on the southern point. Yet for all the superficial damage caused by wind and rain, clusters of incense burned at every household shrine in gratitude for all the lives not taken. Pescadero Village was still safe for the moment, though the storm showed little sign of abating quickly.

★   ★   ★

SINCE CONTINUED TRAVEL WAS OUT OF THE QUESTION, the elder Fat decided that another day's confinement would best be served with a period of review, instruction, and study.

In part the elder Fat wanted to gauge his pupil's level of distraction. It was hardly uncommon for young men in his condition to forget their own names when a woman clouded their purpose.

He was pleasantly surprised when Sing Fat recited the twenty-six principles of diagnosis, the forty-eight primary and the thirty-two secondary pressure points of nerve distraction, and the formulas for compounding medicines beneficial to the treatment of female postnatal melancholia.

In fact, every question the old man posed, Sing Fat answered with sure and confident responses. This pleased and reassured his teacher. If indeed his apprentice was besotted with the comely Sue May Yee, at least it had not addled his brain beyond the point of usefulness. Perhaps there was still some room for hope and aspiration. At least Sing Fat exhibited a healthy glow of intelligence. Even if his pupil was truly infatuated, it was to be hoped that he wasn't moronic enough to let it hobble his future. The signs looked good, but who could tell with the young?

The storm passed on to the north sometime after one in the afternoon. An hour later, Chow Yong Fat decided it was an appropriate time to continue their errand of mercy. After saying farewell to Jung San Choy and receiving a gift of food for the journey, the elder Fat directed the cart toward the highland mines. The roads were not heavily littered with debris and there were no downed trees or deep mud to block the way, so they suffered only minor inconveniences here and there. The sky grew clearer and brighter as the track climbed up into the hills.

The cart was but a short distance from the mines when Sing Fat noticed a two-horse freight wagon coming down the track from the opposite direction. It was obvious that both vehicles could not pass at once, so the elder Fat suggested that they pull the cart off to one side and let the larger wagon pass. As the wagon came closer, the elder Fat recognized his friend Han Foo Yeung, the man who had called him upon this particular errand.

Han Foo Yeung appeared totally preoccupied. A dark, introspective sadness hung about him like a mourning cloak. The elder Fat hailed his friend, who instantly came to life with a start as he looked about for the caller. When he noticed Chow Yong Fat, his eyes lightened for a moment and then fell back in upon his preoccupation. He pulled his wagon to a stop next to the cart and shook his head.

When the elder Fat asked what had happened to cause his friend's distress, Han Foo Yeung almost cried. Though deeply troubled, Han Foo Yeung said that the purpose of his friend's generous attendance no longer existed. His prospective patients had all died, expired like so many diseased dogs.

He turned and spoke something toward the bed of the wagon. From under a soiled tarpaulin two Chinese laborers appeared, looking frightened and bewildered. Han Foo Yeung looked back to his friend and said that only these two men had escaped the deadly illness. He was now helping them to flee the mines and find refuge among their own people, possibly in Watsonville. He admitted that he was afraid the miners would discover his complicity in the escape. They would do anything to see that the story did not circulate. He expected grave trouble in any event.

Han Foo Yeung apologized for any inconvenience the elder Fat might have endured on his journey and reached behind the wagon bench to retrieve a large bundle and a big, wicker hamper. He passed them over to Chow Yong Fat. He said that these were the items he had mentioned in his letter, but that now the venerable apothecary was to consider the articles as gifts in compensation for his compassionate but fruitless journey.

Han Foo Yeung said that he had intended to deliver them personally when he came through Salinas, but now was as good a time as any since he didn't know when they should next meet.

Sing Fat could not put his finger on the exact reason, but there was something in the man's story that didn't exactly ring true. It was more a quality of voice than a point of fact, as if the story had been rehearsed for believability. But since he had no justifiable cause to doubt the account, he kept his suspicions to himself. After all, he had never met Han Foo Yeung, and he certainly had no wish to cause trouble for a stranger. Sing Fat looked to his teacher for a response and was surprised by his reply to the situation.

The elder Fat thought for a moment and suggested that he take the refugees back north with him. They could hide in his cart until Salinas and then make their way to Watsonville without the worry of pursuit. Relieved of his dangerous burden, Han Foo Yeung could return to the mines with no one the wiser. He thanked the apothecary profusely and promised to send on important discoveries as they came into his hands. He then instructed the two laborers to hide in Master Fat's cart and to do as they were instructed. Safety depended upon instant obedience to their benefactor.

The miners bowed, shouldered their meager bundles, and complied immediately. Then Sing Fat turned the cart around, not without some difficulty, and headed back in the direction from which they had come. Han Foo Yeung did the same with a parting wave and a blessing.

At an accessible but otherwise hidden clearing three miles down the road, the four men made camp for the night. The elder Fat gauged their distance from the mines to be sufficient to avoid notice for one night. Sing Fat hoped he was right.

The two frightened Chinese miners fabricated a shelter for themselves from a piece of spare canvas Sing Fat always carried in the cart; then they were instructed to gather firewood for the night. While they were occupied, Sing Fat prepared a simple meal from the rations they carried. The apothecary sat by the little charcoal brazier opening the basket Han Foo Yeung had given him. Suddenly Sing Fat heard a deathly moan and looked up to find his teacher, head in hands, obviously the victim of some emotional distress.

A small sheet of paper he had been reading had fallen to the ground. At first Sing Fat thought his mentor had succumbed to some ailment. When his apprentice asked what pained his master, the elder Fat just shook his head and pointed to the paper. Sing Fat retrieved the handwritten note, but could not decipher what it said. The penciled characters were Chinese, to be sure, but not written in a manner he understood. It might just as well have been code, which in fact it proved to be.

When the elder Fat had recovered his composure, he took back the paper and looked at it again as though he thought he might have misread the message. Again he shook his head. An expression of profound melancholy settled on his brow, and he moaned sadly once more. Again Sing Fat asked the cause of his teacher's distress.

With a voice broken by emotion, the elder Fat said that

Han Foo Yeung had written to say that the ailing miners had indeed died, but not in a manner he could have spoken of openly. He stated that the Italian and Portuguese miners, an ignorant, suspicious, and dangerous gang of barbarians, had not understood the cause of the illness afflicting their Chinese counterparts and feared imminent contagion. As a result they had perpetrated a terrible villainy that would more than likely go unpunished. Since the Chinese had been illegally imported, no one even knew the victims existed, so the barbarians were hardly likely to report the incident. It appeared the miners, fearing a foreign plague at their doorstep, had callously herded the ailing Chinese down an abandoned shaft into what they believed to be safe isolation. There had supposedly been an accident, according to the barbarians, and a mysterious explosion had collapsed the tunnel. The Chinese had all been killed or buried alive. No one knew for sure which.

The implication was so obvious that Han Foo Yeung felt no need to address the sorrowful circumstances further. He wrote that he was in the process of helping some of his compatriots to escape. He feared for their lives as witnesses to the crime.

For safety's sake the note was not signed. The elder Fat committed the evidence to the flames just as the two mine coolies returned with arms full of firewood. As an aside, the elder Fat cautioned his pupil to speak about this matter with no one.

Han Foo Yeung had written his message in code for a reason. If the information it contained fell into the wrong hands, misery and bloodshed would most certainly ensue.

These were special circumstances and required a veil of silence. Ignorance was the best defense against suspicion. If the miners surmised that outsiders knew the truth, the lives of the Chinese wouldn't be worth the price of a pauper's prayers. Sing Fat vowed never to speak of the matter without permission.

At first light the cart was on its way once more. Happily, there was no one on the road to take any interest in their movements, and a day later they made the outskirts of Monterey. It was there, and against all sound advice, that the two coolies decided to part company with the elder Fat and his apprentice.

The older laborer said that he had been a fisherman in his youth. He felt he could make a better living for himself jigging squid than he could hoeing weeds in a sugar beet field.

His young companion chose to follow his friend rather than endure hardship alone in a strange community where he knew no one. Life among the barbarians was difficult enough, but to labor without friends was more than he was willing to contemplate.

The elder Fat allowed his own arguments to fall away. These were men who retained their long-braided queues, which meant that they expected to return to China one day with money for their families. They had a right to choose their own destinies, but the apothecary reminded them that life in the fishing camps was hardly a step toward longevity.

The two men acknowledged this fact, but begged the elder Fat's indulgence and advice all the same. Chow Yong Fat agreed to write a short introduction to a friend who owned squid boats that worked out of McAbee Beach and Point Alones, but beyond that he was unable to make any promises. The two coolies agreed this was the best course of action and thanked the venerable elder for his assistance. They said that if it was at all possible they would repay the master's kindness one day.

Sing Fat, though he kept his sentiments to himself, had been deeply moved by the plight of these men. He remembered the perpetual suffering of his fellow laborers in the placer mines. He knew the loneliness that came from facing death every day without the support of friends or family. He too had become determined that this would not happen to him. He would not, if the fate could be avoided, allow his line to wither in lonely servitude. He needed a family if his line were to survive the cruelties of an uncertain future, and thus visions of Sue May Yee came flooding back into his thoughts once more.

After they had deposited the two men near McAbee Beach with a note of introduction to Ng Tung, the fishing master, Sing Fat turned the cart east toward Salinas. He had wanted to ask the elder Fat for permission to visit Sue May Yee at nearby Point Alones, but his teacher seemed so anxious to return to his business that Sing Fat did not press the point.

He did, however, determine to broach the subject of his marital future as soon as possible. Sing Fat had more than enough gold on deposit to acquire a wife and go into business for himself without asking permission from anyone, but he liked the prospect of studying medicine under his teacher's astute tutelage and would do nothing to unsettle his benefactor's faith in him.

Sing Fat and his teacher reached Salinas late in the evening to find eight important messages pinned to the door of the shop. It seemed as though everyone had waited until their departure to come down with one illness or another. There would be no rest that night. The elder Fat instructed his apprentice to go and tell the various people who had left notes that he had returned. He said they would keep the shop open all night, if necessary, to accommodate their patients, and that was just what they did.

Sing Fat was allowed to retire from his labors just before dawn, but even then, sleep was a long time in coming. Haunting daydreams of Sue May Yee now occupied every waking moment not dedicated to the concentration required by his work. He could not afford the distraction since his movements and decisions lay under the constant vigilance of his eminent teacher.

As the fates would have it, Sing Fat was not forced to broach the subject of Sue May Yee first. The following evening, while the elder Fat's silent and aged housekeeper prepared a modest supper of vegetables and spiced rice, the apothecary cleared his throat and asked his student what ambitions he nurtured for the future. He said that his position required him to understand the depth of a student's dedication to so complex a study as the one that now lay before him.

Sing Fat looked surprised, but blessed this invited opportunity to express his hopes candidly. At the very least he could not be accused of forcing personal considerations upon his generous benefactor. Here bloomed a chance for Sing Fat to accommodate his own visions without causing offense.

Sing Fat took a few moments to order his thoughts, bracing his purpose with solid reasoning so as not to sound like a mooncalf or an infatuated bumpkin. He then spoke his heart with the honesty and respect due a sincere question, but he spoke like one determined to prevail against all intervening demons of opposition. When it came to ways and means, hopes and dreams, Sing Fat was any man's equal.

He began, as one might expect, with a catalog of gratitude and obligations. Sing Fat felt a profound responsibility to maintain his studies in his present capacity. His ambition embraced accreditation eventually, if he proved worthy.

But there was one caveat, one consequential key that was necessary to bind him to a world of measureless professional obligations. Sing Fat must anchor himself within the security and domestic joys of his own family, and to accomplish this he must have a wife. That wife could never be any other than the woman who helped save his life, Sue May Yee. The incomparable Sue May Yee and no other.

The elder Fat affected an expression of modest amazement and deep consideration. He set down his rice bowl and chopsticks and contemplated his pupil's bearing and composure. He had been prepared for love's heartfelt enthusiasm, of course, but not the rationality of purpose, the vehemence of assertion.

It was obvious at once that Sing Fat would have all or nothing. But nothing, in the company of Sue May Yee, was far preferable to everything without her. It seemed his student was willing to take on the responsibility of both worlds and, indeed, he possessed the funds to support his ambitions. Chow Yong Fat lifted his cup, sipped his tea, and closed his eyes, savoring its fragrance and flavor.

So be it, thought Chow Yong Fat. This distant clansman had showed undeniable courage in the raw process of simply surviving a world turned upside down, and he had done it using his wits as well as his back. Any bride would presume the fortunes of heaven had blessed her with a husband of character, intelligence, and tenacity of purpose.

The elder Fat set down his tea, picked up his rice bowl, and ate a small portion of vegetables. He took his time chewing and all the while he clasped eyes with his young pupil in a noncommittal fashion. His hooded gaze betrayed no sentiment whatsoever. Sing Fat could feel the tension raising hairs at the back of his neck. His teacher eventually swallowed, allowed himself another sip of green tea, and waited a long moment. He then bowed his head and asked Sing Fat if he might be accorded the honor of presenting the future bride with her wedding regalia.

Though he could not permit himself the tears of relief and joy that he felt welling, Sing Fat bowed, sniffed back the catch in his voice, and said that such an honor was beyond his worthiness. He warranted that his own merits were of little significance in the schemes of heaven, but the virtuous and noble Sue May Yee would certainly imbue the gift with appropriate grace and radiance.

Sing Fat bowed again and in a stronger voice declared that his master's sponsorship had given him the greatest pleasure he had known since his father had trusted him with his first book and taught him to read.

Chow Yong Fat rose and retrieved a beautiful bottle of golden rice wine and two translucent jade cups. He insisted that tradition demanded that the two men toast the occasion. He bowed slightly and said he would be delighted to stand proxy for Sing Fat's noble father. He would give the first customary invocation of matrimonial longevity and heaven's blessing of many strong and virtuous sons. Sing Fat gave the next toast, and after a few such rounds of celebratory wine the room took on a warm glow of familial commemoration. Sing Fat had missed the presence of such feelings, such moments. He laughed wholeheartedly at the thought of his prospective fulfillments as the head of his own family.

A few more libations to the gods of hearth and home and Chow Yong Fat insisted that it would be best to set about the wedding preparations at once. He suggested Sing Fat withdraw a small sum of money to purchase gifts for Sue May Yee and her relatives. It would be a small expense since her relations had dwindled to but a pitiful few. Her father-in-law would, of course, act on Sue May Yee's behalf and, if Sing Fat approved, Chow Yong Fat would represent the groom in the customary negotiations. There could be no question of a dowry, unfortunately. The Yee clan had been forced to live from hand to mouth since the ocean demons had taken so many of their sons and brothers.

Sing Fat smiled and interjected that he would insist upon a dowry. A dowry of six seashells. One for every son he hoped to rear to flourishing manhood.

Sing Fat said he would take a small house near the shop and continue his duties and studies as before. Sue May Yee might then help with the shop business as well. The prospects shimmered with implied prosperity and good fortune. The rich soil of his dreams now possessed true spiritual roots and purpose, and Sing Fat was the happiest young man on earth.

The following week was crowded with activity. First Sing Fat discovered a great deal of shop work to snatch from disaster, and then there were the daily excursions with his nuptial sponsor to purchase the appropriate gifts for his prospective relations.

Some of these presents were deemed traditional, while other offerings were meant to fulfill appropriate needs. But the most important and thoroughly considered gifts were meant to turn the head of any young woman of modest qualities, and Sue May Yee was all that and much more.

To symbolize his singular affection, Sing Fat purchased an ancient, filigreed ivory fan set with numerous gold dragons and hinged with a silver monkey carrying a staff. It cost one hundred dollars, and Sing Fat would happily have paid twice the price without blinking an eye had it not been for the elder Fat's firm and considerate intervention.

Sing Fat had the fan wrapped in white rabbit fur and purple silk and then placed in a sandalwood box carved all about with cranes in flight. The box, together with a beautifully ornamented tortoiseshell comb, was wrapped inside an expensive embroidered shawl. Then it amused the prospective groom to package the lot in a wrapping of Japan paper and string, as though the parcel's contents were of no particular value. Last, he packaged six small tins of cooked goose livers for Sue May Yee's white cat. Sing Fat thought this a humorous detail and hoped the cat would enjoy the gift and not presume it an out-and-out bribe, which it was.

Dawn of the following Saturday found master and pupil smartly dressed and sitting upon a freshly painted cart. Even the mule's tack and brass furnishings had been polished to a high luster.

Sing Fat had accomplished it all personally in what time he could spare from work. He hadn't slept soundly all week, for obvious reasons, and had decided not to waste the hours in fretful anticipation, so he repainted the cart at his own expense by the light of kerosene lamps.

The elder Fat thought the prospective groom quite moonstruck and prescribed cold baths in the river. Sing Fat merely smiled at the suggestion and went about his business doing just as he pleased. The apothecary shrugged, shook his head, and focused upon his own affairs. He knew from experience that only the simplest tasks could be expected from his pupil until the whole marriage-contract business was settled one way or another. Under the circumstances, the elder Fat saw no reason to postpone the inevitable union. The sooner accomplished, within the constraints of propriety and custom, the sooner everyone could go back to more important matters.

The cart had been stripped of the usual trappings. Instead, numerous wrapped parcels and packages lay in light crates bedded with chopped straw to protect them from breakage. A case of fine rice wine, each bottle mantled in a coat of woven straw, rested on a bed of its own. The traveler's kits and extra clothes were neatly packed within their sleeping quilts. The apothecary's small medicine chest, the one he assembled for emergencies on the road, was tucked under the driver's bench. The elder Fat assessed their absence at three days and left a sign on the shop door indicating the time of their return.

The autumn of the year, though clear and sunny, carried occasional chills from the coast that caught one in midbreath like the stab of needles. These cold currents became more persistent as the travelers neared Monterey Bay. The sun was but a few degrees from the horizon when the rickety village of Point Alones came into sight. It looked even more fragile with the sun setting behind the spindle-legged shanties.

By now the Pacific winds had mastered a northern bite that had both men wearing their black quilted topcoats. With youthful compassion, Sing Fat had even stopped the cart long enough to blanket the mule against the ocean chills as well. The apothecary just rolled his eyes and contemplated the full moon rising in the east. It seemed genuinely propitious, to his way of thinking. He felt confident the marriage-contract negotiations might well be concluded the following afternoon.

Given one extra day of modest celebration, they could be back at work by Tuesday afternoon at the latest.

SUE MAY YEE AND HER AGING FATHER-IN-LAW WERE quite surprised to find the venerable apothecary standing at their door with his arms full of gifts. Sing Fat, as instructed, moved the cart out of the wind behind the shanty and stayed with the precious cargo. He was prepared to camp out under the shelter of its canvas cover for the duration of their visit.

He felt so unsure of himself that at first he didn't even bother to unhitch the mule in case his suit was spurned out of hand. He couldn't think why such a thing should happen, but he was prepared for that eventuality, painful as it would be.

The elder Fat, as tradition dictated, had promised to make all preliminary introductions to the subject of marriage. If there should be an instant refusal to the proposition, at least the prospective groom would not lose face publicly. Once the subject had been entertained seriously, and if the future bride acquiesced to the arrangement, then the blushing groom could be introduced into the company and generally made great sport of for his callow understanding of what lay in wait for his future.

Eventually the prospective groom and his sponsor would distribute gifts and pour wine to seal the verbal contract. The more formal acknowledgments would be made the following day in the presence of what few relatives Sue May Yee could claim. Then the rest of the gifts would be given, and wine would be generously poured out to all.

Hopefully, the intended couple might share a few words, but they would have to steal the time since such things were not customary. In such confined quarters it was to be expected that they would exchange little more than furtive, shy glances.

Sing Fat had made himself comfortable upon a quilt laid out on the straw in the bed of the cart. The laced-up canvas covers kept him from the wind and the curious gaze of neighbors. The one thing he did not possess at that moment was peace of mind. He would have given anything to know what was happening inside the house. On second thought, perhaps not.

Sue May Yee or her father-in-law might have assembled embarrassing objections to the match. What if her relatives refused to let her leave Point Alones? Could he move here and take up the life of a fisherman or squid broker? The idea made him ill. He gestured a magic sign against the demons of self-doubt and tucked himself down for a nap.

Sing Fat awoke with a start at the sound of someone knocking on the side of the cart. He cautiously lifted the canvas and looked over the lip of the cart to see Sue May Yee's father-in-law smiling up at him by the light of a lantern.

His toothless mouth formed a few words that were lost on the wind, and then he waved for Sing Fat to follow. Once dismounted, Sing Fat cupped his hand to his ear. Old Jong Yee said that he had called cousin Choo to look after the mule. Cousin Choo's son would unload the cart at once. Sing Fat was to enter the house and attend to his master's counsel. Jong Yee nodded and, talking to himself mostly, praised the wisdom and skill of Master Chow Yong Fat as though Sing Fat had never met the man before. Cousin Choo and son appeared out of nowhere and began unharnessing the mule and leveling the cart with a yoke brace.

When Sing Fat had straightened his clothing and brushed

the few wisps of straw from his coat, he entered the house and was surprised to find only the elder Fat occupying the front room. He sat on a cushion at a low table illuminated by little brass oil lamps. When Sing Fat entered, his teacher indicated a cushion to his right and then placed a finger against his lips to caution silence. Confused at first, Sing Fat sought out his mentor's eyes and received a confident nod and a smile. The scales of dark foreboding fell away, and Sing Fat could perceive the very marrow in his bones throb with delighted expectation. But where was everyone? Had he done something inappropriate already? The elder Fat would not let his eyes be drawn away again.

The front door sailed open with the force of the wind, and there stood Sue May Yee's father-in-law. He entered with a swift bow followed by the Choos, father and son. Each was burdened with brimming baskets of neatly wrapped packages that they deposited and arranged at the far end of the room where they would remain secure, but on display for all to see.

It required two trips to unload all the groom's gifts. The Yee clan was duly impressed by the generous abundance just as the elder Fat had said they would be. So far, all was progressing according to the oldest traditional protocols, regardless of the strained and humble setting.

Meanwhile, Sing Fat was prompted by his mentor to sit quietly, eyes cast to a small bowl of wildflowers on the table as if meditating on the beneficence of nature's symmetry. He was advised, at all costs, to remain detached from the present for the sake of modesty. Sing Fat felt confident he could hold that mental posture and was coasting along rather nicely until Sue May Yee entered from the next room looking like the Princess of the Jade Moon, despite her simple garments.

Sing Fat couldn't take his eyes from her, and his resolve to remain aloof from the situation dissolved like sugar in hot tea.

From under Sue May Yee's long coat emerged the serene figure of the white cat. When her mistress knelt on a cushion set near the stack of gifts, the white cat took on a formal pose at her knees like a guardian temple lion. Through half-closed eyes the animal stared directly at Sing Fat with a feline expression that bordered on implied criticism. Sue May Yee straightened her posture, clasped her hands on her lap, but never raised her eyes to the room.

The position she occupied was purposely set to indicate symmetry. The prospective bride on one side, the groom's gifts on the other. In the eyes of the world, the value of the gifts brought honor to the family, but at the very bottom stood the ancient abstraction of barter. The estimated benefit of one counterbalanced the worth of the other, and thus one resolved upon a fair medium of exchange.

The insensitive formality of negotiation made Sing Fat uncomfortable. All he desired was to look into Sue May Yee's gentle eyes and know that the proposed marriage was something in which she could find favor. But she would not meet his gaze. It was a matter of respect and tradition, he knew, but it made him uncomfortable not to be able to speak with her. He desperately wanted to know her heart's voice on the matter. His self-confidence sorely needed a leg up, but it seemed he was to be left hanging for some time to come. Only the elder Fat knew how the cards were spread, and he wasn't talking just yet.

Eventually Jong Yee returned to the table, bowed to both his guests with a broad nervous smile, and shakily poured out Sing Fat's gift of golden rice wine. Conversation was kept to topics superficial or humorous, and no mention of the fate of the nuptials was even broached. In a short while they were joined by cousin Choo and Sue May Yee's youngest brother-in-law, Jong Po Yee. More wine was poured and more light conversation exchanged. All the while, Sue May Yee knelt on her cushion and communed silently with her elegant cat. Everyone ignored her presence just as they politely ignored the stack of wrapped parcels arranged opposite the kneeling girl.

Two weathered fishermen arrived. They were both cousins of Sue May Yee's father-in-law and, though well advanced in years, proved to be rather sprightly gentlemen with very active imaginations. They held sway over the company with wonderful tales of sea dragons and shipwrecks.

More wine flowed, and with every cup of wine, Sing Fat settled more comfortably into the pace of the evening. There was really very little for him to say, as most questions of consequence were addressed to his sponsor, Master Chow Yong Fat.

The esteemed protégé and petitioning suitor might have been a wooden mannequin for all anybody cared. Upon reflection, he allowed that he and his capital resources were undoubtedly as much on display as was Sue May Yee. The only difference lay in the fact that he had been obliged to pay for the privilege of feeling this uncomfortable and unnecessary.

Sing Fat looked over to gaze at his intended bride and was surprised to find Sue May Yee and the white cat gone. Only the indentation of her legs upon the cushion remained as evidence that she had ever been there at all.

Sing Fat could hardly wait for this interminable evening of meandering small talk to come to an end so that he might speak freely with his teacher. He still didn't possess the slightest clue of where he really stood in the matter at hand, and it was driving him crazy.

As fixed by tradition, when all the relatives had consumed six cups of wine as well as the proffered sweetmeats and steamed buns, they began to leave in the order they had arrived. The farewell was kind and marginally formal, broad smiles and deep bows being exchanged all around with nothing really said beyond common pleasantries. Not a hint of an opinion from anyone. The whole business was enough to make one's head swim with the meaningless minutiae of it all.

No sooner had the last inquisitive guest withdrawn than Sing Fat caught the piquant scent of hot food wafting from the back of the house. He suddenly realized he hadn't had a decent meal all day. In the tracks of these thoughts came Sue May Yee with a first course of smoked eel and grilled salmon with green onions, black mushrooms, and hot ginger. The rice was steaming and done to perfection.

After five minutes Sue May Yee returned with wine-steamed prawns and grilled rock pigeons with a red-pepper-and-honey glaze. Last served was a young sea bass beautifully crosshatched and deep-fried in ginger-scented oil and brought to the table leaping from a pond of broth and steamed vegetables arranged to emphasize composition. Even Sue May Yee's old father-in-law, normally reticent in such matters, said with pride that his daughter-in-law had outdone herself. The more exotic items on the menu had been provided by the expectant suitor, but it had been beautifully prepared for all that, and with golden rice wine served throughout, who would offend the kitchen gods with even so much as a breath of reproach?

Sing Fat had rarely been exposed to anything like abundance since childhood, and the surfeit of wine and rich food sent his head spinning. Knowing the hour to be late, Sing Fat begged to be excused to his bed. Sue May Yee's father-in-law laughed, nodded, and said that the cart had been especially prepared for his comfort. Master Chow Yong Fat would sleep in the house near the hearth. Jong Yee rose, took up a lantern, and offered to light the young man's way. Sing Fat humbly accepted, bowed to his teacher, and followed the old man out into the night. Sue May Yee was nowhere to be seen.

The cart had been turned so that the canvas-enclosed tail faced away from the cold, onshore breezes. The yoke had been lashed to a long sawhorse to make the vehicle rest level. When his host held up the lantern, Sing Fat saw that the cart had been completely cleaned and a small carpet had been laid. Upon the carpet a quilted mattress and cover had been spread, and at the foot of the cart a small iron brazier containing hot coals had been set on bricks to help ward off the damp air. Sing Fat thanked his host, bid him good night, and after taking the proffered lantern, climbed into the cart.

He settled himself down on the soft bed and began to change into his sleeping robe when he noticed something bright on his pillow. It was a small bouquet of wildflowers bound with a narrow red ribbon. The ribbon also entwined a child's gold ring set with a small amethyst. Next to this treasure lay one of even greater importance. A small embroidered cloth purse containing six beautifully matched seashells.

Sing Fat knew at once who had placed the gift there. It was all Sue May Yee possessed in the way of a dowry, but he wondered how she had learned about the seashells. Only his sponsor could have mentioned it to her.

Obviously these tokens indicated Sue May Yee's acceptance of his proposal and no gift on earth could have made him happier. Nonetheless, it was her relatives who would have the last word in the matter. Sing Fat tossed and turned on the edge of an impassioned sword until exhaustion and a bellyful of wine sent him into a deep dreamless sleep.

In the morning, Sing Fat awoke abruptly to the sound of a loud knocking on the exterior of the cart; then his master's voice called him to arise at once. The hour was late, and there was much to discuss and do. When he had finished his ablutions, Sing Fat was to join his teacher, and the sooner the better. Sing Fat arose to find two trays set on the cart's bench.

One held a bowl of hot water and a cloth to wash with, and the other held a small pot of tea and a dish of sweet rice cakes. On the side of the tea tray lay a small wild rose upon a napkin. Sing Fat smiled and began to wash.

Sing Fat found his teacher fending off the incessant, bird-like queries of village children who thought there might be something in all this adult business that would interest them. They clustered like hungry sparrows in the hope that sweet buns and honey cakes might fall from heaven as their portion of the impending celebrations. When the elder Fat caught sight of his apprentice, he waved him on impatiently and started to walk toward the center of the village like a man escaping mosquitoes.

Sing Fat raced to catch up with a heart full of anxious questions, but before he could utter a syllable his mentor congratulated his pupil on the successful conclusion of the marriage contract. He said that his young friend's generosity quite overwhelmed any possible objection Sue May Yee's relatives might have proposed. In fact, since the future bride was a widow, his protégé's liberal munificence might be perceived, under dissimilar circumstances of course, as slightly conspicuous. As he had said before, strained circumstances precluded any question of a dowry in return.

Here Sing Fat stopped and politely contradicted his teacher. A dowry had indeed been offered, he said, and happily accepted. The apothecary turned on his heel with a look of perplexed astonishment. He had heard no mention of a dowry offer. How had this come about? Sing Fat beamed, reached beneath his tunic, and withdrew the bouquet of wildflowers with the attached child's ring and the little embroidered bag of seashells. These he showed to his teacher. The elder Fat nodded, laughed, and patted his pupil on the back with expressions of admiration and approval. His student was obviously a great soul with a poet's heart, he said. Such fellows made the finest of medical men, he declared. Chow Yong Fat, master apothecary, was well pleased and proud of his enterprising pupil, and he said as much.

Near the center of the village stood a small outdoor shrine erected by the Chee Kong Tong and dedicated to the peace, longevity, and general felicity of the community. Here the elder Fat stopped and suggested that it might be appropriate to light a small bundle of incense to honor the Tong and ask blessings for the afternoon's portentous ceremony.

Sing Fat agreed and placed a few coins in the donation box. Then pupil and teacher each took a bundle of incense, lit the sweet-smelling sticks from a small brazier of coals, and placed the smoking offering in the sand filled bowl under a calligraphic invocation that asked heaven to bless and preserve the people of the village.

This done, the elder Fat suggested a walk to the shore and perhaps taking something to eat at one of the small, rickety food stalls near the bay. While there, the elder Fat would instruct his pupil on the procedures of the betrothal ceremony, the stipulations of the marriage contract, and other pertinent protocols that needed attention.

They found a suitable bayside noodle shop and sat down at a table made of an old hatch plank. The wood still bore part of the name of the unlucky ship that had last been in possession of the goods: SAINT PAUL is all it said.

Master and student ate fresh-steamed urchin and roe directly from the shell and watched the activity on the shore. Though the weather was still sunny and bright, the fishermen were hauling all their sampans high on shore where several old women were cleaning and butchering sharks.

It seemed odd to Sing Fat that, in spite of the early hour of the day, there was no one intent on fishing.

Quite the opposite. Men were busy unbaiting and coiling hundreds of feet of the many hooked trawl lines that were used for bottom fishing, and the squid boats were being divested of their booms and fire baskets. When the sampans were drawn far enough on shore, they were turned upside down on their rollers and secured with rope and large wooden pegs driven into the sand almost two feet. It was as though the fishermen feared that their boats would be drawn mysteriously into the sky if they were not thus fastened to the earth.

Sing Fat's curiosity was piqued when he saw men hauling their drying nets from their trestles and bundling them into the net shacks that bordered the shore. He asked a passing fisherman what all the activity was about and was informed that two ships, recently arrived, had just barely outraced another storm that was bearing up from the south.

It had been a very strange and unlucky year for such things, the fisherman said. Storms at odd seasons, and fish that normally could only be found much farther south had shown up in the bay, while the salmon and herring, which were usually abundant at this time of year, had moved farther north.

The fisherman said that the last big storm, but a week past, had caught the village off guard and they had lost a number of valuable sampans. This time they were taking no chances.

This exchange stirred the elder Fat to insist that they should also conclude their business as soon as possible. He wanted to be on their way back to Salinas before the weather turned foul.

Instructing Sing Fat to appear promptly at one o'clock, the apothecary rushed off to complete preparations for the afternoon. This allowed Sing Fat time to wander about as he pleased until the appointed time. He decided to make his way back by the shore and observe the people at their labors.

Walking south along the beach Sing Fat watched a woman gut and skin a sea lion with such skill that within a span of only five minutes the whole operation was complete. He observed as the people drying squid gathered in their harvest so the coming storm would not destroy their fetid treasure. He also witnessed the seaweed gatherers hurriedly rake up their dried produce to be packed away in sacks and stowed undercover.

As he came to the south end of the village, Sing Fat looked up to see Sue May Yee sitting on her back porch with her white cat. She was shelling soybean pods and singing softly to herself. This was the opportunity he had longed for.

He climbed up the shore and over the rocks and came to stand just below her perch. When she saw him, Sue May Yee smiled and invited her intended bridegroom to come up and sit with her while she worked. Sing Fat needed no coaxing, and within seconds he was sitting on the flimsy boards with only the white cat separating the couple.

The cat took little notice of Sing Fat. The animal seemed quite devoted to the subtle movements of a praying mantis that had taken up a perch on a sprig of rosemary growing in a little broken mustard pot on the edge of the porch.

At first the couple became entangled in a flutter of self-conscious smiles, blushes, and half-finished sentences, each apologizing for interrupting the other. Then they fell into a happy silence and watched the colliding waves on the rocks below. In that contented silence Sing Fat reached down to stroke the cat. It seemed to accept his caresses without taking its eyes from the insect's fastidious preening. The mantis scoured its forelegs, a sign a recent feast had been consumed. Sing Fat reflected that perhaps the cat might be next to indulge in a savory bit should the mantis dally much longer.

As a means of incidental conversation, Sing Fat asked Sue May Yee if the cat had a name. She looked up and giggled with a modest flush on her cheeks. She said that the cat had been named after herself. Not her real name, of course, but the pet name her father used to call her when she was a child. Sue May Yee confessed that her father had spoiled her terribly. He had called her "the Imperial Duchess of Woo."

When she acquired the white kitten from a cousin, she had thought of those distant cheerful days, and in honor of her father, as well as the lost pleasures of childhood, she had named the cat the Imperial Duchess of Woo.

Sing Fat grinned broadly and nodded. He said that he thought it was a most appropriate name for such a patrician creature. With that, the cat looked up at Sing Fat as though it had understood every word. It rose, stretched with an exaggerated yawn, and moved to rest contentedly across Sing Fat's lap. He in turn stroked the pure white fur with pleasure. This was a great triumph for the prospective groom, according to Sue May Yee.

This act of trust and acceptance on the part of her companion seemed to give Sue May Yee great pleasure. She commented on the fact, since it was not the Duchess' habit to accept anyone but her mistress. Sue May Yee felt that this guileless gesture held profound and fortuitous significance. If the Duchess of Woo, who was closer to the gods of insight and fortune than humans, could willingly accept Sing Fat, then perhaps their future union was already blessed.

Sue May Yee was content to let the fates draw out her path as they would. The wheel of destiny had turned once more, and she was pleased with the lot she had drawn. The gods had smiled upon her loneliness at last. She would know the joy of children and the strength imparted by love and family.

The couple sat together for an hour discussing seemingly trivial questions, but all the while warming slowly toward the subject of their impending nuptials. With each passing moment they became more comfortable with the theme, and this opened the way for Sing Fat to discuss his plans for the couple's future.

He said that when he returned to Salinas he would take a modest house with a small piece of land for a kitchen garden. Sing Fat knew of just the right place a little north of the town toward the beautiful Gabilan Mountains. The property belonged to an aging friend of his master. This old gentleman was forced by the constraints of passing years and failing health to move back to Castroville to live with his oldest son. The dutiful son ran a small emporium on the corner of McDougall and Speegle Streets. The elderly father was willing to lease the property, with a promise of purchase, at a very reasonable rate.

His master, the apothecary, had kept the old gentleman alive and well for a number of years, and the arrangement might be accomplished with his patient's gratitude to grease the wheels.

After a moment, Sing Fat added that if Sue May Yee approved and thought it appropriate, he would also be most happy to look after her aging father-in-law as well. It was much warmer in Salinas. Far from the chilled ocean winds and fog of the bay, the old man's bones would limber up a bit, and Sing Fat and his master would be available to look after Jong Yee's health when necessary. Sing Fat saw no reason why the elder Yee would not be far more comfortable and satisfied working in his own garden than contorting his ancient frame stacking dried squid for pennies.

Sue May Yee looked up, and Sing Fat could see tears well up in the corners of her eyes. She said that Sing Fat's consideration for the well-being of her father-in-law was a singular honor and the finest gift he could bestow. It was evidence that her future husband was a man of high moral and philosophical principles, as worthy of the blessings of good fortune as any child of heaven. Only a great soul, she said, values compassion above prosperity. She bowed her head and said formally, for the first time, that she would be honored to be his wife and friend in all adversity. This time it was Sing Fat's turn to blush and tear.

Perhaps this was what the poets and singers meant when they spoke of abiding devotion. Whatever it was, Sing Fat knew at once that this strong but demure young woman now possessed every particle of his existence. Sing Fat looked down at the cat and was surprised to find the creature staring up into his eyes. After a moment it blinked and then, to Sing Fat's total surprise, the creature licked his hand once and went back to sleep in his lap.

Into the heart of their companionable reverie came animated voices from within the house. One of the voices he knew to be that of his teacher. Sing Fat felt the intrusion like a bee sting. He selfishly wished these joyful moments to last all day. He shook his head as if throwing off an unwanted dream. Sing Fat knew at once that it would be thought inappropriate for him to be found alone with Sue May Yee, so he gently lifted the cat from his lap and delicately rested the drowsing animal next to her mistress.

Sing Fat patted Sue May Yee's hand in a reassuring manner, smiled with confident cheer, and jumped off the rickety porch to the rocks below. He looked up to see Sue May Yee beaming at him with a winsome expression. It was as if she could read his thoughts. He reflected for a moment that he had not experienced such joy since childhood. For the first time in many years he could say to himself that he was truly happy to be alive. With a parting wave Sing Fat bounded away around the house so as to make it appear that he had just arrived at the front door.

THE AFTERNOON'S MODEST BETROTHAL CEREMONY, with its further distribution of gifts and considerations, went well. After the signing of the marriage contract, an unpretentious celebratory feast was served to one and all. Again the couple was kept apart, but Sing Fat suffered the whole affair with forbearance. His youthful impatience had been assuaged by the knowledge that in two weeks' time he and Sue May Yee would be husband and wife. The elder Fat had suggested the two-week interval so that everything could be prepared properly in Salinas. The couple would have worlds of time to rejoice in each other's company then.

Toward the end of the feast the elder Fat instructed his apprentice to have the cart ready to travel by first light the next day. He had originally planned to leave after the contract ceremony, but a fisherman's wife came tearfully to Jong Yee's door begging the apothecary to visit her ailing husband. The poor fisherman had been snared in his own trawl line when a shark had hit the bait prematurely. The man had been pulled from his sampan by his own lines and had suffered numerous wounds inflicted by the sharp hooks.

Unfortunately, many of the wounds had festered, and the poor fisherman now suffered from a high fever brought on by the infections. His wife despaired for his life and tearfully implored the learned healer to attend her husband, which he did until late into the evening.

Though distressed for the fisherman, Sing Fat was secretly pleased by the delay in departure. It gave him further opportunity to see and speak with his prospective bride.

THE FOGGY DAWN HAD LIFTED to reveal clear sparkling weather with no sign of the impending storm. Though the journey back to Salinas took most of the day, the time seemed nothing to Sing Fat. He chirped and chatted away like a magpie the whole trip. The apothecary noted this change in disposition. It appeared his pupil's long years of brutal disappointment and hardship had slipped away and left behind a happy young man with a world of fortuitous opportunities awaiting him. He reconsidered Sing Fat's impending nuptials with an eye toward the stability such a union would impart. Now that Sing Fat had taken on matrimonial responsibilities, it was hoped he would strive even more diligently to improve his condition for the sake of his new family.

They arrived back at the shop at dusk, and Sing Fat attended to the mule and cart before taking himself home for a well-deserved rest. The next day he was at the shop before his time with a song on his lips and a flutter of anticipation in his youthful breast. It pleased the apothecary to see his apprentice take on his labors with such cheerful diligence and enthusiasm.

The shop was busy all day. The elder Fat's absence had created a backlog of requests so great that neither master nor student found time to take a meal all day long. That evening the rains came, and they came with a vengeance. The water poured from the sky in torrents and turned the unpaved streets to avenues of deep, sticky mud.

It rained in this manner for two days and nights. The winds occasionally gusted to amazing velocities, causing considerable damage to the poorer buildings of the town. Signs were torn from their fittings, and the slightest imperfection in a roof allowed channels of water to stream through every seam and fissure. But none of this seemed to affect the buoyant and cheerful apprentice.

Sing Fat walked through the rain as through sunlight. His heart and mind rested far away in the company of his bride to be, and no veil of gloom or concern could prevail against his optimistic glow. His mood became infectious, and even the elder Fat found himself laughing and joking more than was his habit.

The storms eventually subsided, and warm sunlight began to dry out the town. Steam rose from the sodden streets as though the earth blistered and bubbled with heat. Every puddle became a raucous birdbath for migrating starlings. As far as Sing Fat was concerned, all was right with the world and the gods were at peace in their jade palace of heaven.

When he was not in attendance at the shop, Sing Fat rushed about making detailed preparations for the wedding. The nuptial party would be small, consisting of Sue May Yee's immediate family; the elder Fat, of course; and the Taoist priest who would conduct the ceremony.

A modestly elaborate banquet was arranged, but to celebrate his true happiness and the pride he took in his new bride, Sing Fat also contracted a three-piece orchestra to play traditional Chinese music. The musicians proved more expensive than he had expected. But Sing Fat knew that the music would delight Sue May Yee, so he refused to haggle and paid one-third of the cost up front to secure the musicians' enthusiastic participation.

He also made contributions to the Taoist temple to guard against spiritual carelessness during the ritual. As a boy, Sing Fat had often heard the dictum that stated one only received the equivalent of true value from hard cash, so he concluded that largesse in these matters was hardly impetuous or foolhardy. The elder Fat agreed. In such important essentials it did not recompense one to be frugal, he said.

The gods detested miserly inclinations and only gave as good as they got. Sing Fat was determined not to be found wanting when it came to the open hand of liberality and saw to it that everything would be concluded according to the best traditions of the Middle Kingdom. His new bride would want for nothing that might be in his power to provide for her. The very thought of bringing a smile to the lovely face of his intended made him happy. The apothecary was inclined to rein in Sing Fat's more elaborate inclinations in favor of modesty. After all, Sing Fat was to marry a widow, and as such, the wedding hinged on different protocols.

These well-intended admonitions did little to dampen Sing Fat's ardor, and he continued to spend his hard-gleaned gold on presents for his bride to be.

He did it, he said, because it gave him pleasure and he had experienced few real pleasures in his life. It wasn't asking too much to be indulged in this one instance.

The elder Fat appeared to understand and ceased applying cautions to every purchase. He acknowledged his protégé's right to do as he pleased with his gold and praised his generosity. He had seen, he said at last, far greater folly explored in the name of mere infatuation, and Sing Fat's relationship with Sue May Yee could hardly be characterized as thoughtless infatuation. He had come to trust Sing Fat as a compassionate young man of sober and established experience. He was hardly the kind of person to fall prey to irresponsible or dissipated influences.

ON THE SIXTH DAY AFTER THEIR RETURN TO SALINAS, Sing Fat and his teacher were working in the shop. The day was luminous and lovely. The recent storm had burnished the air like jewels, and the odor of recently harvested hay and alfalfa drifted through the town with a sweet, earthy fragrance. Sing Fat thought he had never experienced such a wonderful day, though even he had to admit that much of this sensation had to do with his own newfound perception of happiness and prospective fulfillment. Nothing could have altered his mood.

He was above the assault of sordid or mean-spirited prejudices. He was in the grip of devotion and altruism toward his fellow man and nobody could shake his spiritual enthusiasm and good humor.

About two o'clock, while Sing Fat graded and sorted a shipment of red ginseng root and Indian gotakola leaves, a somewhat disheveled figure entered the shop carrying a covered wicker basket over his arm. The man looked to have been journeying on the road for quite some time, as he was blanketed with road dust cast up by passing wagons.

Sing Fat couldn't identify the traveler at first and so returned to his labors. The man came forward and stood in the center of the shop. Sing Fat looked up when the traveler addressed his master as his "kind benefactor." It was then that Sing Fat recognized the man as one of the miners they had rescued and spirited to Monterey. He had wanted to become a fisherman, and from his appearance had accomplished his aim.

The elder Fat greeted the fisherman kindly and asked of what service he could be. A wave of profound sadness overcame the man before he could speak. Tears flowed over his dirty cheeks, creating muddy streaks down his face, but he was beyond speech.

Suddenly the man's grief broke forth in a pained and prolonged moan, and he fell to his knees and sobbed bitterly. The apothecary quickly came from behind his counter and knelt to help the man rise, but the poor fellow was inconsolable and just bowed his head and cried. The first words that could be elicited from the pitiful creature slumped on the floor were appeals for forgiveness and pardon, and for a few moments, that was all he could say.

When the elder Fat insisted that the fisherman had done nothing that should warrant forgiveness, the dusty figure only wailed louder and shivered, while his tears rained all about the wooden floor.

Sing Fat was riveted by the scene. Never in his life had he seen a man so distraught with grief and anguish, not even in the mines.

At last the fisherman gained some slight semblance of self-control and again begged forgiveness. When the elder Fat at last insisted that the man explain himself, the road-weary figure lifted himself up, clutched his basket, and through a broken voice tripped by intermittent sobs, began to explain that no one should carry the burden of such dreadful tidings. But he felt that he owed the two venerable gentlemen his life, so he had walked all the way from Point Alones to bring the news.

He had feared that his information might come to them from a stranger, and that would have been the unkindest wound of all. He had traveled on the errand himself out of respect. Suddenly Sing Fat felt a premonition, and his blood ran like fire through his veins. He demanded to know what had happened and to whom.

The fisherman sobbed once more and then began his story. He said that the day after their departure from Point Alones the expected storm had struck with frightening winds and monstrously steep seas. He said that although no one could be absolutely sure of the true facts, the little fishing village had experienced something like an earthquake about three in the morning. The waves had pounded the shore with such ferocity that no one was quite sure if it was truly the earth or the sea that had created the disturbance. The people had run out into the driving storm to avoid being crushed in their own houses. It was but a few moments later that a great wave rose from the bay like an avenging sea dragon.

It grew to an appalling height and drove straight for the village. Because of the darkness the size of the wave could only be judged by its white luminous crest. It seemed to reach for the clouds.

The fisherman wept once more and attempted to finish his disturbing narrative. Before anyone could give the alarm, the rogue wave crashed down on the rocks, destroying the three southernmost dwellings in the village. Sadly the house of Jong Yee disappeared under the breakers with two others. The shattered remains were dragged into the surge like so much kindling.

By dawn the broken figure of Sue May Yee was discovered on the rocks. Nobody else had been found. Seven adults and six children had disappeared completely. Sue May Yee lived only a short while before joining her honorable ancestors, but she had gathered strength enough to request that a legacy be forwarded to her intended husband with a message. They were to tell the young master that he was not to grieve. She would return to him one day. It was the will of heaven and love's commandment. Until then, Sing Fat was to take guardianship of her emissary. With that, the Imperial Duchess of Woo pushed open the hinged lid of the basket, shook her head, looked at Sing Fat, and voiced a long meow of recognition.

The sobbing fisherman said that the cat had been found in a cypress tree far from the shore, wet and angry but uninjured. He had brought the animal here at once as Sue May Yee had requested, but no one could understand how the poor creature had survived when all the others had been lost.

The elder Fat looked up at his apprentice and was startled

by what he saw. The frame and form of his pupil stood there, to be sure, but the soul, the heart of Sing Fat, had vanished in an instant, had raced away upon the wings of shock, disbelief, and anger.

Sing Fat stood looking down at the beautiful white cat, but he said not a word, nor expressed the least emotion whatsoever.

Again the distraught traveler asked the gentlemen's pardon for being the bearer of such lamentable news. He would rather have lost his right arm than act the courier for such tragic tidings, but such were the ways of heaven.

Still Sing Fat said nothing, disclosed nothing.

Chow Yong Fat was deeply troubled to find that his protégé's expression betrayed no normal human response. Nothing remotely emotional could be perceived behind Sing Fat's stony countenance. The young man's spirit-light had vanished, and in his experience, this signaled a dangerous ledge. Another step and Sing Fat might easily stumble into a bottomless crevasse of anguish-goaded madness.

The elder Fat had witnessed such effects of shock and grief before, and he knew this was beyond his medical skills. This was an affliction that no tincture or compound could assuage and no sacrifice or concern would alleviate. The healer felt totally powerless to alter the course of events.

Whatever was to happen in the next few moments, no matter how extreme or drastic, would define the parameters of response. Chow Yong Fat gripped the counter, held his breath, and waited. The fisherman looked up in fear and waited. A universe of time and stars waited. The last gasp of reason waited as well.

Sing Fat stood motionless for a few moments and then, without saying a word or altering expression, reached down and gently lifted the cat to his breast. He caressed the purring creature's head with his cheek and then walked out of the shop.

THE WHOLE INCIDENT DISTRESSED THE ELDER FAT in the extreme. He even felt that perhaps his own participation in the affair might be assessed as too meddlesome. Since, obviously, the will of heaven was not in harmony with events as planned, he could be rightly criticized for stunted professional insight. He might have acted sooner. If he had not cautioned Sing Fat to exercise patience and wait, the couple would have been married by now, and this fate would have passed from their door. He should have sensed disaster from the sea and guided the couple to safety. Many similar self-reproaches haunted his thoughts and daydreams.

Chow Yong Fat waited a week for his young friend's return, but no word or sign of his whereabouts turned up. The apothecary then began to make broad inquiries. Some said a young man of similar description had been seen in Watsonville, in an opium den. Others heard it said that the young man had taken work as a railroad laborer. But all these accounts proved false. Then one day, an old customer recounted witnessing a person of Sing Fat's description purchase a small spring wagon, mule, and burro from a livery stable in Monterey. This observer also reported that the man in question no longer wore Chinese garb, but rather dressed in overalls, seaboots, and a long, canvas duster. He had also taken to wearing a black derby hat. It was additionally rumored that he carried a twelve-gauge coach gun on a shoulder strap under his duster.

The elder Fat found these stories difficult to believe. None of this sounded like the Sing Fat he knew, but they were the only reports that came to light. Perhaps they were true. Perhaps madness had come to roost in the young man's soul after all.

The one piece of evidence that finally convinced the apothecary that this identification might prove valid was a report that just such an individual, described just as he had heard, always traveled in the company of a beautiful white cat. This last piece of intelligence corked the bottle of speculation.

Chow Yong Fat, apothecary and healer of local distinction, at last buried any hopes that his talented pupil and friend would ever return to him as the man he once knew. The affliction that claimed victims of such cataclysm had consumed his most promising student, and there was no remedy for such misfortune save prayer. One either survived or withered into the grave of love's despair.

The old man assumed, with good reason, that he would never see Sing Fat again. After all was said and done, Sing Fat would not be the last child of the Middle Kingdom to go mad in the land of the barbarians.

It was sad to think upon, but no consecrated soil would claim his bones, and his grave would go uncherished by the generations of family he had hoped to sire.

Chow Yong Fat was alone once more. He despaired of ever finding someone to whom he could pass on his knowledge and practice, but disappointments were part of the currency traded with heaven for the gift of life. He was altogether resolved to accept this fact and went about his business as usual. Out of respect for his loss, no one ever mentioned his tragic apprentice again.

★   ★   ★

SEVEN MONTHS HAD PASSED since the death of Sue May Yee, and on New Year's Day of the Chinese calendar, Master Chow Yong Fat traveled to the Brooklyn district of Watsonville to witness the celebrations as a guest of his old friend, Dr. Lee Wah. It was tradition to render up debts on New Year's Day, and that had prompted one of his reasons for the journey. He maintained business relationships with the elders of the Fon Lee Look Company, the Ling Fook Company, and the Quong Wo Company, and there were important debts to be collected as well as paid during this propitious time of the year.

He had also pledged to visit his onetime benefactor, T. M. Shew, who now owned a general store on San Juan Road. Shew had acquired part ownership of a Chinese nickelodeon down by the Pajaro River, and the elder Fat was curious to see this strange new oddity.

The apothecary arrived back in Salinas two days after the New Year celebrations. It was late in the evening, and not a soul moved on the streets. He had no sooner closed the shop and gone up to his rooms when there came a loud knocking on his front door.

Chow Yong Fat naturally assumed it was a minor medical emergency and went downstairs to answer the summons. When he opened the door he received a shock, for there stood an ominous-looking brigand who resembled the cowboy villains he had seen illustrated in the cheaper periodicals. He was about to slam the door in the man's face when he noticed a beautiful white cat step out from under the man's full-length trail duster.

He looked up in the dim light and saw that behind the wispy beard, mustache, and long, unkempt hair burned the eyes of his erstwhile apprentice, Sing Fat. He had changed to such a degree that the apothecary barely recognized him at all.

Behind Sing Fat, in the street, stood a mule-drawn wagon with a little gray burro haltered to the tailgate. At Sing Fat's feet lay a number of large sacks packed to bursting and a small ironbound strongbox. The elder Fat swung open the door and warmly invited his former pupil to enter. The Duchess of Woo made her entrance first, followed by Sing Fat, who dragged in the sacks and the strongbox.

There followed a few moments of embarrassed silence before Sing Fat spoke a greeting. The elder Fat noticed at once that more than appearance had changed. Sing Fat no longer spoke in his usual fast-paced, youthful manner. His voice had sunk to a low baritone, and he talked in a slow, studied cadence that left one with the impression that he had only just learned his own language.

Sing Fat apologized for the lateness of the hour. He had come by on New Year's Day, as tradition mandated, to repay his debts, but he was told that Master Chow Yong Fat had gone to Watsonville. He said that he would have waited until morning, but he had business to attend to, and he wished to be back on the road as quickly as possible.

The old man shook his head in confusion and said that he didn't recall any debts owed him. His former apprentice had paid his own way and owed him nothing. But Sing Fat said that some debts were a matter of opinion and it was his considered belief that a substantial debt was owed for all the elder Fat had taught him. He appraised the services rendered by his teacher to be of the greatest value and, as such, worthy of remuneration even if his former teacher did not consider it so.

Pulling a large knife from under his duster, Sing Fat began to open the sacks and lay their contents on the counter.

Chow Yong Fat was surprised and dismayed by the variety and value of the gifts. There were bags of wild Indian ginseng, rare mountain herbs by the pound, pickled sea urchins, dried juniper berries by the quart, and rare deepwater shark fins in dried bundles of ten pounds each. He also presented his old teacher with rolls of beautifully smoke-tanned buckskin, dried cobra root, best-quality willow bark, and the cured gall-bladders of wild mountain boar as well as their curled tusks, the luster of which rivaled the finest ivory. Along with these he stacked wax sealed crocks of pickled green eels and jars of wild mountain honey still in their wax combs as well as big black wood bees preserved in their own honey. Finally Sing Fat lifted the sturdy strongbox onto the counter and opened it with a large, iron key. He withdrew eight large goose quills packed with gold dust, approximately five ounces in all. The gold, he said, was to help his teacher's business and might finance the recruitment of qualified assistants for the shop.

Sing Fat paused, looked at the Duchess perched on a tea chest, and then said it was the least he could do since he had left his master's employ on such short notice. He went on to remark that every few months he would return with more goods appropriate to the arts of medicine. Whatever profits were to accrue from his contribution were to be reinvested in the business. Sing Fat let a sad smile cross his lips. He said he no longer had much need for ready cash. His life was simpler now and required little in the way of money.

The elder Fat asked what he did and where he now lived, but his ex-pupil avoided the question by apologizing for any undue inconvenience, disappointment, or distress he might have caused his revered teacher. Sing Fat said that, though he still took great interest in medicine and collecting specimens useful in those arts, he could no longer abide the company or fellowship of other people.

He preferred to live away from human society and craved no companionship save that of his beloved Duchess of Woo. Together with his mule, Po Lin, and his burro, General Sing, he was blessed with all the comradeship he needed.

For habitation he preferred the mountains of the Big Sur. They sheltered him from the ravages of an unjust world and the soul-stripping flails of heaven.

With that, Sing Fat made a soft clicking sound with his tongue and the Duchess reappeared from her feline explorations and jumped nimbly up into his arms. Then Sing Fat bowed to his mentor and wished him a prosperous and fruitful new year.

Clutching his strongbox under one arm and cradling the Duchess in the other, Sing Fat disappeared into the night, leaving his bewildered benefactor to contemplate the power of grief over men's lives. It seemed to him that the older he grew, the less he really understood about the intricacies and frailty of the human heart. For him it was enough to know that the organ pumped blood and kept one alive against the odds of nature.

FOR ALL INTENTS AND BY DESIGN, Sing Fat slipped from the weave of Chinese society and, indeed, from the fellowship of humanity in general. For thirty-nine years he wandered the mountains and coasts of the Big Sur. Everyone living in the area remembered having seen him on one or another of his enigmatic foraging expeditions, always accompanied by his white cat. Nobody knew what he did for money, where he lived, nor did they really care. He was always fastidiously polite to everyone, but never went out of his way to seek their company. He made no close friends and rarely spoke unless spoken to.

There were a few odd souls that Sing Fat counted as helpful and worth the time of day. West Smith, Horace Hogue, J. W. Gilkey, and the Posts fell into that category, but the rest were shadow acquaintanceships and of little real importance aside from infrequent instances of trade.

After the death of Master Chow Yong Fat, his erstwhile pupil bought a bigger spring wagon and went into the seaweed trade. Sometimes he would stop by the Post ranch and trade for apples, sugar, tobacco, or a portion of beef if the deer proved scarce. But other than that, the Chinaman and his reasons for living such an isolated life on the wild coast of the Big Sur remained a mystery to everyone.

ONE DAY IN SPRING, a passing cowhand discovered Sing Fat, by then an old man, sitting under a broad oak near his spring wagon. He looked asleep but was, in fact, dead of natural causes. He appeared quite tranquil and at peace with the world at last. He was buried on a gentle hillside not far from where he was found.

Some years later Sing Fat's little cabin was discovered in the mountains. In a well-preserved clearing overlooking the sea near his rude shelter, a tiny ornate grave was discovered. It was just big enough for a cat. It was surmounted by a simple Chinese shrine cleverly constructed of wood and cut stone. The legend, intricately carved and painted on the marker, was in Chinese. Translated, it said, "Here reposes the truest Heart and Spirit of

Sing Fat. The humblest servant of the Imperial Duchess of Woo."

Below that, carved and painted in gold, was a sentiment in English: "That which the compassion and glory of heaven has united, no power in the universe shall ever divide."

About the Author

Thomas Steinbeck began his career in the 1960s as a motion picture cinematographer and photojournalist in Vietnam. Along with his writing, speaking, and producing obligations, Mr. Steinbeck has taught college-level courses in American literature, creative writing, and communication arts. He serves on the board of directors of the Stella Adler Theatre Los Angeles and the National Steinbeck Center. He has written numerous original screenplays and documentaries, as well as adaptations of his father's work. Thomas Steinbeck lives on the central coast of California with his wife. He is currently at work on his first novel.